494102C

S0-CFO-351

WITHDRAWN
Alhambra Library

The Heart's Victory

NORA ROBERTS

The Heart's Victory

Thorndike Press • Chivers Press
Waterville, Maine USA   Bath, England

ALHAMBRA PUBLIC LIBRARY
ALHAMBRA, CALIFORNIA

This Large Print edition is published by Thorndike Press, USA and by Chivers Press, England.

Published in 2002 in the U.S. by arrangement with Harlequin Books S.A.

Published in 2002 in the U.K. by arrangement with Harlequin Enterprises II BV.

U.S. Hardcover 0-7862-3979-4 (Americana Series)
U.K. Hardcover 0-7540-7402-1 (Chivers Large Print)
U.K. Softcover 0-7540-7403-X (Camden Large Print)

Copyright © 1982 by Nora Roberts.

All rights reserved.

All the characters in this book have no existence outside the imagination of the author and have no relation whatsoever to anyone bearing the same name or names. They are not even distantly inspired by any individual known or unknown to the author, and all incidents are pure invention.

The text of this Large Print edition is unabridged.
Other aspects of the book may vary from the original edition.

Cover used by permission of Harlequin Books.

Set in 16 pt. Plantin.

Printed in the United States on permanent paper.

British Library Cataloguing-in-Publication Data available

Library of Congress Cataloging-in-Publication Data

Roberts, Nora.
    The heart's victory / Nora Roberts.
      p. cm.
    ISBN 0-7862-3979-4 (lg. print : hc : alk. paper)
    1. Automobile racing drivers — Fiction.   2. Large type books.   I. Title.
PS3568.O243 H425 2002
  813'.54—dc21   2002019930

The Heart's Victory

ALHAMBRA PUBLIC LIBRARY
ALHAMBRA, CALIFORNIA

Chapter One

Foxy stared at the underbelly of the MG. The scent of oil surrounded her as she tightened bolts. "You know, Kirk, I can't tell you how much I appreciate your lending me these coveralls." Her smooth contralto voice was touched with sarcasm.

"What are brothers for?" Foxy heard the grin in his voice though all she could see were the bottoms of his frayed jeans and his grimy sneakers.

"It's wonderful you're so broad-minded." She gritted her teeth on the words as she worked with the ratchet. "Some brothers might have insisted on fixing the transmission themselves."

"I'm no chauvinist," Kirk returned. Foxy watched Kirk's sneakers as he walked across the concrete floor of the garage. She heard the click and clatter of tools being replaced. "If you hadn't decided to be a photographer, I'd have put you on my pit crew."

"Fortunately for me, I prefer developing fluid to motor oil." She wiped the back of her hand over her cheek. "And to think if I hadn't been hired to shoot the photos for Pam Anderson's book, I wouldn't be here right now up to my elbows in car parts."

When Foxy heard his quick, warm laugh, it struck her how much she had missed him. Perhaps it was because their two-year separation had worked no change on him. He was precisely the same, as if she had closed the door and opened it again only minutes later. His face was still weathered and bronzed with creases and dents that promised to grow only deeper and more attractive with age. His hair was still as thickly curled as her own, though his was a dark gold and hers a rich russet. The familiar mustache twitched above his mouth when he smiled. Foxy couldn't remember him ever being without it. She had been six and he sixteen when it had first appeared, and seventeen years later it was a permanent fixture on his face. Foxy had seen, too, that the recklessness was still there. It was in his smile, in his eyes, in his movements.

As a child, she had worshiped him. He had been a tall, golden hero who allowed her to tag behind and pay homage. It had been Kirk who had absently dubbed her Foxy, and the ten-year-old Cynthia Fox had clung to the name as if it were a gift. When Kirk left home to pursue a career in professional racing, Foxy had lived for his occasional visits and short, sporadic letters. In his absence, he grew more golden, more indestructible. He was twenty-three when he won his first major race. Foxy had been thirteen.

This tender, testing, learning year of her life had been one of indescribable pain. It had been late when Foxy had driven home from town with her parents. The road was slick with snow. Foxy watched it hurl itself against the windows of the car while the radio played a Gershwin tune she was too young to either recognize or appreciate. She had stretched out on the backseat, closed her eyes, and begun to hum a tune popular with her own generation. She wished briefly that she was home so that she could put on her records and call her best friend to talk about things that were important — *boys.*

There had been no warning as the car began its skid. It circled wildly, gaining speed as the tires found no grip on the slick, wet snow. There was a blur of white outside the car windows and she heard her father swear as he fought to regain control of the wheel, but her fear never had the chance to materialize. Foxy heard the crunching impact as the car slammed into the telephone pole, felt the jerk and the quick pain. She felt the cold as she was tossed from the car, then the wet swish of snow against her face. Then she felt nothing.

It had been Kirk's face that Foxy saw upon awakening from the two-day coma. Her first wave of joy froze as she remembered the accident. She saw it in his eyes — the weariness, the grief, the acceptance. She shook her head to deny what he had not yet told her. Gently, he bent down to rest his cheek on hers. "We've got each other now, Foxy. I'm going to take care of you."

And so he had, in his fashion. For the next four years, Foxy followed the circuit. She received her education from a series of tutors with varying degrees of success. But during her teenage years, Cynthia Fox learned more than American history or algebra. She learned about piston displacement and turbo engines; she learned how to take an engine apart and how to put it back together; she learned the rules of pit lane. She grew up in what was predominantly a man's world, with the smell of gasoline and the roar of engines. Supervision at times had been lax, at others, nonexistent.

Kirk Fox was a man with one consuming passion: the race. Foxy knew there were times he forgot her existence completely, and she accepted it. Seeing the dents in his perfection only caused her to love him more. She grew up wild and free and, inconsistently, sheltered.

College had been a shock. Over the next four years, Foxy's world had expanded. She discovered the eccentricities of living in a dormitory with females. She began to learn more about Cynthia Fox. Having a discerning eye for color, cut, and line, she had developed her own distinctive taste in clothes. She found that clubs and sororities were not for her; her childhood had been too freewheeling to allow her to accept rules and regimentation. It had been easy for Foxy to resist college men because they seemed to her to be foolish, immature boys. She had entered college a gangling, awkward girl and graduated a willow-slim woman with her own innate grace and a passion for photography. For the two years following college, Foxy poured every ounce of her talent and effort into building her career. The assignment with Pam Anderson was a two-fold gift. It allowed her to spend time with her brother while nudging the crack in the door of opportunity yet wider. Foxy knew the first part of the gift was still more important to her than the second.

"I suppose you'd be shocked to learn I haven't seen the underside of a car in over two years." Foxy made the admission as she tightened the last of the bolts.

"What do you do when your transmission needs work?" Kirk demanded as he took a final look under the MG's hood.

"I send it to a mechanic," Foxy muttered.

"With your training?" Kirk was appalled enough to bend down and glare at the top of her head. "You can get twenty years to life for a crime like that."

"I don't have time." Foxy sighed, then continued, as if to make amends, "I did change the points and plugs last month."

"This car is a classic." Kirk closed the hood gently, then wiped the surface with a clean rag. "You're crazy if you let just anybody get their hands on it."

"Well, I can't send it out to Charlie every time it gets the sniffles, and besides . . ." Foxy stopped her justifications at the sound of a car pulling up outside.

"Hey, this ain't no place for a businessman." Foxy heard the smile in her brother's words as she set down the ratchet.

"Just checking on my investment."

Lance Matthews. She recognized the low, drawling voice instantly. Just as instantly her hands clenched into tight balls. Heat bubbled in her throat. Slowly, Foxy forced herself to remain calm. *Ridiculous,* she thought as she flexed her fingers; *resentments shouldn't survive a six-year separation.*

She saw from her vantage point that he, too, wore jeans and sneakers. While his showed no streaks of grease, they were frayed and worn. *He's just slumming,* she thought and suppressed an indignant sniff. Six years is a long time, she reminded herself. He might be almost tolerable by now. But she doubted it.

"I couldn't get here for the practice run this morning. How'd she do?"

"200.558." She heard the click and fizz of a beer being opened. "Charlie wants to give her a last going over, but she's prime, absolutely prime." From the tone of her brother's voice, Foxy knew he had forgotten she was there, forgotten everything but the car and the race.

"He's got his mind fixed on setting a pit record Sunday." There was a faint snap and a pungent aroma drifted to Foxy. It annoyed her that she recognized it as the scent of the slender cigars Lance habitually smoked. She rubbed her nose with the back of her hand as if to erase the fragrance from her senses. "New toy?" Lance asked, walking over to the MG. Foxy heard the hood lift. "Looks like the little number you bought your sister after she got her license. She still playing with cameras?"

Incensed, Foxy gave a push and rolled out from under the car. For the instant she lay on the creeper, she saw a look of surprise cross Lance's face. "It's the same little number," she said coldly as she struggled to her feet. "And I don't play with cameras, I work with them."

Her hair was pulled in a ponytail back from her grease-smeared face. The coveralls left her shapeless and sloppy. In one oil-splattered hand, she held the ratchet. Through her indignation, Foxy noted that Lance Matthews was more attractive than ever. Six years had deepened the creases in his rawboned face, which, by some odd miracle, just escaped being handsome. Handsome was too tame a word for Lance Matthews. His hair was richly black, curling into the collar of his shirt and tossed carelessly around his face. His brows were slightly arched over eyes that could go from stone-gray to smoke depending on his mood. The classic, aristocratic features were offset by a small white scar above his left brow. He was taller than Kirk with a rangier build, and there was an ease in his manner that Kirk lacked. Foxy knew the indolent exterior covered a keen awareness. Through his twenties he had been one of the top drivers in the racing world. She had heard it said that Lance Matthews had the hands of a surgeon, the instinct of a wolf, and the nerve of the devil. At thirty, he had won the world championship and abruptly retired. From her brother's less than informative letters, Foxy knew that for the past three years Lance had successfully sponsored drivers and cars. She watched as his mouth formed the half-tilted smile that had always been his trademark.

"Well, if it isn't Fox." His eyes ran down the coveralls and back to her face. "Six years hasn't changed you a bit."

"Nor you," she retorted, furious that their first meeting would find her so attired. She felt like a foolish, gangling teenager again. "What a pity."

"Tongue's as sharp as ever." His teeth flashed in a grin. Apparently the fact that she was still a rude, bad-tempered urchin appealed to him. "Have you missed me?"

"As long as I possibly could," she replied and held the ratchet out to her brother.

"Still hasn't any respect for her elders," Lance told Kirk while his eyes lingered on Foxy's mutinous face. "I'd kiss you hello, but I never cared for the taste of motor oil."

He was teasing her as he had always done and Foxy's chin shot up as it always had. "Fortunately for both of us, Kirk has an unlimited supply."

"If you walk around like that for the rest of the season," Kirk warned as he replaced his tool, "you might as well work in the pits."

"The season?" Lance's look sharpened as he drew on his cigar. "You going to be around for the season? That's some vacation."

"Hardly." Foxy wiped her palms on the legs of the coveralls and tried to look dignified. "I'm here as a photographer, not as a spectator."

"Fox is working with that writer, Pam Anderson," Kirk put in as he picked up his beer again. "Didn't I tell you?"

"You mentioned something about the writer," Lance murmured. He was studying Fox's face as if to see beneath the smears of grease. "So, you'll be traveling the circuit again?"

Foxy remembered the intensity of his eyes. There were times when they could stop your breath. There was something raw and deep about the man. Even as an adolescent, Foxy had been aware of his basic sensuality. Then she had found it fascinating, now she knew its dangers. Willpower kept her eyes level with his. "That's right. A pity you won't be along."

"Not a pity," he countered. The intensity disappeared from his eyes and Foxy watched them grow light again. "Kirk's driving my car. I intend to tag along and watch him win." He saw Foxy frown before he turned to her brother. "I suppose I'll meet Pam Anderson at the party you're having tonight. Don't wash the grease off, Foxy." He patted a clean spot on her chin before he walked to the door. "I might not recognize you. We should have a dance for old time's sake."

"Stuff it in your manifold," Foxy called after him, then cursed herself for trading dignity for childish taunts. After shooting Kirk a glare, she stepped out of the coveralls. "Your taste in friends eludes me."

Kirk shrugged, glancing out the window as Lance drove away. "You better test-drive the car before you drive to the house. It might need some adjustments."

Foxy sighed and shook her head. "Sure."

The dress Foxy chose for the evening was made of paper-thin crepe de chine. The muted pastels of lavender and green clung and floated around her slender, curved figure. With a draping skirt and strapless bodice covered by the sheerest of short jackets, it was a romantic dress. It was also very alluring. Foxy thought with grim satisfaction that Lance Matthews was in for a surprise. Cynthia Fox was not a teenager any longer. After placing small gold hoops in her ears, she stood back to judge the results.

Her hair was loose, left to fall below her shoulders in a thick mane of gleaming russet curls. Her face was now clear of black smudges. Her prominent cheekbones added both elegance and delicacy to the piquant quality of her triangular face. Her eyes were almond-shaped, not quite gray, not quite green. Her nose was sharp and aristocratic, her mouth full and just short of being too wide. There was a hint of her brother's recklessness in her eyes, but it was banked and smoldering. There was something reminiscent of the wilds in her, part deer, part tigress. Much more than beauty, she possessed an earthy, untapped sensuality. She was made of contradictions. Her willowy figure and ivory complexion made her appear fragile while the fire in her hair and boldness of her eyes sent out a challenge. Foxy felt the night was ripe for challenge.

Just as she was slipping into her shoes, a knock sounded at her door. "Foxy, can I come in?" Pam Anderson peeked through a crack in the door, then pushed it wider. "Oh, you look marvelous."

Foxy turned with a smile. "So do you."

The dreamy pale blue chiffon suited Pam's china-doll looks perfectly. Studying the petite blond beauty, Foxy wondered again how she had the stamina for as demanding a career as that of a free-lance journalist. How does she manage to get such in-depth interviews when she speaks like a magnolia blossom and looks like a hothouse orchid? They had known each other for six months, and though Pam was five years Foxy's senior, the younger woman was developing maternal instincts toward the older.

"Isn't it nice to start off a job with a party?" Pam moved to the bed and sat as Foxy ran a comb through her hair. "Your brother's home is lovely, Foxy. My room's perfect."

"It was our house when we were kids," Foxy told her, frowning over her perfume bottle. "Kirk kept it as sort of a base camp since it's so close to Indianapolis." Her frown turned upward into a smile. "Kirk's always liked to camp near a track."

"He's charming." Pam ran her fingers over her short, smooth page boy. "And very generous to put me up until we start on the circuit."

"Charming he is." Foxy laughed and leaned closer to the mirror as she added color to her lips. "Unless he's plotting track strategy. You'll notice, sometimes he leaves the rest of the world." Foxy stared down at the lipstick tube, then carefully closed it. "Pam . . ." Taking a quick breath, she glanced up and met Pam's eyes in the mirror. "Since we'll be traveling so closely, I think you should understand Kirk a bit. He's . . ." She sighed and moved her shoulders. "He's not always charming. Sometimes he's curt, and short-tempered, and downright unkind. He's very restless, very competitive. Racing is his life, and at times he forgets people aren't as insensitive as cars."

"You love him a lot, don't you?" The clear insight and hint of compassion in the quiet blue eyes were a part of the reason for Pam's success in her field. She was not only able to read people, but to care.

"More than anything." Foxy turned until she met the woman's face rather than the reflection. "More still since I grew up and discovered he was human. Kirk didn't have to take on the responsibility of raising me. I don't think it occurred to me until I was in college that he'd had a choice. He could have put me in a foster home; no one would have criticized him. In fact" — she tossed her head to free her shoulders of her hair, then leaned back against the dresser — "I'm sure he was criticized by some for not doing so. He kept me with him, and that's what I needed. I'll never forget him for that. One day perhaps I'll pay him back." Smiling, Foxy straightened. "I suppose I'd better go down and make sure the caterer has everything set. The guests will be arriving soon."

"I'll come with you." Pam rose and moved to the door. "Now, what about this Lance Matthews you were grumbling about earlier? If I did my homework properly, he's a former driver, a very successful driver, now head of Matthews Corporation which among other things designs racing cars. He's designed and owns several Formula One cars, including the ones your brother will be driving this season. And yes . . . the Indy car too. Isn't he . . . ?" She made a small cluck of frustration as her inventory of facts grew sketchy. "He's from a very old, wealthy family, isn't he? Boston or New Haven, shipping or import-export. Disgustingly rich."

"Boston, shipping, and disgusting," Foxy affirmed as they moved down to the first floor. "Don't get me started on him tonight or you'll have nightmares."

"Do I detect a smidgeon of dislike?"

"You detect a ton of dislike," Foxy countered. "I've had to rent a room to hold my extra dislike of Lance Matthews."

"Mmm, and rent prices are soaring."

"Which only makes me dislike him more." Foxy moved directly to the dining room and examined the table.

Lacquered wooden dishes were set on an indigo tablecloth. The centerpiece was an earthenware jug filled with sprays of dogwood and daffodils. One look at the setting, at the chunky yellow candles in wooden holders, assured Foxy that the caterer knew his business. "Relaxed informality" was the obvious theme.

"Looks nice." Foxy resisted dipping a finger into a bowl of iced caviar as the caterer bustled in from the kitchen.

He was a small, fussy man, bald but for a thin ring of hair he had dyed a deep black. He walked in quick, shuffling steps. "You're too early." He stood protectively between Foxy and the caviar. "Guests won't be arriving for another fifteen minutes."

"I'm Cynthia Fox, Mr. Fox's sister." She offered a smile as a flag of truce. "I thought perhaps I could help."

"Help? Oh no, good heavens, no." To prove his words, he brushed at her with the back of his hand as though she were an annoying fly threatening his pâté. "You mustn't touch anything. It's all balanced."

"And beautifully, too," Pam soothed as she gave Foxy's arm a warning squeeze. "Let's go have a drink, Foxy, and wait for the others to arrive."

"Silly, pompous man," Foxy mumbled as Pam urged her into the living room.

"Do you let anyone else set your f-stops?" Pam asked with bland curiosity as she sank into a chair.

Foxy laughed as she surveyed the portable bar. "Point taken. Well, there seems to be enough liquor here to keep an army reeling for a year. Trouble is, I don't know how to fix anything more complicated than the gin and tonic Kirk drinks."

"If there's a bottle of dry sherry, pour some in a very small glass. That shouldn't tax your ingenuity too far. Going to join me?"

"No." Foxy scouted through the bottles. "Drinking makes me just a little too honest. I forget the basic rules of survival — tact and diplomacy. You know the managing editor of *Wedding Day* magazine, Joyce Canfield?" Pam gave an affirmative response as Foxy located and poured sherry. "I ran into her at this cocktail party a few months back. I'd done several layouts for *Wedding Day*. Anyway, she asked me what I thought of her dress. I looked at her over the rim of my second spritzer and told her she should avoid yellow, it made her look sallow." Foxy crossed the room and handed Pam her glass. "Honest but dumb. I haven't taken a picture of a wilted bouquet for *Wedding Day* since."

Pam laughed her quiet, floating laugh and sipped her sherry. "I'll remember not to ask you any dangerous questions when you have a glass in your hand." She watched Foxy run a finger over a high, pie-crust table. "Does it feel strange being home?"

Foxy's eyes were dark, the green merely sprinkled over the gray. "It brings back memories. Strange, I really haven't thought of my life here in years, but now . . ." Walking to the window, she pulled back the sheer ivory curtain. Outside, the sun was dipping low in the sky, shooting out sprays of red and gold light. "Do you know, this is really the only place I could define as home. New York doesn't count. Ever since my parents died, I've moved around so much, first with Kirk, then with my career. It's only now that I'm here that it occurs to me how rootless my life has been."

"Do you want roots, Foxy?"

"I don't know." When Foxy turned back to Pam, her face was puzzled. "I don't know," she repeated. "Maybe. But I want something. It's out there." She narrowed her eyes and stared at something she could not yet see.

"What is?"

Foxy jolted as the voice shattered her thoughts. Kirk stood in the doorway studying her with his easy smile, his hands thrust into the pockets of dun-colored slacks. As always, there was an aura of excitement around him.

"Well." Giving him a considering look, Foxy crossed to him. "Silk, huh?" With sisterly prerogative, she fingered the collar of his shirt. "Guess you don't change too many engines in this." Kirk tugged on her hair and kissed her simultaneously.

In her heels, she was nearly as tall as he, and their eyes were level with each other's. As Pam watched she noticed how little family resemblance they shared; only the curling heaviness of their hair was similar. Kirk's eyes were a dark true green, and his face was long and narrow. There was nothing of his sister's elegance or her delicacy about him. Studying his profile, Pam felt a tiny quiver chase up her spine. Quickly she glanced down at her drink. Long-term assignments and quivering spines didn't mix.

"I'll fix you a drink," Foxy offered, drawing away from her brother and moving to the bar. "We don't dare go into the other room for another two and a half minutes. Oops, no ice." She closed the lid on the ice bucket and shrugged. "I'll be heroic and challenge the caterer. Pam's drinking sherry," she called over her shoulder as she left the room.

"Want a refill?" Kirk asked, turning his attention to Pam for the first time.

"No, thanks." She smiled and lifted her glass to her lips. "I haven't had a chance to thank you yet for putting me up. I can't tell you how nice it is not to be sleeping in a hotel."

"I know all about hotels." Kirk grinned and sat across from her. For the first time since they had met the day before, they were alone. Pam felt the quiver again and ignored it. Kirk took a cigarette from the holder on the table and lit it. For those few seconds, he studied her.

Class, he thought. *And brains.* This was no racing groupie. His eyes lingered an instant on the soft pink mouth. *She looks like something in a store window. Beautiful, desirable, and behind a wall of glass.*

"Foxy's spoken of you so often, I feel I know you." Pam immediately cursed herself for the inanity and took another sip of sherry. "I'm looking forward to the race."

"So am I," Kirk answered, then leaned back in his chair and studied her more openly. "You don't look the type to be interested in pit stops and lap speeds."

"No?" Pam countered as she collected her poise. "What type do I look like?"

Kirk smoked in long, deep drags. "The

type who likes Chopin and champagne."

Pam swirled the remaining sherry in her glass and held his gaze. "I do," she answered, then relaxed against the cushions of her chair. "But as a journalist, I'm interested in all kinds of things. I hope you'll be generous with your thoughts and feelings and your knowledge."

A smile lifted the corners of his mustache. "I've been known to be generous with all manners of things," he mocked, wondering if the dewy texture of her skin was as soft as it looked. The doorbell broke the silence. Kirk rose, took the drink from Pam's hand, and pulled her to her feet. Though she told herself it was a foolish reaction, her heart thundered. "Are you married?" he asked.

"Why . . . no." She frowned, confused.

"Good. I never like sleeping with married women."

He spoke so matter-of-factly, it took Pam a moment to react. Angry color flooded her porcelain cheeks. "Of all the presumptuous —"

"Listen," Kirk interrupted. "We're bound to sleep together before the season's finished. I'm not much on games, so I don't play."

"And would it shock you very deeply,"

Pam returned with the coldness only a southern-bred voice can achieve, "if I decline your generous invitation?"

"Seems like a waste," Kirk concluded with a careless shrug. He took Pam's hand as the doorbell pealed a second time. "We'd better answer it."

Chapter Two

Over the next hour, the house filled with people and grew noisy. As the room filled, the patio doors opened to allow guests to spill outside. The night was warm and still.

For Foxy, there were both new faces and old friends. She wandered from group to group, assuming the role of unofficial hostess. The caterer's proud balance had been long since shattered as trays and bowls were scattered throughout the house. People milled in every corner. Still, the breezy informality of the party was linked with a common bond. These were racing people, whether they were drivers, wives, or privileged fans.

Flushed and laughing, Foxy answered the door to admit a late arrival. Her smile of greeting faded instantly. There was some satisfaction to be gained from seeing a look of surprise in Lance's gray eyes. It came and went with the lift and fall of his brow. Slowly he took his gaze over the length of her. There was a look of consideration on his face, which Foxy equated with a man about to purchase a piece of sculpture for his den. Instantly the ease fled from her stance as her chin lifted and her shoulders straightened. Annoyed, she gave him the same casual appraisal he gave her.

Both his turtleneck and slacks were black. The night apparel lent him a mysterious, dangerous look only accentuated by his leanness and reckless looks. About him was the odd air of calm Foxy remembered. It was an ability to remain absolutely motionless and absorb everything. The true hunter possesses it, and the bullfighter who survives. Now, as she knew he was absorbing her, Foxy challenged him with her eyes though her heart beat erratically. *Anger,* she told herself. *He always makes me so angry.*

"Well, well, well." Lance's voice was quiet and oddly intimate over the hum of the party. He met her eyes, then smiled at her sulky pout. "It seems I was wrong."

"Wrong?" she repeated and reluctantly shut the door behind him rather than in his face.

"You have changed." He took both her hands, ignoring her sharp jerk of protest.

31

Holding her away from him, he let his eyes roam down the length of her again. "You're still ridiculously thin, but you've managed to fill out a bit in a few interesting places."

Her skin trembled as if a cool breeze had caressed it. Furious with the sensation, Foxy tried to snatch her hands away. She failed. "If that's a compliment, you can keep it. I'd like my hands back, Lance."

"Sure, in a minute." Her anger and indignation rolled off him as he continued to study her. "You know," he said conversationally, "I always wondered how that funny little face of yours would turn out. It had an odd appeal, even when it was splattered with transmission fluid."

"I'm surprised you remember how I looked." Resigned that he would not let her go until he was ready, Foxy stopped struggling. She took a long, hard look at him, searching his face for any flaws that might have developed during the past six years. She found none. "You haven't changed a bit."

"Thanks." With a grin, he transferred his hold to her waist and led her toward the sounds of the party.

"That wasn't intended as a compliment." Foxy had a strange reaction to his

32

quick grin and intimate touch. The wariness remained with her, but it was tempered with amusement. Foxy drew firmly away from him as they entered the main room. It was, she reminded herself, always so simple for him to charm her. "I imagine you know just about everyone." She made a quick sweep of the room with the back of her hand. "And I'm certain you can find your way to the bar."

"Gracious to the last," Lance murmured, then gave her another measuring stare. "As I recall, you didn't always dislike me so intensely."

"I was a slow learner."

"Lance, darling!" Honey Blackwell bore down on them. Her hair was short and fluffed and silver blond, her face pretty and painted, her body all curves and dips. She had money and an unquenchable thirst for excitement. She was, in Foxy's opinion, the classic racing leech. As her arms circled Lance's neck he rested his hands on her generous hips. She kissed Lance with single-minded enthusiasm as he watched Foxy's disdainful smirk over Honey's bare shoulder.

"Apparently, you two have met." Inclining her head, she turned and moved to the center of the party. *And apparently,* she added to herself, *you can manage to amuse yourselves without me.* Feeling a hand on her arm, Foxy glanced up.

"Hi. I knew you'd stand still long enough eventually for me to introduce myself. I'm Scott Newman."

"Hello. Cynthia Fox." Her hand was taken in a very proper shake.

"Yes, I know. You're Kirk's sister."

Foxy smiled at him as she completed her study of his features. His face was well formed, just escaping fullness. His eyes were deep brown, his nose straight, his mouth long and curved. He wore his brown hair at a conservative length, neither long nor short. They stood eye to eye, as he was a few inches short of six feet. He was handsomely tanned and trim without being lean. His three-piece suit was well cut, but the jacket had been casually left unbuttoned. He was, Foxy decided, the perfect model for a study of up-and-coming young executives. She thought briefly that it was a pity he hadn't dressed up the beige suit with a deep-toned shirt.

"We'll be seeing a lot of each other over the next few months," he told her, unaware of the trend of her thoughts.

"Oh?" She gave him her full attention as she eased out of the way of someone bearing a tray of crackers and Gouda cheese.

"I'm Kirk's road manager. I see to all the traveling arrangements, accommodations for him and the crew, and so forth." His eyes smiled over to hers while he lifted his glass to his lips.

"I see." Foxy tilted her head, then tossed back her hair. "I haven't been around for a few years." Catching a glimpse of her brother out of the corner of her eye, Foxy focused on him, then smiled. He had the animated look of a knight-on-quest as a brunette hung on his arm and a small tangle of people hung on his words. "We didn't use a road manager when I was on the team," she murmured. Foxy remembered more than once falling asleep in the backseat of a car in a garage that smelled of gasoline and stale cigarettes. Or camping on the infield grass, waiting for the morning and the race. *He's a comet,* she thought, watching her brother. *A brilliant, flaming comet.*

"There've been a number of changes in the past few years," Scott commented. "Kirk began winning more important races. And of course, with Lance Matthews' sponsorship, his career has come more into focus."

"Yes." She gave a quick laugh and shook her head. "Money talks after all, doesn't it?"

"You haven't got a drink." Scott noticed the lack of glass, but not the sarcasm in her voice. "We'd better fix that."

"Sure." Foxy linked her arm in his and allowed him to lead her to the bar. *I don't care one way or the other about Lance Matthews' money.*

"What would you like?" Scott asked.

Foxy glanced at him, then at the short, graying professional bartender. "A spritzer," she told him.

Moonlight shone through the young leaves. The flowers in the garden were still new with spring, their colors were muted with night. Their fragrance was light and tender, only whispering of the promise of summer.

With a mighty sigh, Foxy dropped on one seat of a white glider and propped her feet up on the other. Dimly over the stretch of lawn, she could hear the sounds of the party ebb and flow. By slipping into the kitchen and out the back door, she had escaped to steal a few moments of quiet and solitude. Inside, the air was thick with smoke and clashing perfumes. Foxy took a long, greedy breath of spring air and pushed with her feet to set the glider into motion.

Scott Newman, she decided, was handsome, polite, intelligent, and interested. And, she admitted, ordinary. Rolling her eyes on a sigh, Foxy stared up at the sky. Wisps of dark clouds were edged in gray. As they passed lazily across the moon the light shifted and swayed. *There I go,* she mused, *being critical again. Does a man have to stand on one foot and juggle for me to consider him entertaining? What am I looking for? A knight?* Foxy frowned and rejected the choice. *No, knights are all polished and shiny and pure. I think my taste runs to something with a bit of tarnish and maybe a few scratches. Someone who can make me laugh and cry and make me angry and make my knees tremble when he touches me.* She laughed quietly, wondering how many men she was looking for. Leaning her head back, she crossed her ankles. The hem of her dress lifted to tickle her knee. Tossing up her arms, she gripped the slender poles on either side of the glider. I want someone dangerous, someone wild and gentle and strong and smart and foolish. With another laugh for her own specifications, she stared up at the stars. With a hazy blue light, they peeked and glimmered through the shifting clouds.

"Which star do I wish on?"

"The brightest is usually the best."

With a quick gasp, Foxy dropped her hands and searched for the owner of the voice. He was only a dark shadow, tall and lean. As it moved she thought of the steady stalking grace of a panther. Lance's black attire blended with the night, but his eyes caught the luminescence of the moon. For a moment, Foxy felt an eeriness, a displacement of the quiet suburban garden into a primitive, isolated jungle. Like a large cat of prey, his eyes glowed with their own light and conquered the dark. Shadows fell over his face and deepened its chiseled lines. She thought Lucifer must have looked equally dark and compelling as he fell from heaven into the flames.

"What are you wishing for?" His voice was so quiet, it shook the air.

Suddenly Foxy became aware that she was holding her breath. Carefully she released it. It was only the surprise, she insisted, that had made her skin quiver. "Oh, all I can get," she returned flippantly. "What are you doing out here? I thought you'd be knee-deep in blondes."

Lance swung onto the glider. "I wanted

some air," he told her as he stood staring down at her, "and some quiet."

Disturbed that his motives mirrored hers, Foxy shrugged and closed her eyes as if to ignore him. "How did you manage to tear yourself away from Miss Lush Bust?"

The sounds of the party penetrated the quiet of the night. Foxy felt his eyes on her face but stubbornly kept hers closed. "So," he murmured, "you've grown claws. You shouldn't sharpen them on someone's back, Foxy. The face is cleaner."

She opened her eyes and met his. Reluctantly she admitted that she had been nasty from the moment she had seen him again. Unprovoked nastiness was out of character for her. Foxy sighed and shrugged. "I'm sorry. I don't usually make a habit of snarling and spitting. Sit down, Lance, I'll try to behave." A small smile accompanied the invitation. He did not, as she had expected, sit across from her. Instead, he dropped down beside her. Foxy stiffened. Either unaware of or unconcerned by her reaction, Lance propped his feet next to hers on the opposite bench.

"I don't mind sparring, Fox, but a rest between rounds is always refreshing." Pulling out his lighter, he flicked it at the end of a long, thin cigar. The flame licked and flared. Strange, she thought as she relaxed her muscles, how clearly I remember that scent.

"Let's see if we can manage to be civilized for a few minutes," Foxy suggested and twisted slightly to face him. A smile hovered on her lips. She was an adult now, she reminded herself, and could meet him on his own terms. "Shall we discuss the weather, the latest best-seller, the political structure of Romania? I know" — she propped her cheek on her palm — "the race. How does it feel to be designing cars instead of racing them? Are you more hopeful for the Indy car you designed, or the Formula One for the Grand Prix races? Kirk's done very well on the GP circuit since the season opened. The car's supposed to be very fast and very reliable."

Lance saw the mischief in her eyes and lifted a brow. "Still reading racing magazines, Foxy?"

"If I didn't keep up to date, Kirk would never forgive me." She laughed, a low, heavy sound.

"I see that hasn't changed," Lance commented. She gave him a puzzled smile. "Even at fifteen, you had the sexiest laugh I'd ever heard. Like something stealing through the fog." He blew out a stream of smoke as she shifted in her seat. Moonlight showered on her hair, shooting out hundreds of tiny flames. She felt just the smallest hint of his power tempting her.

"The main branch of your company is in Boston," Foxy began, navigating to safer ground. "I suppose you live there now."

Lance smiled at her maneuver and tipped off the ash at the end of his cigar. "Most of the time. Ever been there?" He tossed his arm over the back of the seat. The gesture was so casual Foxy was barely aware of it.

"No." The glider's motion continued, slow and soothing. "I'd like to. I know there are fabulous contrasts. Brownstones and ivy, and steel and glass. I've seen some very effective pictures."

"I saw one of yours not too long ago."

"Oh?" Curious, she turned her head toward him and was surprised to find their faces nearly touching. His warm breath touched her lips. The power was stronger this time, and even more tempting. As she inched cautiously away his eyes never flickered from hers.

"It was taken in winter, but there was no snow, only a bit of frost on naked trees. There was a bench, and an old man was sleeping on it wrapped up in a gray and black topcoat. The sun came low through the trees and fell right across him. It was incredibly sad and quite beautiful."

Foxy was for the moment at a total loss. She had not expected Lance Matthews to possess any sensitivity or appreciation for the fine points of her craft. As they sat in silence something was happening between them, but she knew neither how to resist or encourage it. It was something as elemental as man and woman and as complex as emotion. His eyes continued to hold hers as his fingers tangled in the tips of her hair.

"I was very impressed," he went on as she remained silent and perplexed. "I noticed your name under it. I thought at first it couldn't be you. The Cynthia Fox I remembered didn't have the ability to take a picture with that much depth, that much feeling. I still knew you as a wide-eyed adolescent with a vile temper." When Lance broke the look to flick away the stub of his cigar, Foxy let out a quiet, shaky breath.

Relax, she ordered herself. *Stop being an idiot.*

"In any case, I was curious enough to do some checking. When I found it was you, I was doubly impressed." As he turned back to her one brow lifted and disappeared under the tousled front of his hair. "Obviously you're very good at what you do."

"What? Play with cameras?" But she smiled with the question. The evening air had mellowed her mood.

His grin was quick. "I've always thought a person should enjoy their work. I've been playing with cars for years."

"You can afford to play," she reminded him. Her voice cooled without her being aware of it.

"You've never forgiven me for having money, have you?" There was a light amusement in his voice that made her feel foolish.

"No." She shrugged. "I suppose not. Ten million always seemed so ostentatious."

He laughed, a low rumble, then tugged on her hair until she faced him again. "Only new money is ostentatious in Boston, Foxy. Old money is discreet."

"What constitutes 'old,' financially speaking?" Foxy found she enjoyed his laugh and the friendly hand on her hair.

"Oh, I'd say three generations would be the bare minimum. Anything less would be suspect. You know, Fox, I much prefer the lily of the valley to the gasoline you used to wear."

"Thanks. I do wear unleaded now and

again, but only when I'm feeling reckless."
She rose with a sigh. It surprised her that
she would have preferred sitting with him
to rejoining the party. "I'd better get back
in. Are you coming?"

"Not yet." He took her hand and with a
swift jerk spun her around until she tumbled into his lap.

"Lance!" With a surprised laugh, she
pushed against his chest. "What are you
doing?" Her struggles were halfhearted,
though his hands were still firm on her
waist. Foxy's mood was still mellow.

"I never kissed you hello."

Laughter died on her lips as she sensed
danger. Quickly she jerked back, but he
cupped his hand around the base of her
neck. She managed a startled "no!" before
his mouth closed over hers.

The kiss began light and teasing. Indeed,
she could feel the curve of a small smile on
the lips that touched hers. Perhaps if she
had struggled, perhaps if her protest had
continued, it would have stopped at a careless brush of lips. But as their mouths met,
Foxy froze. It seemed her heart stopped
pumping, her lungs stopped drawing and
releasing air, her pulse stopped beating as
her blood lay still. Then, in a sudden wild
fury, her blood began to swim again.

Who deepened the kiss first she would never know. It seemed instantaneous. Hot and hungry, their mouths took from each other in a moist, depthless, endless kiss. The muffled groan that touched the air might have come from either of them or both. Her breasts were soft and yielding against his chest as she used tongue and teeth and lips to take the kiss still deeper. He explored all the intimate recesses of her mouth while she wallowed in his flavor, his scent, in the feel of his skin against hers. His hand moved once in a long, bruising stroke down her back and waist and over her hip and thigh. The thin material of her dress was little more than air between them. At the rough caress, Foxy strained closer, nipping his lip to provoke more heat. His answer was to crush her mouth savagely, desperately, until her senses tangled into ecstatic confusion. With a quiet sound of pleasure, she went limp in his arms. Their lips clung for an instant longer as he drew her away.

Her eyes seemed as gray as his as they watched each other in silence. Her arms were still locked around his neck. Foxy could no longer smell the flowers but only his warm, male aroma, she could no longer hear the laughter of the party for the quiet sound of his breathing, she could no longer feel the breeze, but only the spreading heat of his hands. Only he existed. An owl swooped from the tree behind them and hooted three times. Instantly the spell was shattered. Foxy shuddered, swallowed, and struggled to her feet.

"You shouldn't have done that." As tingles continued to race along her skin she avoided his eyes and brushed distractedly at the skirt of her dress.

"No? Why not?" Lance's voice was as calm as a shrug. "You're a big girl now." He stood, and she was forced to tilt her head to see his face. "You enjoyed that as much as I did. It's a little late to play the flustered maiden."

"I'm not playing the flustered maiden," Foxy denied hotly as her eyes shot back to his. "Whether I enjoyed it or not is beside the point." Realizing she was fitting his description precisely, she tossed her hair behind her back in annoyance. She planned to make a dignified exit as she stepped from the glider, but Lance stopped her with a hand on her arm before she had taken two steps across the grass.

"What is the point, Fox?" He no longer sounded amused or calm but irritated.

"The point is," she said between her

teeth, "don't do it again."

"Orders?" he murmured softly. "I don't take orders very well."

"I'm not asking for a ham on rye," she countered. "I was off guard." Foxy tried to reason out her response to him while justifying it. "And — and tired and perhaps a bit curious. I overreacted."

"Curious?" His laugh was male and again amused. "Did I satisfy your curiosity, Foxy? Maybe like Alice, you'll find it 'curiouser and curiouser.'" He trailed his fingers lightly up her arm. Foxy shied away as her skin trembled.

"You're impossible!" She pushed the hair from her face in impatient fury. "You've always been impossible." With this, she whirled and ran toward the safety of the party. Lance watched her dress float and swirl around her.

Chapter Three

The Indianapolis 500 is an event that transforms Indianapolis from an ordinary midwestern city into the focus of the racing world. More people watch this one race than any other single sporting event in the country. It is for car racing what Wimbledon is for tennis, what the Kentucky Derby is for horse racing, what the World Series is for baseball — prestige, honor, excitement.

Foxy was relieved that the sky was empty of clouds. There was not even the smallest wisp to hint of rain. The mixture of rain and racing always made her uneasy. A breeze teased the ends of the ribbon that held her hair in a ponytail. Her jeans were old friends, nearly white with wear at the knees and snug at the hips. A baseball-style shirt in red and white pinstripes was tucked neatly into the waist. Around her neck hung the secondhand Nikon she had purchased while in college. Foxy would not have traded it for a chest of gold. From her vantage point in the pits, she could see that the grandstands were empty. Reporters, television crews, drivers, mechanics all milled about attending to business or drinking coffee from foam cups. The air was quiet enough to allow an occasional bird song to carry, but it was not calm. A current ran through the air, stirring up waves of tension and excitement. In less than two hours, the stands and infield would be swarming with people. When the green flag was waved, Indianapolis Motor Speedway would hold four hundred thousand people, a number that rivaled the population of some American cities. The noise would explode like one long roar of thunder.

During the hours that followed, there would be a continuous drone of engines. The pits would grow steamy with heat and thick with the smell of fuel and sweat. Eyes would be glued to the small, low-slung cars as they tore around the two-and-a-half-mile oval. Some would think only of the thrill of the race.

Foxy's feelings were more complicated. It had been two years since she had stood near a racetrack and six since she had been a part of the racing world. But it was, she discovered as she stared around her, like

49

yesterday. The feelings, the emotions inside her, had not been altered by her absence. There was anticipation, excitement. She was almost light-headed with it, and she knew it would grow only more intense after the race began. There was a wonder and pride at knowing her brother's skill, a talent which seemed more innate than learned. But underlying all was a deep-rooted fear, a terror so rich and sharp, it never dulled with the years. All the sensations scrambled inside of her, and she knew when the green flag was waved, they would all merge together into one heady, indescribable emotion. Nothing had changed.

Foxy knew the ropes. There were some drivers who would grant interviews and speak cheerfully, casually, about the race to come. Others would be technical or abstract, some belligerent. She knew Kirk would grant early interviews, answering questions with his patented brand of appealing arrogance. To Kirk each race was the same and each race was unique. It was the same because he drove each to win, unique because each race presented problems unlike any before or after. Foxy knew after the interviews that he would disappear and remain alone until it was time to be strapped into the cockpit. From long experience, she knew how to be unobtrusive. She moved among drivers and timers and mechanics and the dozens of other photographers, letting her camera record the prerace routine.

"What are you poking around here with that thing for?"

Foxy recognized the grumble but finished her shot before turning. "Hiya, Charlie." With a grin, she tossed her arms around his neck and nuzzled his grizzled cheek. She knew he would protest and grumble as well as she knew the hug pleased him.

"Just like a female," he muttered, but Foxy felt the slight squeeze of his hands on her back before he pulled away.

For the next few minutes, they studied each other openly. She saw little change. There was a bit more gray in his beard, a bit less hair on his head, but his eyes were the same clear blue she had first seen ten years before. He had been fifty then, and she had thought him ancient. As Lance Matthews' chief mechanic, Charlie Dunning had ruled the pits like a despot. He continued to do so now as the head of Kirk's team.

"Still skinny," he said in disgust. "I

should've known a few years wouldn't put any weight on you. Don't you make enough money to eat by taking pictures?"

"No one's been leaving chocolate bars lying around for me lately." She pinched his cheek as she spoke, knowing he would suffer torture and death before admitting he had planted chocolate bars for a skinny kid to find. "I missed you at Kirk's party the other night," she added as he shuffled and grumbled.

"I don't go to kids' parties. So you and the fancy lady are going to take in the Indy and the rest of the Grand Prix races this season." He sniffled and set his mouth in a disapproving line.

"If you mean Pam, then yes, we are." Foxy decided Charlie had nearly perfected irascibility. "And she's a journalist."

"You just mind that neither of you gets in the way."

"Yes, Charlie," Foxy said demurely, but his eyes narrowed at the gleam in hers.

"Still sassy, too. If you hadn't been so puny, I'd have taken a strap to you years ago."

Grinning, Foxy lifted the camera and shot a full-faced picture. "Smile," she suggested.

"Sassy," Charlie repeated. As his lips

started to twitch he turned and lumbered away.

Foxy watched until he had disappeared into the crowd before she turned around. She gave a small gasp as she bumped into Lance. He rested his hands briefly on her shoulders as his eyes locked with hers. She had managed to completely block out the interlude on the glider, but now it all came flooding back in full force. The mouth, which had been hungry on hers, twitched in a half smile.

"He always did have a soft spot for you."

Foxy had forgotten everything but the dark gray eyes that watched her. As his smile grew, touched now with arrogance, she jerked out of his hold. He was dressed in much the same manner as herself, in jeans and a T-shirt. His hair danced on his forehead as the breeze caught it. Mentally she cursed him for being so wickedly attractive.

"Hello, Lance." Her voice was marginally friendly with overtones of aloofness. Foxy was pleased with it. "No reporters dogging your footsteps?"

"Hello, Foxy," he returned equally. "Taking a few snapshots?"

"Touché," Foxy muttered. Turning away, she lifted the Nikon to her face and became absorbed in setting the aperture. She thought she must have gained an extra sense where Lance Matthews was concerned. His presence could be felt on the surface of her skin. It was both uncomfortable and arousing.

"Looking forward to the race, Foxy, or has it lost its charm?" As he spoke Lance tangled his fingers in the thick softness of her ponytail. Foxy wasted four shots.

"I heard Kirk won the pole position in the time trials. He knows how to cash in on that kind of advantage." When she turned back to him, her face was calm, her eyes cool. One kiss, she told herself, was nothing to be concerned about. They were still the same people. "I imagine as the owner, you're pleased." His smile was not the answer Foxy was looking for. "I've seen the car. It's very impressive." When he still did not reply, Foxy let out a frustrated breath and squinted up at him. "This conversation is fascinating, Lance, but I really must get back to work."

His hand curled firmly around her upper arm as she turned to go. He watched her in silence, and she was forced to toss up a hand to shield her eyes from the sun. "I'm having a small party tonight." His voice was quiet. "In my suite at the hotel."

"Oh?" Foxy employed the arched-brow look she had perfected in college.

"Seven o'clock. We'll have dinner."

"How small a party?" Foxy met his eyes steadily, though hers were shadowed by her hand.

"Very small, as in you and me."

"Smaller," she corrected evenly, "as in just you." Two mechanics, clad in the vivid red shirts of Kirk's team, moved past them. Lance's gaze never wandered from hers. "I have a date with Scott Newman."

"Break it."

"No."

"Afraid?" he taunted, bringing her an inch closer with a slight movement of his hand.

"No, I'm not afraid," Foxy retorted. The green in her eyes shimmered against the gray in his. "But I'm not stupid either. Maybe you've forgotten, I'm not a newcomer where you're concerned. I've already seen your string of — ah — ladies," she said with a dash of scorn. "It was quite a boost to my education, watching you pick and shuffle and discard. I do my own picking," she added, growing angrier as he remained silent. "And I do my own discarding. Go find someone else to feed your voracious ego."

Abruptly Lance smiled. His voice was light and amused. "You still have a vile temper, Foxy. You've also got a bright, inquiring mind and energy in every cell. You'll outdistance Newman in an hour, and he'll bore you to distraction."

"That's my problem," Foxy snapped, then remembered to jerk her arm free.

"That it is," Lance agreed cheerfully. He deprived her of having the last word by walking away.

Infuriated, Foxy whirled around, prepared to stomp off in the opposite direction. With a small shock, she saw that the grandstands were filling with people. Time was moving quickly. Annoyed, she swiftly walked down into the pit area.

As she interviewed a rookie driver, Pam watched the entire scene between Lance and Foxy. It wasn't possible for her to hear what passed between them, but she had clearly seen the variety of emotions take possession of Foxy's face. She watched them with the objectivity and curiosity peculiar to her trade. There was something physical between them, she had only to see them together to be certain. She was certain, too, that Foxy was kicking out against it like an ill-tempered mule and that she had come out second best in the battle that had just taken place.

Pam had liked Lance Matthews immediately. She was prone to judge people quickly, then calculate the most direct and productive approach to them. The consistent accuracy of her judgment had helped her climb to success in her profession. She had judged Lance Matthews as a man who did not so much shun convention as make his own. He would attract both men and women simply because he had so much to offer. He had strength and arrogance and a rich sensuality. Pam thought he would be indispensable as a friend and terrifying as a lover.

The rookie, blissfully unaware of her preoccupation, continued to answer her questions as she wound up the interview. With one eye cocked on Lance's back, Pam thanked him graciously, wished him luck, and hurried off.

"Mr. Matthews!"

Lance turned. He watched a small, delicate-faced blond dressed impeccably in gray slacks and a blazer running toward him. A tape recorder was slung over one shoulder, a purse over the other. Curious, he waited until she caught up with him. Pam paused and offered Lance a breathless smile.

"Mr. Matthews, I'm Pam Anderson." She held out a hand whose nails were polished a baby-pink. "I'm doing a series of articles on racing. Perhaps Foxy mentioned me."

"Hello." Lance held her hand a moment as he studied her. He had expected someone sturdier. "I suppose we missed each other at Kirk's party the other night."

"You were pointed out to me," Pam told him, deciding to use flat-out honesty as her approach. "But you disappeared before I could wrangle my way over to you. Foxy disappeared, too."

"You're very observant." Though the annoyance in his voice was only slight, Pam recognized it and was pleased. She knew she had his full attention.

"Our friendship is still at the apprentice stage, but I'm very fond of Foxy. I also know how to mind my own business." She brushed absently at her hair as the wind teased it into her eyes. "Professionally, I'm only interested in the race and any and all aspects thereof. I'm hoping you'll help me. Not only do you know what it's like to design and own a Formula One, you know what it's like to compete in one. You also know this track and the specifics of an Indy car. The fact that you're a well-known figure not only in racing circles but in society will add tremendous readability to the series."

Sometime during Pam's speech, Lance had stuck his hands in his pockets. He waited for a full ten seconds to see if she was finished before he started to chuckle. "A few minutes ago, I was trying to figure out how you could be the same Pam Anderson who wrote that blistering series on foul-ups in the penal system." He inclined his head in a gesture she took as a seal of approval. "Now I know. We'll have plenty of time to talk over the next few months." Pam watched his gaze shift and focus to where Foxy leaned against a fence and fiddled with lenses. She saw the birth of his patented smile. "Plenty of time." When his attention darted back to Pam, his grin widened and settled. "What do you know about the 500?"

"The first 500 was in 1911, and the winning car had an average speed of 74.59 miles per hour. The track was originally paved in brick, hence the nickname the Old Brickyard. It's a full-throttle race where a driver moves to high gear and stays there. It's not a Grand Prix race because no points are given, but there are many similarities between the Formula

One car and the Indy car. There are also a number of drivers who have competed in both the 500 and the Grand Prix circuit . . . like Kirk Fox. The cars here are fueled by alcohol. An alcohol fire is particularly dangerous because there's no flame."

"You've done your homework." Lance grinned at the computerlike flow of information.

"Oh, I have the facts," she agreed, liking the directness of his gaze. "But they don't tell the whole story. Forty-six people have died at this race, but only three in the last ten years. Why?"

"Cars are safer," Lance answered. "They used to be built like battleships, and in a crash they stayed solid and the driver absorbed all the power. Now it's the fragility of the cars that saves lives. Cars self-destruct around a driver, diffusing the power away from him. The restraint systems have been improved, and the drivers wear fire-resistant clothes from the shoes up." Sensing that the starting time was drawing near, Lance led her back toward the start-finish line.

"So racing has become fairly safe?" Pam asked. Her look was as candid as her voice was soft.

Again Lance gave her his full attention.

She was a very sharp lady. "I didn't say that. It's safer, but there will always be the element of risk. Without it, a race like the Indy would just be some cars going in a circle."

"But a crash doesn't bring the fear it once did?"

He grinned again and shook his head. "I doubt if many drivers think about crashing. If they did, they wouldn't get in a cockpit. It's never going to happen to you, always to someone else. When you do think about it, you accept it as part of the rules. A crash is never the worst fear in any case. It's fire. There isn't a driver alive who doesn't have a gut fear of fire."

"What about when you're driving and another driver crashes? What do you feel then?"

"You don't," he answered simply. "You can't. There isn't room in the cockpit for emotion."

"No." She nodded. "I can understand that. But there is one thing I don't understand. I don't understand why."

"Why?"

"Why do people strap themselves into a car and whirl around a circuit at earth-shattering speeds. Why do they risk injury or death? What's the motivation?"

Lance turned and frowned at the track. "It varies. I imagine there're as many motivations as there are drivers — the thrill, the competition, the challenge, the money, the prestige, the speed. Speed can be addicting. There's the need to prove your own capabilities, to test your own endurance. And, of course, there's the ego that goes with any sport." As he turned back to Pam he saw Kirk step out into the sunlight. "Drivers all have different degrees of need, but they all need to win."

Foxy moved around the car, crouching and snapping as Kirk was strapped into the cockpit. He pulled the balaclava over his head, and for the moments before he fixed the helmet over it, he looked like an Arthurian knight preparing to joust. He answered Charlie's questions with short words or moves of his head. Already, his concentration was consumed by the race. Beneath his helmet visor, his eyes were unfathomable, his expression neither relaxed nor tense. There was an air about him of being separate, not only from the people crowded around the car, but from himself. Foxy could sense his detachment, and her camera captured it. As she straightened she watched Lance walk over and bend close to her brother's head.

"I got a case of scotch says you won't break the track record."

She saw Kirk's imperceptible nod and knew he had accepted the challenge. He would thrive on it. From the opposite side of the car, Foxy studied Lance, realizing he knew Kirk better than she had imagined. His eyes lifted and met hers as the engine roared to life between them. As Kirk cruised onto the track to take his pole position Foxy disappeared inside the garage area.

As the last strands of "Back Home Again in Indiana" floated on the air, the crowd roared with approval at the release of the thousands of colored balloons. For miles, those who were not at the Motor Speedway would see the drifting orbs and know that the 500 was under way. The order was official, ringing out over the rumble of the crowd. "Gentlemen, start your engines." On the starting grid, tension revved as high as the engines.

The stands were a wave of color and noise as the cars began their pace lap. The speed seemed minimal. The cars themselves, low splashes of color and lettering, were in formation and well behaved. They shone clean and bright in the streaming light of the sun. No longer could bird songs be heard. Suddenly the pace car pulled away and sped off the track.

"This is it," Foxy murmured, and Pam jumped slightly.

"I thought I'd lost you." She pushed her sunglasses more firmly on her nose.

"You don't think I'd miss the start, do you?" There was a long sports lens on her camera now, and she had it trained on the track. "They'll get the green flag any second now." Pam noticed that she seemed a bit pale, but as she opened her mouth to comment, the air exploded with noise. With professional ease, Foxy drew a bead on the white flash of Kirk's racer.

"How can they do it?" Pam spoke to herself, but Foxy lowered her camera and turned to her. "How can they keep up that pace for five hundred miles?"

"To win," Foxy said simply.

The afternoon wore on. The noise never abated. The heat in the pits was layered with the smell of fuel, oil, and sweat. Out of a field of thirty, ten cars were already out of the running due to mechanical failure or minor crashes. A broken gearbox, a failed clutch, a split-second error in judgment brought the curtain down on hope. Pam had discarded her blazer, rolled up the sleeves of her white lawn blouse, and now stalked the pit area with her tape recorder. Trickles of dampness worked their way down Foxy's back. Her shirt clung to her skin, and her hair curled damply around her face. But there was another tickle between her shoulder blades, one that had her stiffening and turning away from the track. Lance stood directly behind her. He spoke first but looked beyond her. The track was a valley cupped inside the mountains of the grandstands.

"He's going into lap 85." He had a cold drink in his hand and held it out to her without shifting his gaze. Foxy took it and drank, though his thoughtfulness confused her. "Yes, I know. He's got nearly a full lap on Johnston. Have you timed his average speed?"

"Just over 190."

Foxy watched Kirk maneuver through a tight cluster of cars. She held her breath as he passed a racer in the short chute between turns three and four. She stared down into floating chunks of ice, then drank again. "You've set up a tremendous pit crew. I timed the last fuel stop at under twelve seconds. They've given Kirk an edge. And it's obvious the car's fast and handles magnificently."

Slowly Lance lowered his eyes and looked down at her. "We both know racing is a matter of teamwork."

"All but this part," Foxy countered. "Out there it's really up to Kirk, isn't it?"

"You've been standing a long time." The softness of Lance's voice brought Foxy's attention back to him. "Why don't you sit down for a while." He could nearly see the headache that was drumming inside her skull. Surprising them both, he lifted a hand to her cheek in a rare gesture of tenderness. "You look tired." He dropped his hand, then stuck it in his pocket.

"No, no, I can't." Foxy turned away, oddly moved by the lingering warmth on her cheek. "Not until it's over. You're going to lose that scotch, you know."

"I'm counting on it." He swore suddenly, causing her to turn back to him. "I don't like the way number 15 handles turn one. He gets closer to the wall every time."

"Fifteen?" Foxy narrowed her eyes as she searched the streaking stream of cars. "That's one of the rookies, isn't it? The kid from Long Beach."

"The *kid*'s a year older than you are," Lance muttered. "But he hasn't the experience to go that high in the groove. He's going to lose it."

Seconds later, number 15 approached turn one again, only to challenge the unforgiving wall too closely. Sparks flew as the rear wheels slammed into the solid force, then were sheared off and tossed into the air as the car began to spin out of control. Pieces of fiberglass began to spray the air as three cars swerved, maneuvering like snakes around the wounded racer. One nearly lost control, its wheels skidding wildly before gripping the asphalt. The yellow flag came down as number 15 flipped into the infield and lay still. Instantly it was surrounded by emergency crews and fire extinguishers.

As always when she witnessed a crash, a frozen calm descended over Foxy. She did not think or feel. From the instant the car connected with the wall, she had lifted her camera and recorded each step of the crash. Dispassionately she focused, set speed and depth of field. One of her shots would be a classic study of a car in distress. She felt only a shudder of relief when she saw the driver crawl from the wreckage and give the traditional wave to assure the crowd he was unharmed.

"My God. How can a man walk away from a wreck like that?" Foxy heard Pam's voice behind her but continued to shoot the routine of the emergency crew in the infield.

"As I told you before, the very fragility of the racer and the improved restraints have saved more than one life on the grid." Lance answered Pam but his attention was on Foxy. Her face was without color or expression as she lowered her camera.

"But not all of them," she stated as she caught the blur of Kirk's car as it whizzed by. "And not every time." She felt the cold passing as warmth seeped back under her skin. "You'd better go interview that driver. He'll be able to give you a firsthand report on what it's like to see your life pass before your eyes at two hundred miles an hour."

"Yes, I will." Pam gave her a searching look but said nothing more before she moved away.

Foxy pushed a stray hair from her face, allowing her camera to dangle by its strap. "I suppose number 15 will have more respect for turn one the next time."

"You're very professional and unflappable these days, aren't you, Fox?" Lance's eyes were cold as steel under his lowered brows. Foxy remembered the look and felt an inward tremor.

"Photographers have to have good nerves." She met his look of annoyance without flinching. She knew if annoyance turned to genuine anger, he could be brutal.

"But feelings aren't necessary," he countered. He gathered the strap of her camera in one hand and pulled her closer. "There was a man in number 15. You never missed a frame."

"What did you expect me to do?" she tossed back. "Get hysterical? Cover my eyes with my hands? I've seen crashes before. I've seen them when they haven't walked away, when there hasn't been anything to see but a sheet of fire. I've watched both you and Kirk being dragged out by the epaulettes. You want emotion?" Her voice rose in a sudden torrent of fury. "Go find someone who didn't grow up on the smell of death and gasoline!"

Lance studied her in silence. Color had shot back into her face. Her eyes were like a raging sea under a haze of clouds. "Tough lady, aren't you?" His tone was touched with amusement and scorn, a combination Foxy found intolerable.

"Damn right," she agreed and tossed her chin out further. "Now, take your hands off my camera."

At first, the only thing that moved was his left brow. It rose in an arch which might have indicated humor or acceptance.

In an exaggerated gesture, he lifted both hands, holding them aloft, empty palms toward her. Still, he did not back off, and they stood toe to toe. "Sorry, Fox." She knew him well enough to detect the dregs of temper in his voice. Her own anger forced her to ignore it.

"Just leave me alone," she ordered and started to brush by him. To her fury, he stepped neatly in her path and blocked her exit.

"I'll just be another minute," he told her. Before she had grasped his motive, Lance had shifted the camera to her back and pulled her into his arms.

As she opened her mouth to protest he closed his over it and plundered its depths. She was caught fast. Instead of pushing against him, her hands gripped desperately on his upper arms. They would not obey the command her brain shot out to them. Her mouth answered his even as she ordered it to be cold and still. The flame sparked and burned just as quickly, just as intensely, as it had the night on the glider. She could not deny that even if her mind and her heart were her own, her body was his. Never had she known such perfection in a touch, such intimacy, such hunger. She lifted her arms to lock them around his neck as her body melted into his. The whine of finely tuned engines whirled in her brain, then was lost in a flood of need and desire. The people who milled around them faded, then disappeared from her world as she strained closer. She demanded more of him even as she gave all of herself. Ultimately it was Lance who drew away. They were still tangled in each other's arms, their faces close, their bodies molded. With his quiet, probing intensity, he stared down at her.

"I suppose you'll tell me I shouldn't have done that."

"Would it make any difference if I did?" Her knees wanted badly to tremble, but Foxy forced them to be still.

"No," he answered. "It wouldn't."

"Will you let me go now?" Foxy was pleased at the cool, impersonal timbre of her voice. Inside her stomach dozens of bats were waging war.

"For now," he agreed. Though he loosened his grip, he kept his hands light on her hips. "I can always pick up where I left off."

"Your conceit is threatening to outweigh your arrogance these days, Lance." Firmly Foxy drew his hands from her hips. "I don't know which is more unappealing."

Lance grinned at the insult and tweaked her nose in a brotherly fashion. "You're cute when you're dignified, Foxy." His glance wandered over her head as he saw Kirk veer off the track and onto the pit lane. "Kirk's coming in. With any luck, the second half of the race will run as smoothly as the first."

Refusing to dignify any of his comments with an answer, Foxy dragged her camera back in front of her and walked away. Tucking his hands in his pockets, Lance rocked gently on his heels and watched her.

Only half of the starters finished the race. Foxy had known Kirk would win. She had studied his face during his brief, final pit stop and had seen the confidence mixed with the strain and tension. Cars no longer looked shiny in the sun but were dull with grime. After the checkered flag came down, Foxy watched Kirk take his victory lap as the roars of the crowd and the crew washed over her. She knew he would come into the pits ready for adulation. His eyes would no longer be opaque. His mouth would be lifted in that easy boyish grin, and all the lines of strain would have magically vanished. Tirelessly he would grant interviews, sign autographs, accept congratulations. The layers of sweat and grime that covered him were his badge of success. He would take it all in, recharging his system. Then it would be over for him, a thing of the past. In two days, they would be on their way to Monaco for the qualifying races. The Indianapolis 500 would be to Kirk no more than a newspaper clipping. For him, it was always the next race.

Chapter Four

Monte Carlo is cupped between the high, forested peaks of the Maritime Alps and the brilliant blue waters of the Mediterranean Sea. Buildings are packed together; a dense pattern of skyscrapers and elegant old homes. It has the feel and look, if not the size, of a great city while maintaining a fairy-tale aura.

It was the colors that appealed to Foxy. The whites and pastels which dominated the buildings, the rich, ripe greens and browns of the mountains, and the perfect blue of the sea. Lush flowers and palms added a taste of the exotic. It was a country of culture and castles, warm sea breezes, and barren peaks. The romantic in Foxy instantly fell in love with it.

With Kirk immersed in qualifying races and practice sessions and Pam involved with interviews and local color, Foxy often found herself thrown together with Scott Newman. She found him kind, considerate, intelligent, and — though she detested Lance for being right — dull. He planned too thoroughly, considered too carefully, and followed through too accurately for Foxy's taste. Each of their dates, no matter how casual, was given an itinerary. He dressed perfectly, even elegantly, and his manners were identical. With Scott, Foxy knew there would be no disasters, no dangers, no surprises. More than once, she felt a twinge of guilt, knowing her character would never be as untarnished as his. He was a knight on a white charger who rescued his quota of damsels in distress each day then polished his armor.

Restlessly Foxy wandered from window to window mulling over her analysis. There was a light staccato clicking from Pam's typewriter. She could see boats of all sizes and descriptions docked in the Bay of Monaco or moving out to sea. She recalled that during one of the qualifying races, a car had taken a turn badly and joined the boats in the water. Foxy turned from the window and watched Pam's fingers fly over the keys. The table where she worked was strewn with notes and paper and cassettes. There was a unique organization to it all, but only Pam had the solution.

"Are you going to the casino tonight?" Foxy asked. She felt restless and dissatisfied.

"Mmm, no . . . I want to finish this segment." Pam's rhythm never altered. "You going with Scott?"

Frowning, Foxy threw herself into a chair and draped her feet over the arm. "Yes, I suppose."

At the sulky tone, Pam sighed and stopped typing. Foxy's long mouth was pursed in a pout, and her brows were drawn together over moody eyes. Russet curls tumbled without design over her shoulders. All at once, Pam felt very old.

"All right." She propped her elbows on her table and laid her chin on her laced hands. "Tell Momma." Quite purposely, her tone was mild and patronizing. Foxy's chin shot out. Met with Pam's amused, affectionate smile, however, her defiance melted.

"I'm being an idiot," Foxy confessed with a self-deprecating laugh. "And I don't know why. I'm absolutely crazy about Monte Carlo. It has to be one of the most romantic, exotic, perfect spots in the universe. More, I'm getting paid to be here. I even have a terrific-looking man dancing attendance on me, and I'm . . ." She drew a deep breath and swept her arms in a huge circle.

"Bored," Pam supplied. She lifted her cup, sipped cold coffee, and grimaced. "You've been left almost entirely in Scott's company. Though he is nice, he isn't the most stimulating companion. Kirk's not available, I'm tied up, Lance is —"

"I don't need Lance's company," Foxy said too quickly. Her frown became more pronounced. Not having Lance Matthews to contend with was a blessing, not a problem.

Pam said nothing for a moment, recalling the tempestuous kiss she had seen them exchange at the Indianapolis Speedway. "In any case," she said carefully, "you've been deserted."

"Scott really is very nice." Somehow, Foxy felt the statement defended both Scott and herself. "And he's not pushy. I made it clear from the beginning that I wasn't interested in a serious relationship and he accepted it. He didn't argue." Foxy swung herself out of the chair and began to pace. "He hasn't tried to lure me into the bedroom, he doesn't lose his temper, he doesn't forget the time, he doesn't do anything outrageous." Foxy remembered that both times Lance had kissed her, it had been over her protests. "He makes me feel comfortable," she added tersely. She glared at Pam, daring her to comment.

"My fuzzy blue slippers do the same thing for me."

Foxy wanted badly to be angry, but a gurgle of laughter escaped. "That's terrible."

"You're not built to be satisfied with comfortable relationships." Pam twirled a pencil between her fingers and frowned at the eraser. "Like your brother, you thrive on challenges of one sort or another." Shaking off a quick moodiness, she lifted her eyes and smiled. "Now, Lance Matthews . . ."

"Oh no," Foxy interrupted, holding her hand up like a traffic cop. "Stop right there. I might not be looking for comfort, but I'm not looking for a bed of nails either."

"Just a thought," Pam said mildly. "I seriously doubt he would ever make you feel bored or comfortable."

"Comfortable boredom begins to sound more appealing," Foxy commented. "In fact," she added as she headed for the door, "I'm going to thoroughly enjoy myself tonight. In all probability I'll win a fortune at roulette. I'll buy you a hot dog out of my winnings at the race tomorrow." With a wink, she shut the door behind her.

Alone, Pam allowed her smile to dissolve. For the next few minutes, she stared down at the typewritten page in her machine. *Kirk Fox,* she decided, *is becoming a problem. Not that he has made even the slightest advance since his arrogant declaration the night of his party,* she mused. *He's been much too involved with the races to do any more than vaguely acknowledge my presence.* Pam ignored the annoyance the fact brought her and straightened a pile of blank typing paper. *And of course, he's had all those women hanging around him.* Pam sniffed and shrugged and went back to her typing. *With any luck,* she thought as she attacked the keys, *he'll be just as busy throughout the entire season.*

Feeling guilty over her discussion of Scott, Foxy dressed with special care for the evening. Her dress was a stretchy black jersey that clung to her curves and left her shoulders bare. The neckline was cut straight, secured with elastic just above the subtle swell of her breasts. She swept her hair off her neck into a chignon, letting loose tendrils fall over her brow and cheeks. With the addition of a thin silver chain around her neck and a quick spray of cologne, she felt ready for the elegance of the Monte Carlo casino.

Just as she was transferring the bare necessities into a small silver evening bag, the knock sounded on her door. With one quick glance around the hotel room, Foxy went to admit Scott. She found herself face-to-face with Lance Matthews.

"Oh," she said foolishly as she recalled her success in avoiding him since Indiana. Abruptly it occurred to her that she had never seen him in evening dress before. His suit was impeccably cut, fitting over his broad shoulders without a wrinkle. He looked different, if no less dangerous. He was, for a moment, a stranger: the Harvard graduate, the longtime resident of Beacon Hill, the heir to the Matthews fortune.

"Hello, Fox, going to let me in or do I have to stand out in the hall?" The tone, and the ironic lift of his mouth made him Lance again. Foxy straightened her shoulders.

"Sorry, Lance, I'm practically on my way out."

"Prompt as well as beautiful?" There was an amused light in his eyes. "The two rarely go together." He stepped forward and cupped her chin in his hand before she had time to start evasive action. "We'll have to have a cocktail before dinner. The reservation isn't until eight."

Foxy backed up, then noted with disgust that the action only brought Lance further into the room. "You'll have to run that by me again." She lifted a hand to the one on her chin but found it unbudgeable.

"We've nearly an hour before dinner," Lance stated simply. His eyes roamed her face with a hint of a smile. "Perhaps you've an idea how we might pass the time."

"You might try a few hands of solitaire," Foxy suggested evenly. "In your *own* room. Now, I'd like my face back."

"Would you?" Amusement was smooth and male in his tone. "Pity. I'm quite taken with it." With the barest of pressure, he brought her an inch closer as his gaze dropped and lingered on her mouth. "Newman sends his regrets," Lance said softly as his eyes moved back to hers. "Something — ah — came up. Do you have a wrap?"

"Came up?" Foxy repeated. She found no relief when her chin was released as his hands moved to her bare shoulders. She felt the temperature of the room rise ten degrees. "What are you talking about?"

"Newman discovered he didn't have the evening free after all. It's a pity to cover up such elegant shoulders, but the nights here can be cool in June." They were closer than they had been a moment before, but Foxy didn't know how he had contrived it. His hands were still light on her shoulders.

"What do you mean, didn't have the evening free?" she demanded. She started to back away but his hands tightened on her shoulders slightly but meaningfully. The mockery in his smile caused her temper to soar along with her heart rate. "What did you do? What did you say to him? He's much too polite to break a date without telling me himself. You intimidated him," she finished hotly, glaring into Lance's smile.

"I certainly hope so since that was my intention." He confessed to the crime so easily, Foxy could only splutter. "Fetch your wrap."

"My — my . . . I certainly will not!" she managed in a choked voice.

"Suit yourself." Lance shrugged and took her hand.

"If you think I'm going out with you," Foxy began as she tugged furiously at her hand, "you're not running on all your cylinders. I'm not going anywhere."

"Fine." Lance's hands spanned her waist. "I find the idea of staying here very appealing." Before she could move away, he lowered his mouth to the gentle incline between her neck and shoulder. Her skin trembled.

"No." Hearing the waver in her voice, Foxy fought to steady it. The room was already swaying. "You can't stay."

"Room service is excellent here," Lance murmured as he caught the lobe of her ear between his teeth. "You smell like the woods in spring, fresh and full of secrets."

"Lance, please." It was becoming very difficult to think as his mouth roamed over her skin, leaving a soft trail of quick kisses.

"Please what?" he whispered. Lightly he rubbed his lips over hers. His tongue teased the tip of hers before she could answer. Foxy could feel the quicksand sucking and pulling at her legs. Desperately she pushed away from him and filled her lungs with air.

"I'm starving," she said abruptly. She considered the statement a tactical retreat. Hoping to hide her vulnerability, she brushed casually at the curls that rested on her flushed cheeks. "Since you frightened off my escort, I suppose I should make you pay for my dinner. At a restaurant," she added hastily as he cocked a brow. "Then you'll have to take me to the casino as

Scott was going to do."

"My pleasure," Lance replied with a faint bow.

"And I," she said, feeling stronger with the distance between them, "shall take pains to lose as much of your money as possible." Lifting a thin silk shawl from the bed, Foxy tossed it over her shoulders and flounced from the room. She managed for nearly an hour to remain cool and aloof.

Moonlight spilled over the Bay of Monaco. A breeze that had been born far out to sea drifted easily into shore. It carried its own perfume. The terrace of the restaurant was canopied by stars and palm fronds. Music floated by the secluded table, but it was too soft for Foxy to distinguish any words. Only the melody flickered like the lights of the twin white candles on the tablecloth. Between these was a red rose in a slender vase. The murmur of other diners seemed more a backdrop than a reality. Foxy was finding it difficult to maintain an indifference to an ambience which called so strongly to her romantic soul. Above all else, she wanted Lance to see her as a mature sophisticated woman and not a silly child who melted at soft music and starlight. Still, she trod carefully with the iced champagne. So far she had managed to keep the conversation impersonal and safe.

"I noticed the car gave Kirk a bit of trouble yesterday." Foxy speared her steamed shrimp and dipped it absently in its sauce. "I hope it's been worked out."

"An engine ring; it's been replaced." As he spoke Lance watched her over the rim of his glass. There was a light in his eyes which had Foxy doubling her guard.

"It's amazing, isn't it? So often it's a tiny thing, a twenty-five-cent part or an overlooked screw that can be the deciding factor in a race where hundreds of thousands of dollars are at stake."

"Amazing," Lance agreed in a somber tone that was belied by his half smile.

"If you're going to laugh at me," Foxy said as her chin tilted, "I'll simply get up and leave."

"I'd just bring you back." With narrowed eyes, she studied Lance for a full minute. Her prolonged examination did not appear to disturb him as he kept his eyes steady on hers. His mouth was still curved in an annoying half smile.

"You would, too," Foxy conceded with grudging admiration. Chivalrousness was simply not one of Lance's qualities, and

Foxy knew that she had had enough of chivalrousness for a while. "And if I kicked up a scene that landed us both in a cell, you wouldn't be a bit bothered . . . not as long as you had your way." She sighed and shook her head, then took a sip of wine. "It's hard to gain an edge on a man who's so utterly nerveless. You drove that way. I remember." Her mouth moved in a pout as she looked back in time. "You drove with the same single-minded intensity as Kirk, but there was a smoothness he still lacks. You stalked; he charges. He's all fire and thrust, you were precise and ruthlessly steady. There was an incredible ease in your driving; you made it look simple, so effortless. But then you raced because you enjoyed it." Foxy twirled the stem of her glass between her fingers and watched the starlight play on the swirling wine.

Intrigued, Lance studied her with more care. "And Kirk doesn't?"

"Enjoy it?" Her surprise was evident in both her eyes and her voice. "He lives for it, and that's entirely different. Enjoyment comes much lower on the list." She tilted her head, and her eyes caught the flicker of the candles. "You didn't live for it or you couldn't have given it up at thirty. If Kirk lives to be a hundred, they'll have to carry him to the cockpit, but he'll still race."

"It appears you had more perception as a teenager than I gave you credit for." Lance waited until their steak Diane was served, then thoughtfully broke a roll in half. "You've always hated it, haven't you?"

Foxy met his eyes levelly. "Yes," she agreed and accepted the offered roll. "Always." Her silence grew pensive as she spread butter on the roll. "Lance, how did your family feel about your racing?"

"Embarrassed," he said immediately. Foxy was forced to laugh as she met his eyes again.

"And you enjoyed their embarrassment as much as you enjoyed racing."

"As I said" — he lifted his glass in toast — "you are perceptive."

"Families of drivers all seem to have different ways of dealing with racing. It's more difficult standing in the pits than driving on the grid, you know," she said softly, then sighed and deliberately shook off the mood. "I suppose now that you're in the business end of it, your family's no longer embarrassed." Foxy bit into the crusty roll. "It's more acceptable, though you hardly need the money."

"You took an oath to see that I do after tonight," he reminded her. "You'd better eat all of your steak. Losing money takes more energy than winning it."

Sending him a disdainful smirk, Foxy picked up her knife and fork.

The evening was still young when they entered the casino. Foxy found her indifferent veneer dissolving. The combination of elegance and excitement was too potent.

"Oh!" She took in the room with a long, sweeping glance and squeezed Lance's arm for emphasis. "It's fabulous."

Clothes in a kaleidoscope of hues and the glitter and gleam of jewels caught her eye. There was a hum of voices in a hodge-podge of languages accented by the quick precise French of the croupiers. There was a mix of other sounds: the click and clatter of the roulette balls jingling in the wheels, the soft scrape of wood on baize as markers were drawn in, the flutter and whoosh of cards being shuffled, the crackle of new money and the jangle of coin.

With a laugh, Lance tossed an arm around her shoulders. "Foxy, my love, your eyes are enormous and shockingly naive. Haven't you ever been to a den of iniquity before?"

"Stop teasing," she demanded, too impressed to be properly insulted. "It's so beautiful."

"Ah, but gambling's gambling, Fox, whether you do it in a plush chair with a glass of champagne or in a garage with a bottle of beer."

"You should know." Tilting her head, she shifted her eyes to his and smiled. "I remember the poker games. You would never let me play."

"You were a very precocious brat." He slid his hand up her neck and squeezed.

"You were just afraid that I'd beat you."

His grin was quick and powerful. Guiltily Foxy admitted that she was glad to be there with him instead of with Scott. Lance Matthews exuded an excitement Scott Newman would not even understand.

"What big eyes you have," Lance murmured as his fingers lingered on her skin. "What goes on behind them, Foxy?"

"I was thinking how furious I should be with you because of the maneuvering you did with Scott, and how guilty I am that I'm not."

He laughed, then gave her a hard, brief kiss. "Too guilty to enjoy yourself?"

"No," she said immediately, then shrugged. "I suppose I'm basically selfish and not very nice."

Lance's mouth twisted into a grin. "Then we should suit each other well enough." He laced his fingers with hers, then led her to a roulette table.

Seated, Foxy moved her attention instantly to the wheel as the tiny silver ball bounced and jumped. When it stilled, she watched the croupier scoop in the losing markers and add them to those of the winners. Foxy thought the table a Tower of Babel. As she glanced from face to face she heard lilting Italian, precise London-style English, low, guttural German, and other languages that she could not distinguish. Faces were varied as well; some old, some young, some bored, some animated, many carrying the unmistakable polish of wealth. But it was the face directly across from her that fascinated her.

The older woman was beautiful. Her hair was like white silk swept around a fine-boned oval face. The lines in her skin were far too much a part of it to detract from the beauty. Rather, they matured and gave character to what had once been a delicate elegance. Her eyes were like sharp green emeralds, but it was diamonds she wore at her throat and ears. They seemed more fire than ice. She wore flaming red silk with absolute confidence. Foxy watched in fascination as she lifted a long, slender black cigarette and drew gently.

"Countess Francesca de Avalon of Venice," Lance whispered in Foxy's ear as he followed her gaze. "Exceptional, isn't she?"

"Fabulous." Turning to Lance, Foxy was vaguely surprised to see him offer her a glass of champagne. As the stem passed from his fingers to hers she noticed the tidy pile of markers in front of her. "Oh, are these the chips?" Tracing a fingernail down the edges, she looked back at Lance. "How much do you bet at a time?"

He shrugged and cupped his hands around the end of his cigarette as he lit it. "I'm just along for the ride."

With a laugh, Foxy shook her head. "I have a hard enough time with plain francs, Lance. I don't even know how much these little things are worth."

"An evening's entertainment," he said easily and lifted his glass.

Sighing, Foxy chose five chips and unwittingly bet five thousand francs on black. "I don't suppose I should lose all your money at once," she said confidentially.

"That's generous of you." Repressing a smile, Lance settled back and watched the wheel spin.

"Vingt-sept, noir."

"Oh!" Foxy said, surprised then pleased. "We've won." Looking up, she caught the blatant amusement on Lance's face. His eyes, she realized, were more silver than gray. "You needn't look so smug." She shook off her preoccupation and sipped the effervescent wine. "That was just beginner's luck. Besides" — she gave him a wicked grin — "it'll hurt more if I win a bit first." Her gaze shifted to the two stacks of five markers on black, but as she started to reach for them, Lance laid a hand on her arm.

"He's started the wheel, Fox. You've let it ride." Her face was so completely horrified, Lance dissolved into laughter.

"Oh, but I didn't mean . . . that must be over a hundred dollars." A glance at the spinning wheel made her giddy, and she swallowed more wine.

"Must be," Lance agreed gravely.

Foxy watched the ball bounce its capricious way around the wheel. She felt a mixture of fear, guilt, and excitement as the wheel began to slow.

"Cinq, noir."

She closed her eyes on a shudder of relief. Remembering herself, she quickly drew the four stacks of five in front of her.

As Lance chuckled she turned and gave him a haughty glare. "It would have served you right if I *had* lost."

"Quite right." Lance signaled for more champagne. "Why don't you bet on one of the columns, Foxy," he suggested as he tapped the ash of his cigar into an ashtray. "You've got to take more than a fifty-fifty chance in life."

She grinned and tossed her head. "Your loss," she announced as she impulsively pushed five chips to the head of column one.

It was, as it turned out, his gain. With uncanny consistency, the stack of markers in front of Foxy grew. Once, she unknowingly lost twenty thousand francs, then cheerfully gained it back on the following spin. Perhaps it was her complete ignorance of the amounts she wagered, or her random betting pattern, or simply the generosity of Lady Luck, but she won, spin after spin after spin. And she found winning was much to her taste. It was a heady experience that left her nearly as giddy as the seemingly bottomless glass of champagne at her side. Lance sat calmly back and watched the flow and ebb and flow of her winnings. He enjoyed the way she used her eyes to speak to him, letting them widen and glisten on a win or roll and dance on a loss. Her laugh reminded him of the warm mists on Boston's Back Bay. Her pleasure in winning was engagingly simple, her nonchalance in losing charmingly innocent. She was a child and woman at perfect balance.

"Are you sure you wouldn't like to bet some of this?" Foxy asked generously, indicating the stacks of markers.

"You're doing fine." Lance twirled a stray curl of russet around his finger.

"That, young man, is a gross understatement."

Foxy twisted her head quickly and looked into sharp emerald eyes. The Countess de Avalon stood behind her, leaning on a smooth, ivory-handled cane. It shocked Foxy momentarily to see that she was so tiny, no more than five feet. Imperiously she waved Lance to sit as he started to get to his feet. Her English was quick and precise, with only a trace of accent. "You have won resoundingly, signorina, and cleverly."

"Resoundingly, Countess," Foxy returned with a wide smile, "but accidentally rather than cleverly. I came determined to lose."

"Perhaps I will change my strategy and

come determined to lose," the countess commented. "Then I, too, might have such an accident." She gave Lance a slow, thorough, and entirely feminine appraisal. Foxy felt a tickle of jealousy and was completely astounded by it. "You appear to know me; might I return the pleasure?"

"Countess de Avalon." Lance gently inclined his head. "Cynthia Fox." Foxy took the extended hand in hers and found it small and fragile. But the quick study the green eyes made of her was full of power.

"You are very lovely," the countess said at length, "very strong." She smiled, showing perfect white teeth. "But even ten years ago, I would have lured him away from you. Never trust a woman of experience." Dismissing Foxy with a mere shifting of the eyes, the countess gave her attention to Lance. "And who are you?"

"Lance Matthews, Countess." He brought the offered hand to his lips with perfect charm. "It's an honor to meet you."

"Matthews," she murmured, and her eyes narrowed. "Of course, I should have seen from the eyes, the 'devil-take-it' look. I knew your grandfather quite well." She laughed. It was a young, sultry sound. "Quite well. You've the look of him, Lancelot Matthews . . . you're named for him. Very appropriate."

"Thank you, Countess." Lance's smile warmed. "He was one of my favorite people."

"And mine. I saw your Aunt Phoebe in Martinique two years ago. A singularly boring woman."

"Yes, Countess." The smile became grim. "I'm afraid so."

With a regal sniff, the countess turned to a fascinated Foxy. "Never relax for a moment with this one," she advised. "He is every bit the rake his grandfather was." She laid her hand briefly on Foxy's, and squeezed. "How I envy you." She turned and walked away in a flash of red silk.

"What a magnificent woman," Foxy murmured. Turning back to Lance, she gave him a wistful smile. "Do you suppose your grandfather was in love with her?"

"Yes." With a gesture of his finger, Lance signaled the croupier to cash in his markers. "He had a blistering affair with her, which the family continues to pretend never happened. It was also complicated because they were both married. He wanted her to leave her husband and live with him in the south of France."

"How do you know so much about it?"

Intrigued, Foxy made no objection when he drew her to her feet.

"He told me." Lance set her shawl around her shoulders. "He told me once he'd never loved anyone else. He was over seventy when he died, and he would still have left everything to live with her if she had permitted it."

Foxy walked slowly through the casino with Lance unaware of how many pairs of eyes watched them; a russet-haired beauty and the man with the dark, brooding attraction. "It sounds so wonderfully sad," she said after a moment. "But I suppose it was dreadful for your grandmother, knowing he loved someone else all those years."

"My dear, innocent Fox," Lance said dryly. "My grandmother is a Winslow of Boston. She was quite content with the Matthews merger, their two offspring, and her bridge club. Love is untidy and plebeian."

"You're making that up."

"As you like," he said easily.

"Let's not take a cab," she said as they stepped outside. She tossed her head back to the stars. "It's so beautiful." Smiling into his eyes, she tucked her hand in his arm. "Let's walk, it isn't far."

They ignored the light stream of traffic and walked under the warm glow of street lamps. Champagne spun pleasantly in Foxy's head and lifted her feet just an inch from the sidewalk. The countess's warning was forgotten, and she was completely relaxed. The walk under the slice of moon and smattering of stars seemed to occur in a timeless realm, full of the scents and mysteries of night.

"Do you know," Foxy began and spun away from him, "I love palm trees." Giggling, she rested her back against one and smiled at Lance. "I always wanted one when I was little, but they don't do well in Indiana. I had to settle for a pine."

Moving closer, he brushed curls from cheeks flushed with wine and excitement. "I had no idea you were so interested in horticulture."

"I have my secrets." Swirling out of reach, she leaned over a sea wall. "I wanted to be a skin diver when I was eight," she told him as she peered out into the dark sea. "Or a heart surgeon, I could never make up my mind. What do you want to be when you grow up, Lance?" She turned back to him, and the wind caught and pulled at her free curls. Her eyes were speared with laughter.

"Starting pitcher for the Red Sox." His eyes dropped to the elegant curve of her neck as she threw back her head and laughed.

"I bet you've got a whole bagful of pitches." She sighed with the pleasure of laughter. "You never told me how much I won in there."

"Hmm?" Lost in the flicker of moonlight in her hair, he listened with half an ear.

"How much did I win in the casino?" she repeated, pushing dancing curls from her face.

"Oh." He shrugged. "Fifty, fifty-five thousand francs."

"What?" The one syllable was half laugh, half choke. "Fifty-five *thousand?* That's — that's more than ten thousand dollars!"

"At the current rate of exchange," Lance agreed carelessly.

"Oh, good grief!" Her hands flew up to cover her mouth as her eyes grew impossibly wide. "Lance, I might have lost!"

"You did remarkably well." Amusement was back in his eyes and in his voice. "Or remarkably poorly considering your desire to lose."

"I had no idea I was gambling with that kind of money; I never would have tossed it around that way. Why . . . you're crazy!"

Helplessly she began to laugh. "You're a lunatic. Certifiable." She dropped her head to his shoulder as her laughter floated warmly on the quiet night. When he brought his arms around her, she made no protest. "I might have lost, you know," she managed between giggles. "And I might easily have fainted cold if I'd have found out how much those chips were worth while the wheel was still spinning." Taking a deep breath, she lifted her brilliant eyes to his. "Now, it seems I've added to your already disgusting fortune."

"The winnings are rightfully yours," he corrected, but Foxy stepped back horrified.

"Oh no, it was your money. In any case . . ." She paused, distracted, and plucked a daisy from a clump of grass at the foot of the sea wall. The champagne was still flowing. "In any case," she repeated as she tucked the flower in her hair. "You wouldn't have expected me to make up your losses." With this logic, she began to walk again, holding out a hand for his. "Of course," she began on a new thought, moving away before Lance could take her hand. "You could buy me something extravagant." She whirled back to him with a smile. "That would be perfectly above-board, I believe."

"Is there anything particular you have in mind?"

Her footsteps clicked on the sidewalk as she continued to circle away from him. "Oh, perhaps a pack of Russian wolf-hounds." Her laughter drifted. "Or a line of those marvelous horses with the sturdy legs . . . Clydesdales. Or a flock of Albanian goats. I'm almost certain they have goats in Albania."

"Wouldn't you rather have a sable?"

"Oh no," she answered. She wrinkled her nose and, either by accident or design, moved just out of his reach. "I don't care much for dead animals. I know! A pair of black Angus so I can start my own herd." The decision made, she stopped. Lance slipped his arms around her. "You will be sure to get one male and one female, won't you? It's very important if you want things to move along properly."

"Of course," he agreed as his lips traced her jawline.

"I shouldn't tell you this." Foxy sighed as her arms encircled his neck. "I'm terribly glad you intimidated Scott."

"Are you?" Lance murmured, gently nipping at the pulse in her throat.

"Oh yes," she whispered and drew him

ALHAMBRA PUBLIC LIBRARY
ALHAMBRA, CALIFORNIA

closer. "And I'd very much like it if you'd kiss me now. Right now." The last word was muffled as their lips found each other.

They seemed to fuse together in one instant of blinding heat. The instant was an eternity. She tangled her fingers in his hair as if she could bring him yet closer when now even the breeze from the sea could not come between them. Her body had molded to his as if it had no other purpose. She could feel his heart beat at the same speeding rhythm as her own. Unnoticed, her shawl slipped to the ground as he explored the smooth skin of her back. Together, they began to taste more of each other. His lips tarried on her throat, lingering and savoring the sweetness before moving to trace her cheekbone and whisper over her closed lids.

She discovered a dark, male flavor along the column of his neck. She wanted to go on tasting, go on learning, but his mouth demanded that hers return to his. The power of the new kiss pierced her like a spear of lightning, shooting a trembling heat through her every cell. With a moan, she swayed against him. Lance plundered her surrendering mouth, drawing more and more from her until she was limp in his arms. When his lips parted from hers, she murmured his name and rested her head on his shoulder.

"I don't know if it's you or the champagne, but my head's spinning." Foxy shivered once, then snuggled closer. Lance moved his hand to the base of her neck and tilted her face back to his. Her eyes were dark and heavy, her cheeks flushed, her mouth soft and swollen from his.

"Does it matter?" His voice was rough as he tightened his grip to bring her closer. She did not resist, but stepped back into the fire. "Isn't it enough to know that I want you tonight?" he murmured against her ear before his tongue and teeth began to fill her senses again.

"I don't know. I can't think." Drawing away, Foxy took two steps back and shook her head. "Something happens to me when you kiss me. I lose control."

"If you're telling me that so I'll play fair, Foxy, you've miscalculated." In one quick motion, he closed the distance between them. "I play to win."

"I know," she replied and lifted a hand to his cheek. "I know that very well." Turning, she walked back to the sea wall and breathed deeply to clear her head. She leaned back and lifted her face to the moon. "I always admired your unswerving determination to come out on top." She lowered her face to look at him, but his was still shadowed by the palm. "I loved you quite desperately when I was fourteen."

He didn't speak for a moment but bent and picked up her wrap. "Did you?" he murmured as he stepped from the shadows.

Moonlight fluttered over her as she tossed windblown curls from her eyes. "Oh yes." Relaxed, Foxy continued with champagne-induced honesty. "It was a wonderfully painful crush, my very first. You were quite impressive and I was quite romantic." Lance was beside her now, and Foxy turned her head to smile at him. "You always looked so indestructible, and very often you brooded."

"Did I?" He answered her smile as he lay the wrap over her shoulders.

"Oh yes. You had this single-minded intensity about you . . . you still do a great deal of the time. It's terribly attractive, but it was more pronounced when you were racing. Then, there were your hands."

"My hands?" he repeated and paused in the act of reaching in his pocket for his lighter.

"Yes." Foxy surprised him by taking both his hands in hers and studying them. "They're quite the most beautiful hands

I've ever seen. Very lean, very strong, very elegant. I always thought you should've been an artist or a musician. Sometimes I'd pretend you were. I'd set you up in a drafty old garret where I'd take care of you." She released his hands and pulled absently at her wrap as it slipped off her shoulders. "I wanted badly to take care of someone. I suppose I should've had a dog." She laughed lightly but was too involved with her memories to notice that Lance did not laugh with her. "I was snarling jealous of all those women you had. They were always beautiful. I remember Tracy McNeil especially. You probably don't remember her at all."

"No." Lance flicked on his lighter and frowned at the flame. "I don't."

"She had beautiful blond hair. It was clear down to her hips and straight as an arrow. I hated my hair as a child. It was all curly and unmanageable and such an awkward color. I was quite certain the only reason you kissed Tracy McNeil was because she had straight blond hair." The scent from Lance's cigar stung the air, and Foxy breathed it in. "It's amazing how naive I was for someone raised in a man's world. Anyway, I languished over you for the better part of a year. I imagine I was a

105

nuisance around the track, and you were very tolerant for the most part." A yawn escaped her as she grew sleepy in the sea air. "After I turned sixteen, I felt I was quite grown up and ready to be treated as a woman. The crush I'd had on you became very intense. I'd find every opportunity to be around you. Did you notice?"

"Yes." Lance blew out a thin stream of smoke, and it vanished instantly into the breeze. "I noticed."

Foxy gave a rueful laugh. "I thought I was being so clever in my pursuit. You were always so kind to me, I suppose that's why when you stopped being kind, it was all the more devastating. Do you remember that night? It was at Le Mans, the twenty-four-hour race," she went on before he could answer. "The night before the race I couldn't sleep so I walked down to the track. When I saw you going into the garage area, I was certain it was fate." With a sigh, Foxy absently fingered the flower in her hair. "I followed you in. My palms were sweating. I wanted you to notice me." Turning her head, Foxy met Lance's eyes with a gentle smile. "As a woman. A girl's right on the border at sixteen, and I wanted so desperately to get to the other side. And my feelings for you were very adult and very real, even though I had no idea how to handle them."

"I was very nonchalant when I came in, do you remember? 'Hello, how are you, couldn't you sleep?' You were wearing a black sweater; black always suited you. You were very remote, you'd been remote off and on for weeks. It only made you more romantic." With a soft, low laugh, she lifted her palm to his cheek. "Poor Lance. How uncomfortable my adulation must have made you."

"Uncomfortable is a mild word for what you were doing to me," he muttered. Turning away, he tossed his cigar over the wall and into the sea.

"I wanted to be sophisticated," she went on, not hearing the annoyance in his tone. "I had no idea how to make you want to kiss me. I tried to remember all the ploys I'd ever seen the heroine use in the movies. It was dark, we were alone. What next? The only thing I could come up with was to keep as close as possible. You were tinkering under the hood of the car, doing your best, I'm sure, to ignore me so that I'd go away and let you get on with it. There was just that one small light on, and the garage smelled of oil and gasoline. I thought it was as romantic as Manderley."

Foxy turned and grinned cheerfully while the wine made her remember. "Romance has always been my big weakness. Anyway, I was standing behind you, trying to think of what to do next, and I began to wonder what in the world you were doing to the car. I started to peek over your shoulder just as you turned around, and we collided. I remember you grabbed my arms to steady me, and my knees turned to water instantly. The physical part of it was incredible, probably because I'd never experienced it before. My heart started pounding, and my skin went hot then cold. It seemed as though I'd be swallowed up by your eyes, they'd gotten so dark, so intense. I thought: *This is it.* I was positive you were going to pull me into your arms and kiss me. I *knew* you were. We were Clark Gable and Vivien Leigh and the garage was Tara. Then you were shouting at me, absolutely livid that I was continually in your way. You swore magnificently, giving me a good shake before you pushed me away. You said some really dreadful things; the worst, to me, was that you called me an annoying child. Anything else, I could have passed off, but that crushed my pride and my ego and my fantasies with one blow. I never gave a thought to the tension you must have been under with the race the next day, or to the simple fact that I *was* in your way. I only thought about what you were saying to me and how it hurt. But I've always been a survivor. As soon as it began to hurt too badly, my defenses came up. When I turned and ran out of that garage, I didn't love you anymore, but I hated you almost as obsessively."

"You were better off," Lance murmured. After a moment, he twisted his head and ran a fingertip down her cheek. "Have you forgiven me?"

Foxy gave him an easy smile. "I suppose. It's been years, and since it cured me of being in love with you, I should be grateful." With another yawn, she rested her head against his shoulder.

"Yes, I suppose you should," he agreed softly. "Come on, I'll get you back before you fall asleep on the sidewalk."

Drowsy but willing, Foxy went with him as he slipped an arm around her waist.

Chapter Five

Monaco's Grand Prix is a classic example of a round-the-houses circuit. The course is short, just under two miles, and in the heart of a crowded civic complex. No part of the circuit is straight for more than a few feet, and among its eleven curves are two hairpins. One lap includes seventeen corners. The course is anything but flat; its ups and downs range from sea level to one hundred and thirty-two feet above. Its hazards include curbs, sea walls, a three-hundred-foot tunnel, utility poles, and, of course, the sparkling Mediterranean. For the driver, there is not a second's rest in the hundred laps. It is short, slow, and unlike any other Formula One course in the world. It stands as a great test of man and machine as its constant demands make it more fatiguing than longer, faster circuits. Here was a course that tested a car's reliability and a man's endurance. Still, it remains romantic and somehow mystical, like a yearly joust before the prince and princess.

Through quick maneuvering, Pam had managed to corner Kirk for an interview. There were just over two hours before race time, and the pits were crowded and noisy. Monaco's pits stood exposed to the course at the head of the small, picturesque harbor. Behind them, the water was crowded with yachts and sailboats. Pam found herself glancing around for Foxy. Though it annoyed her, she knew she would be more comfortable if she did not interview Kirk alone. Pushing this thought aside, she looked directly into his eyes. This type of contact was as essential to her style as her clean-lined, elegant clothes and her calm, unruffled manner. The sharp, probing, tenacious mind was well camouflaged by the fragility of her appearance.

"I've heard a lot of differing opinions on this course," she began, adding her professional smile. "Some, especially the carmakers I've spoken to, consider Monaco a drawing-room circuit. How do you feel about it?"

Kirk was leaning back against a wall, sipping from a foam cup. Thin wisps of smoke rose from it. His eyes squinted against the sun, and he looked completely at ease. Pam felt stiff and formal. It annoyed her that Kirk Fox always caused her to feel stiff and formal and somehow out of place.

"It's a race," he answered simply as he watched her over the rim of his cup. "It's not fast. It's rare a driver goes over a hundred and forty and usual to go less than thirty on the hairpins. But then, it's more a test of stamina and ability than speed."

"The driver's or the car's?" Pam countered.

His eyes crinkled deeper at the corners as he grinned. To her fascination, they seemed to grow greener. "Both. Two thousand or more gear changes in two and a half hours is a strain on a man and a machine. And there's the tunnel. You go from daylight to dim and back to daylight. Do your batteries ever run down?" he asked, taking the tape recorder which hung at her side.

"No," she returned coolly. If he was going to laugh at her, she wasn't going to give him the satisfaction of reacting. She cleared her throat and straightened her shoulders. "You had a crash here two years ago that totaled your car and broke your left shoulder. Will that experience affect your driving today?"

"Why should it?" Kirk countered, then drained his coffee. He was watching her with complete concentration, oblivious to the milling crowds in the pit area.

"Don't you worry about crashing again?" Pam insisted. As the frisky breeze tugged at her hair she tucked it behind her ear with a quick, impatient gesture. There was a tiny turquoise stone on the lobe. "Don't you ever consider that the next time you crash, you might be killed? Doesn't that come home to you, particularly when you pass over the part of the course where you crashed before?"

"No." Kirk crushed the cup between his fingers, then tossed it carelessly aside. "I never think about the next crash, only about the next race."

"Isn't that foolhardy?" Knowing her tone had become argumentative did not prevent her from continuing. She was irritated with him without having a clear reason why. Pam always conducted her interviews craftily, charmingly. Now she knew she had lost the reins but felt no impulse to reach for them again. "Or are you just smug? One instant of miscalculation, one insignificant mechanical flaw, can result in disaster, yet you don't think about it? You've had your share of crashes, been yanked out of wrecks, had your bones broken, and been laid up in hospitals. Tell me," she demanded, "what goes through your mind as you're roasting in the cockpit, hurtling around a track at two hundred miles an hour? What do you think of when they're strapping you into that machine?"

"Winning," Kirk answered without hesitation. The sharpness of her tone apparently bounced off the smooth nonchalance of his. His eyes roamed calmly over her face. The faint pink tint that temper gave her skin emphasized its flawlessness. He wondered how it would feel under his hand. The gold of her hair grew more vibrant as the sun washed over it. Pam watched the journey of his eyes and frowned. His eyes dropped to her lips.

"Is winning really all that important?"

Kirk's gaze shifted from her mouth to her eyes. "Sure. It's all there is."

It was clear from his tone that he was completely sincere. Helplessly Pam shook her head. "I've never known anyone like you." It was unlike her to lose her temper on the job, and she took a long breath to steady it. "Even here among all these other drivers, I haven't met anyone who thinks along the same straight, unswerving line you do. I suppose if you had the choice, you'd like to die on the track in a blaze of glory."

Kirk's grin was quick. "That would suit me, but I'd like to put it off about fifty years, and I'd prefer it to be *after* I'd crossed the finish line."

Pam's lips curved of their own accord. He was outrageous, she thought, but honest. "Are all race-car drivers as mad as you are?"

"Probably." Before she realized his intent, Kirk tangled his fingers in her hair. "I wondered if it was as soft as it looked. It is." The back of his hand brushed her cheek. "Like your skin." Pam's usual aplomb deserted her, leaving her silent and staring. "Your voice is soft, too, and very appealing. I like the way you always look as though you've stepped out of a bandbox. It gives me the urge to muss you up a bit." His voice was as insolent and amused as his grin.

Pam felt her cheeks grow warm and was infuriated. She had thought she had left blushing behind years before. "Is this a pass?" she asked in a scathing voice.

Kirk laughed, and she heard a trace of Foxy in the sound. "No, it's just an observation. When I make a pass, you won't have a chance to ask." Still grinning, he pulled her close and planted a long, hard kiss on her mouth. He thought she tasted like some rich, dangerous dessert and lingered over her longer than he had intended. When he released her, he felt the small whisper of air escape her lips as if she had held it there in surprise. "That," he said easily, "was a pass."

As he turned and sauntered away Pam lifted a finger to trace the place where his mustache had brushed her skin. *A crazy man*, she decided, unwilling to admit how deeply shaken she was. *A truly crazy man.*

Nearly two hours later, Foxy stood in almost the precise spot where her brother had been. Her mood was just short of grim. All too clearly, she remembered every detail from the evening before. The wine had not been kind enough to dull her memory.

I told *him to kiss me,* she thought on a wave of self-disgust. *I practically ordered him to. It wasn't bad enough that I went out with him when I should've known better, but I made certain he knew I was enjoying myself every minute. Blasted champagne!* Letting out her breath in a huff, she crammed the straw hat she wore further down on her head. *Then I babble on about the silly crush I had on him when I was a teenager. Oh boy, when I go out to humiliate myself, I don't do it by halves. All that business about being in love with him and fantasizing about him.* Closing her eyes, Foxy made a strangled sound in her throat. The breeze blew from the harbor, cooling her skin under her white gauze blouse. She set her teeth and lifted her camera as the parade lap began. *I wonder if it's possible to avoid him for the rest of the season? Better,* she added as she worked systematically, *for the rest of my life.*

As the drivers lined up for the green flag Foxy scurried for a new angle. In a moment, the air thundered with engines, and utilizing the motor drive, she shot each row of cars as the flag set the start. Crouched on one knee, she caught the low, fragile sleekness so unique to the Formula One racer. Her movements were calm and professional, absorbing her concentration, lending her an air of efficiency at odds with the sassy straw hat and thin, faded jeans. The lead car was already rounding the first curve before she rose. As she turned back toward the pits she collided with Lance. His hands came out to steady her, bringing her an uncomfortable sensation of déjà vu. Hastily Foxy disentangled herself from his hold, then made a business of adjusting her camera.

"I'm sorry, I didn't know you were behind me." Realizing she would have to meet his eyes sooner or later, she tossed her hair behind her shoulder and boldly lifted her chin. The amusement she had expected to see on his face was absent. There was no mockery in the dark gray depths of his eyes. She recognized the long, thorough study he was making and backed away from it. "You're looking at me as though I were an engine that wasn't responding properly." Frowning, Foxy busied herself by dragging sunglasses out of her camera case. She felt more at ease once they were in place. A shield was a shield, however slight.

"You might say I found a few surprises when I opened the hood."

Foxy was not certain how to take the quiet quality of his voice. His continued unblinking study was unnerving. She knew he was capable of watching her endlessly without speaking. He could be incredibly, almost unnaturally patient when he chose to be. Knowing she would be outmatched in this sort of contest, Foxy took the initiative. "Lance, I'd like to speak with you about last night." Her sophisticated demeanor was hampered by rising color. The roar of engines cut her off, and she turned away to watch the cars hurtle by. The pack was still thick after the first lap. Cheeks cool, Foxy took a deep breath and turned back to Lance. His eyes left the track to meet hers, but he said nothing. He was waiting, composed and contained. Foxy could have cheerfully strangled him. "I wasn't really myself last night, you see," she began again. "Wine . . . liquor has a tendency to go straight to my head, that's why I usually avoid it altogether. I don't want you to think, that is, I wouldn't want you to feel . . . I didn't mean to be so . . ." Frustrated, she jammed her hands into her pockets and shut her eyes. "Oh help," she muttered and turned away again. Lance remained silent as she squirmed and struggled. She wondered how it was possible to cast the line and be the fish at the same time.

That was brilliant, Foxy, she berated herself. *Why don't you try again, maybe you can top your own incoherency record. Get it out quick and stop stammering like an idiot.* Setting her chin, she turned to face him again, meeting his eyes straight on. "I didn't mean to give you the impression I would sleep with you." Once it was said, Foxy let out a hasty breath and plunged ahead. "I realize I might have given that impression last night, and I don't want you to misunderstand."

Lance waited nearly a full minute before he spoke, all the while watching Foxy steadily. "I don't believe I misunderstood anything." His comment was ambiguous and left her floundering.

"Yes, well . . . I know when you took me back to my room you didn't, well, you didn't . . ."

"Make love to you?" he supplied. In a quick move, he stripped off her sunglasses, leaving her eyes vulnerable. Even as she blinked against the change in light, he closed the slight distance between them. His hand came to her arm, warning her not to back away. "No, I didn't, though we're both perfectly aware that I could have. Let's say I had a whim to play by the rules last night." His smile spread lazily, packed with confidence, while his voice became low and intimate. "I don't need champagne to seduce you, Foxy." His mouth lowered to brush lightly over hers before she could move. It was a kiss that promised more.

Infuriated by his calm arrogance, incensed that her pulses had responded instantly, Foxy snatched the glasses back from him and jerked away. "Stuff your seductions." Her suggestion was drowned out by the noise of the second lap. Foxy threw an annoyed glare over her shoulder at the line of cars. Temper sparked in her eyes when she turned back to face Lance. "Just remember that last night was a lapse of intelligence on my part, that's all. And all that — that stuff I talked about . . ." To her greater fury, she felt her cheeks grow warmer. What had possessed her to confess that foolish crush? "All that business about that night in the garage was just as ridiculous as it sounded."

"How ridiculous was that?" Lance asked with an ease in direct contrast to Foxy's agitation. She barely resisted stomping her foot.

"I was sixteen years old and very naive. I'm sure it's not necessary to go into it any further."

"You're not sixteen anymore," Lance commented with a slight inclination of his head that reminded her of the elegant man of the evening before. "But you're still naive."

"I am not," she blurted out indignantly, then saw his brow lift and disappear under his fall of hair. Knowing her dignity was threadbare, she drew herself straight. "That's hardly relevant and strictly a matter of your own opinion." He smiled at that with quick charm, and Foxy hurried on. "I've got work to do, and I imagine you can find something to keep you busy for the next ninety-eight laps."

"Ninety-seven," Lance corrected as the leaders sped by. "Kirk's in third position," he noted absently before he looked back down at Foxy. "My opinion, Fox, might be to your advantage as it should induce me to continue playing by the rules for a while longer. It makes an interesting change." He grinned, a crooked, challenging half grin, and she was instantly wary. "There's no telling when I'll stop being a nice guy, though."

"Nice guy!" Foxy repeated and rolled her eyes at the thought.

Still grinning, Lance took the sunglasses from her and perched them back on her nose before walking away.

Over the next three months, Foxy used all her skill to avoid Lance Matthews. From Monaco to Holland to France to England to Germany, she made certain to stay out of his way. Whenever possible, she coupled herself with Pam. She felt if she was not alone, Lance would not find the opportunity to approach her for a personal conversation. Her pleasure with her success was slightly marred by the fact that he did not appear to be fretting for lack of personal conversations. Their schedule since Monaco had been tight. For the racing team there had been little time for anything but work and travel, meals and sleep. It was a hard, demanding circuit, packed with qualifying heats and practice runs and races. Away from the track, the hotels all began to seem the same. But each grid had a separate identity. Each was different, with its own problems, its own dangers.

With the end of summer came Italy and the Monza circuit. The grueling months in Europe had taught Foxy an important lesson. When the season was over, she would never follow the circuit again. Her days of moving from town to town, from pit area to pit area, were over. With each race her nerves had become more highly strung, her composure more difficult to maintain. It became apparent to her that the two years she had spent away from racing had left their mark. She could never be a part of it again. She knew if she ever came back to Italy, it would be to visit Rome or Venice, not Monza.

With night came utter silence. All during

the day, the track had vibrated with the practice runs. As Foxy sat alone in the deserted grandstands she thought she could hear ghost cars whiz past, feel their phantom breeze. Sixty years of speed. The sky was faultlessly clear with a white moon and gleaming blue stars. The musky scent of the forest drifted to her, almost crowding the air. Behind her came the quiet chirp of crickets and small insects. It was warm, without the burning heat of the long, sunfilled day. There were no harsh fumes, no screaming tires or thundering engines. It was a night for promises and secrets, a night for romance and soft words. With a sigh, Foxy closed her eyes on the thought of Lance. *More than anything else,* she realized wearily, *I need a little peace.*

A hand on her shoulder brought her quickly back to the present. "Oh, Kirk!" She placed a hand to her drumming heart and smiled up at him. "I didn't hear you."

"What are you doing out here all alone?"

"I wanted some quiet," she told him as he dropped down beside her. "There's too much going on back at the hotel. What are you doing here?"

He shrugged. "I like the track the night before a race." Carelessly he leaned back, then propped his feet on the seat in front of him. She saw he wore his old, reliable sneakers. "This is a fast track. We'll set a record tomorrow." He spoke with the absolute confidence of fact, not speculation.

"Did Charlie fix the exhaust problem?" Foxy studied his profile. Her mind was not on the car, not on the race, but on him. As in the past, she tried to draw on his confidence to soothe her own nerves.

"Yeah. Has Lance been bothering you?"

The question was so abrupt and so unexpected, Foxy took nearly a full minute to react. "What?" The one syllable was spoken with complete incredulity.

"You heard me." She heard the annoyance in Kirk's tone as he shifted in his seat to face her. His features were set and serious. "Is he bothering you?"

"Bothering me," Foxy repeated carefully. She ran the tip of her tongue between her teeth, then lifted her brows. "Maybe you should be more specific."

"Damn it, you know what I mean." Exasperated, Kirk rose and stared out at the track. His hands retreated into his pockets. Foxy could feel his discomfort and marveled at it. She understood Kirk well enough to know he rarely put himself into an uncomfortable position. "I've seen the way he's been looking at you," he muttered, and she heard the scowl in his voice. "If he's been doing more than looking, I want to know about it."

Though Foxy clasped both hands over her mouth, the giggle escaped. When Kirk whirled around, his face was a study in fury. Even in the dark, she could see his eyes glitter with temper. She pressed her lips together firmly, but her laughter burst out of its confines. She could only shake her head and struggle to compose herself as he glared at her.

"What the devil's so funny?" he demanded.

"Kirk, I . . ." She was forced to stop and cough, then take several deep breaths before she could trust herself to speak. "I'm sorry, I just didn't expect you to — to ask me something like that." She swallowed hard as another giggle threatened. "I'm twenty-three years old."

"What does that have to do with anything?" he tossed back, watching her eyes shine with good humored affection. He felt like a total fool and scowled more deeply.

"Kirk, when I was sixteen, you never paid a bit of attention to any of the boys who hung around the track, and now you're —"

"Lance isn't a boy." Kirk cut her off furiously, then ran a hand through his hair. The thick locks sprang back in precisely the same manner Foxy's did. "And you're not sixteen anymore."

"So I've been told," she murmured.

Letting out a frustrated breath, Kirk jammed his hands farther into his pockets. "I should've paid more attention to you when you were."

"Kirk." The humor left her voice as she rose to stand beside him. "It's nice of you to be concerned, but it's unnecessary." Touched both by his caring and his discomposure, Foxy laid her head on his shoulder. *What an odd man he is,* she thought, *with such unexpected scraps of sweetness.*

"It is necessary," he muttered, wishing he didn't feel obligated to pursue the matter. He was closer to Lance than to any other person in his life other than his sister. With Lance, there was the added bond of manhood and shared adventures. It was some of these adventures which prodded Kirk on when he wanted nothing more than to drop the entire subject. "You're still my sister," he added, half to himself. "Even if you have grown up a bit."

"A bit?" Foxy grinned again. A reckless mischief gleamed in her eyes, reminding

Kirk uncomfortably of himself. "Kirk, I passed 'a bit' at twenty."

"Look, Foxy," Kirk cut in impatiently. "I know Lance. I know how he . . ." He hesitated and swore.

"Operates?" Foxy supplied and earned a fierce glare. Her laughter was unavoidable, but she tempered it by kissing his cheek. "Stop worrying about me. I learned a little more than photography in college." When Kirk's expression failed to alter, she kissed his other cheek and continued. "If it makes you feel any better, Lance isn't bothering me. If he were, I could handle it quite nicely, I promise you, but he isn't. We hardly speak." She tried to be pleased by the statement, but found herself annoyed.

"He looks," Kirk mumbled. His sister's scent lifted on the faint breeze. Her hair had been soft and fragrant against his cheek. His frown deepened. "He looks a lot."

"You're imagining things," Foxy said firmly, then tried to draw Kirk away from the subject of Lance Matthews. She found speaking of him brought back disturbing memories. "Tell me, Mr. Fox," she began, mimicking the tone of a sports reporter, "are you always so introspective the night before a race?"

He did not answer at once, but simply stared out over the track. Foxy wondered what he saw there that she didn't. "It occurred to me recently that a woman's better off not getting involved with a man like me. She'll only get hurt." Restlessly he shifted, then turned to her. Foxy studied him curiously. There was something in his eyes she could not understand, and it puzzled her that he seemed tense. She sensed it was more than the race that was pulling at his nerves. "Lance is a lot like me," he continued. "I don't want you hurt. He could do that, maybe not meaning to, but he could do it."

"Kirk, I . . ."

"I know him, Foxy." He pushed away the beginnings of her objections and placed his hands on her shoulders. "No woman's ever been more important to him than cars. I don't think it's smart to get mixed up with men like us. There's always going to be another race, Foxy, another car, another track. It pushes everything and everyone else into the backseat. I don't want that for you. I know it's what you've always had. I've never done the things I should've done for you, and I . . ."

"No, Kirk." She stopped him by flinging her arms around his neck. "No, don't."

Foxy buried her face in his shoulder the same way she had years before in her hospital bed. He had been her rock when her world had crumbled away from its foundations. "You did everything you could."

"Did I?" Kirk sighed and hugged her tighter. "If I had it to do again, I know I'd do exactly the same things. But that doesn't make them right."

"It was right for us." She lifted her face to look at him with glistening eyes. "It was right for me."

Letting out a long breath, he tousled her hair. "Maybe." After cupping her face in his hands, he kissed both her cheeks. His mustache whispered along her skin causing her to smile at the old familiarity. "I never expected you to grow up, I guess. And I never thought you'd be beautiful and that I'd have to worry about men. I should've paid more attention while it was happening. You never complained."

"What about? I was happy." When he dropped his hands from her face, she took them in hers. His palms were hard and she felt the faint line of a scar along the back. She remembered that he had gotten it in Belgium eight years before in a minor crash. "Kirk," she spoke quickly, wanting to put his mind at ease, "we were both where we needed to be. I don't regret anything, and I don't want you to. Okay?"

She stood still as he studied her face. His eyes had long since adjusted to the night, enabling him to see her features clearly. He realized she had grown up right under his eyes. Somehow the woman who looked back at him aroused his protective instincts profoundly, while the girl had always seemed somehow indestructible. Perhaps he understood the pitfalls of womanhood, while those of childhood were a mystery to him. It was an uncharacteristic gesture when he lifted her fingers to his lips, yet it was a gesture that flooded Foxy's eyes with warm tears. "I love you," he said simply. "Don't do that," he warned as he brushed a tear from her lashes. "I don't have anything to mop them up with. Come on." He slipped an arm around her shoulders and began to walk with her from the grandstands. "I'll buy you a cup of coffee and a hamburger. I'm starved."

"Pizza," she countered. "This is Italy."

"Whatever," he said agreeably as they moved without haste through the moonlight.

"Kirk." Foxy tilted her face, and now her eyes shone with mischief. "If Lance does bother me, will you beat him up?"

"Sure." Kirk grinned and tugged on her hair. "As soon as the season's over."

Foxy laughed. "That's what I figured."

It was just after eleven when they walked down the hall of the hotel to their rooms. Pam heard Foxy's laugh and the low answering sound of her brother's. Nibbling on her lip, she waited for the sounds of their doors closing. She badly needed to talk to Foxy, to have someone laugh and joke and take her mind off Kirk Fox. For weeks Pam had been able to think of little but him. As they had moved from country to country, from race to race, he had grown remote. He spoke to her rarely, and when he did, he was unmistakably aloof. It became apparent that he had lost interest in the flirtation he had initiated. His coolness might have caused her some minor annoyance or even some amusement under normal circumstances. But Pam had discovered that the circumstances here were far from normal. As Kirk had gradually grown more taciturn she had grown gradually more tense. Sleeping had become a major feat and eating a monumental task. Her tension had come to an unexpected climax when Kirk stepped from his car during the final laps of the race in France.

Their eyes met for only one brief instant, but abruptly the realization had come to her that she was in love with him. The very thought had terrified her; he was so different from any of the men she had been attracted to in the past. But this was not mere attraction, and the old rules were insignificant. Briefly Pam had considered chucking the assignment and returning to the States. Professional pride refused to allow her this convenient escape. Personal pride kept her aloof from him. She did not want to be another of his trophies, another victory for Kirk Fox.

Hearing no sound in the hall, Pam drew a thin robe over her nightgown, deciding to slip down to Foxy's room. The instant she opened the door, she froze. Kirk walked silently down the hall. His head was bent but it snapped up immediately as she made a small sound of surprise. Stopping, he surveyed her carefully with eyes that held no expression. Framed in the doorway, Pam felt her breath backing up in her lungs. She seemed to have lost the power to force it out, just as she had lost the power to command her feet to move back into the room. His eyes held hers as he began to walk again, and though her fingers tightened on the knob, she did not retreat. Calm settled over her suddenly. This, she knew, was what she wanted, what she needed. When he stopped in front of her, they stood unsmiling, studying each other. The light from her room bathed them in a pale yellow glow.

"I've walked by your door a hundred times the last few months."

"I know."

"I'm not walking by tonight." There was a challenge in his voice, a hint of anger around his mouth. "I'm coming in."

"I know," Pam said again, then stepped back to allow him to enter. Her calm acceptance caused him to hesitate. She saw doubt flickering in his eyes.

"I'm going to make love to you," he told her in a statement that reflected a rising temper.

"Yes," she agreed with a nod. A smile touched her lips as she recognized the nervousness in his tone. *He's just as terrified as I am,* she realized when, after a brief hesitation, Kirk stalked into the room. Quietly Pam closed the door behind him. They turned to face each other.

"I don't make promises." His voice was rough as he studied her. His hands stayed firmly in his pockets.

"No." Her robe whispered gently as she

moved to switch off the light. The room was softened by starlight and moonbeams. In the courtyard below her window someone spoke quickly in Italian, then laughed heartily.

"I'll probably hurt you," he warned in a lowered voice.

"Probably," Pam agreed. She walked to him until they were both silhouetted in the moonlight. He found her perfume quiet, understated, and unforgettable. "But I'm much sturdier than I look."

Unable to resist, he lifted a hand to her hair. It was as soft as a cloud under his palm. "You're making a mistake." In the dim light, he watched the sheen of her eyes.

"No." Pam lifted her arms until they circled his neck. "No, I'm not."

On a low groan, Kirk pulled her against him and took the offered mouth. As she felt him lift her Pam melted against him.

Chapter Six

There was the usual crush of people and noise as the starting time approached. The light, insistent drizzle did nothing to hamper attendance. The skies were lead-gray and uncompromising. Slicks were exchanged for rain tires.

Foxy stood before the basin in the empty ladies' room and rinsed the taste of sickness from her mouth. With the absent gestures of habit, she sponged her face and touched up her pallor with makeup. The palms of her hands were still hot and moist, and automatically she ran cool water over them. The drone of the loudspeaker penetrated the walls. Knowing she had only a few minutes until the start, she picked up her camera case and hurried out. The swarming crowd swallowed her instantly. Because she was preoccupied she didn't notice Lance until she was nearly upon him.

"Cutting it a bit closer than usual,

Foxy?" She glanced up just as the thrust of the crowd pushed her against him. His grin faded as his hands touched the still clammy skin of her arms. "You're like ice," he muttered, then pulled her free of the throng and into a narrow hallway.

"For heaven's sake, let me go," she protested. Her legs were still a bit rubbery and nearly folded under her at the sudden movement. "They're going to start in a minute."

Ignoring her, Lance put a firm hand under her chin, then jerked her face to his. His eyes were narrowed and probing. Color had not yet returned to her cheeks, and the camouflage of makeup did not deceive him. "You're ill." The statement came partly as an accusation as he propped her against a wall. "You can't go out there while you're sick." Lance slipped an arm around her waist to lead her away, and she struggled against him. The sound of revving engines filled the air.

"For Lord's sake!" Foxy pushed unsuccessfully against him, frustrated by his interference. "I'm sick before every race, but I don't miss the start. Let me go, will you?"

His expression altered rapidly from surprise to disbelief to fury. Trapped between him and the wall, Foxy saw the changes and realized she had made a mistake. "You'll damn well miss this one," he grated, then half dragged, half carried her away from the pits. Feeling his grip, Foxy conceded and went peacefully. In silence, he led her to the restaurant under the main grandstand. "Coffee," he barked to the waiter as he pushed Foxy into a corner booth.

"Listen, Lance," she began, recovered enough to be indignant.

"Shut up." His voice was quiet, but so full of fury, she obeyed instantly. She had seen him angry before, but she decided she would have to go back some years to find a memory of an anger that sharp. His mouth was set in an uncompromising line, his voice vibrated with temper just under control. But it was his eyes, heated to a smoky gray, which kept her silent. Discretion, she reflected, sometimes is the better part of valor.

The restaurant was empty, silent save for the vibrations of the cars outside on the grid. There was a gray wall of gloom beyond the window, broken only by thin, clear rivulets of rain on the glass. Foxy watched one wind its slow, erratic way down the pane. The waiter set a pot of coffee and two cups on the table between them, then disappeared. The look in Lance's eyes told him he wanted solitude not service. Picking up the angry vibes Lance transmitted, Foxy watched as he poured the coffee into each cup. Curiosity began to temper her annoyance. *What is he so worked up about?* she wondered.

"Drink your coffee," he ordered in clipped tones.

Her brows arched at the command. "Yes, sir," she said humbly and lifted her cup.

A flash of trembling fury sparked in his eyes. "Don't push me, Foxy."

"Lance." She set down her coffee untasted, then leaned toward him. "What's the matter with you?"

He studied the perplexity on her face before drinking half his coffee, hot and black. The pallor clung stubbornly to her cheeks, lending her a look of vulnerability. Her eyes were young and earnest as her own coffee sat cooling in front of her. "How do you feel?" he asked as he drew out a cigar and his lighter.

"I'm fine," she answered cautiously. She noted he didn't light the cigar but merely twirled it between his fingers. Silence spread again. *This is ridiculous*, Foxy decided, and opened her mouth to demand an explanation.

"You're sick before every race?" Lance demanded suddenly.

Foxy hesitated over the question and began to stir her coffee. "Listen, Lance —"

"Don't start with me." The sharp order startled her and she lifted her eyes and encountered dark fury in his. "I asked you a question." His voice was too controlled. Though never timid, Foxy respected a temper more volatile than her own. "Are you ill, physically ill," he repeated in slow, precise tones, "before every race?"

"Yes."

Though soft, his oath was so violent she shuddered. Her wary eyes settled on his face. "Have you told Kirk?" he demanded.

"No, of course not. Why should I?" His temper flared again at the incredulity in her voice. Sensing danger, Foxy quickly laid her hand on his. "Lance, wait a minute. In the first place, at this point in my life, it's certainly my problem. When I was a kid, if I had told Kirk how I reacted to the start of a race, he would have worried, he would have been concerned, he might even have banned me from the track. All of those things would have made me guilty and miserable." She paused a moment and shook her head. "But he wouldn't have stopped. He couldn't have stopped."

"You know him well." Lance drained his cup, then poured more from the pot. His movements were smooth but Foxy was aware that his temper was just below the surface.

"Yes, I do." Their eyes met again, his heated, hers calm. "Racing's first with Kirk, it always has been. But I've always been second." Foxy made an imploring gesture, wanting him to understand her as badly as she had wanted Kirk to understand the night before. "That was enough. If he had put me first, he would have been a different person altogether. I love Kirk just the way he is . . . maybe because of the way he is. I owe him everything." As Lance opened his mouth to speak Foxy rushed on. "No, please listen, you don't understand. He gave me a home, he gave me a life. I don't know what would have happened to me after the accident if I hadn't had Kirk. How many twenty-three-year-old men would choose to be saddled with a thirteen-year-old girl? He's been good to me. He's given me everything he was capable of giving. I know he's not perfect. He's moody, he's self-absorbed. But, Lance, in all these years, he's never asked for anything except that I be there." She let out a long breath, then stared into her coffee. "It doesn't seem like much to ask."

"That all depends," Lance said quietly. "But in any case, you can't be there forever."

"No, I know that." Her shoulders moved with her sigh. Facing the window again, she watched the rain trickle down the glass without seeing her own ghostly reflection. "I realized this time around that I can't cope with it anymore, not in person anyway. I can't handle watching him get into a car and waiting for him to crash, knowing one day he might not walk away from it." She shifted her eyes back to Lance, and for a moment they were drenched in despair. "I won't watch him die."

"Foxy." Lance leaned over to take her hand. His voice was gentle now, without any sign of temper. "You know better than most that not every driver is killed on the track."

"I don't love every driver," she countered simply. "I've already lost two people in a car. No, no," she said quickly as he began to speak. She pressed her fingers to her eyes, simultaneously shaking her head as if to push the words away. "I don't dwell on it. I don't think about any of this often.

You go crazy if you do." After taking a deep breath, Foxy felt more composed and met his eyes. "I'm not morbid about all of this, Lance. I just don't cope with it very well. And it gets harder all the time."

"I know the danger shouldn't be minimized, Foxy," Lance began, frowning at the weariness he saw in her eyes. "But you're aware of the improved safety features. A driver's much more protected than he used to be. Fatalities are the exception, not the rule."

"Statistics are just numbers on paper. They don't mean anything to me." She smiled as his brows drew together, then shook her head. "You can't understand because you're one of them. You're a very unique breed. You all say you race for a variety of reasons, but there's really only one. You race because you love it. It's your mother and mistress and best friend. Drivers flirt with death, break their bones, singe their skins, and get back on the grid before the smoke's cleared. In the hospital one day, in the cockpit the next; I've seen you do it. It's like a religion, and I can't condemn it any more than I can comprehend it. Some people call it a science, but that's a lie. I've lived with it all my life, and it never makes any more sense. That's because it's emotional, and emotions rarely make sense." Foxy leaned her head against the cool glass of the window and stared into the rain. "I keep hoping one day he'll have had enough. Someday he'll find something else to take its place." When she looked back at Lance, her eyes were steady and studying. "I always wondered . . . why did you quit?"

"I didn't love it anymore." With a half smile, he reached over and tucked her hair behind her ear.

"I'm glad," she said simply, smiling back at him. Toying with her coffee, she lapsed into silence a moment. "Lance, you won't say anything about this to Kirk?" Foxy lifted her eyes and used them shamelessly.

"No, I won't say anything." He watched relief flutter over her face before she lifted her cup. "But, Fox." The cup paused at her lips. "I'd like you to skip the last races in the circuit."

"I can't do that." She shook her head as she tasted the coffee. It was strong and cold, causing her to wrinkle her nose and set it back down. "Not only because of Kirk, but because I have a commitment to Pam." Foxy leaned back and watched Lance frown at her through a haze of cheroot smoke. "It's my job to photograph these races, and my work is very important to me."

"And when the season's over?"

It was her turn to frown. Her eyes reflected the gray light coming through the window. "I have my own life, my own work. I have to resolve to myself that I can't be a part of Kirk's life. I'm not equipped for it. My emotions are too near the surface. And I'm a coward," she added briskly, then started to slide from the booth. "I have to get back."

Lance was out of the booth before her and blocking her way. Even as her eyes rose to his in question, his arms came around her. He drew her close, nestling her head against his chest. "Oh, don't," she murmured and shut her eyes. A treacherous warmth flooded through her. "I can't handle you when you're kind." She could feel his lips trail over her hair while his hand moved gently up and down her spine. "Lance, please, if you're not careful I'll start flooding the place with tears, and you've already terrified the waiter."

"Tears?" He spoke quietly, as if considering. "You know, Foxy, I don't believe I've ever seen you cry, not once in all the years I've known you."

"I have an aversion to humiliating myself

in public." She felt cozy and pampered and entirely too right in his arms. "Lance, please don't be nice to me. I could get used to it." She lifted her face, but her smile never materialized. She could read his intent in his eyes. "Oh help," she murmured as his mouth touched hers.

There was no need to brace herself for the explosion because his lips were gentle. There was no demand, no fire, just a lingering tenderness. Even as she felt her bones melt into submission, she felt oddly protected. The slow, soft embrace confused her, disarmed her, seduced her more successfully than his most ardent demand. His lips were warm, tasting hers without pressure, giving only comfort and pleasure. She had not known he was capable of such poignant tenderness. Because he was not asking, she gave more freely. The kiss lengthened, but remained a quiet gift. Reality slipped away leisurely, leaving Foxy with only Lance inside her world. When her mouth was free, she could not speak. Her eyes asked him questions.

"I'm not quite sure what to do with you," he murmured. Taking a handful of her hair, he let it run through his fingers. "It was simpler before I found out you had a fragile side. I doubt that I deal very well with frailty."

Nonplussed, Foxy bent to lift her camera gear. She had not felt fragile until he had touched her so gently. Knowing there was no safety in the feeling, she tried to shake it off. "I'm not frail at all," she denied, then stood straight and faced him.

A smile flickered over his face, lifting his mouth and lighting up his eyes. "You don't like to be."

"I'm not," she countered with a quick shake of her head. No one had ever made her feel that way before, and Foxy was afraid he would touch her, making her feel that way again. She knew from experience that only the strong survived intact.

Lance studied her face before he took the camera case from her. "Humor me then," he suggested, then closed his hand over hers to lead her outside.

When the team returned to the States, Kirk led the competition for the world championship by five points. A win at Watkins Glen would give him the title. But through the high spirits and growing confusion, Foxy noticed subtle changes in the people closest to her. She herself had been preoccupied since the race in Italy. Something seemed to be nagging at the outside

147

of her mind. The sensation did not make her uneasy as much as curious. She was accustomed to being in full control of her thoughts and feelings, but now it seemed part of her mind belonged to someone else. She found herself thinking more and more of Lance.

Since their talk over coffee, he had treated her with a strange gentleness. Oddly the gentleness was mixed with an aloofness that only added to Foxy's confusion. Since the kiss he had given her in the restaurant, Lance had not touched or indeed attempted to touch her again. Having never seen him be gentle or diffident before, Foxy began to wonder if she really knew him as well as she had assumed. Unwillingly she was drawn to him.

She noted a change in her brother. He grew more quiet and more withdrawn. Because she had seen him go inside himself before, Foxy accepted it. She attributed his mood to pressure over the championship. In Pam, she saw a growing serenity. Often during the qualifying races and long practice sessions, Foxy wished for a portion of Pam's absolute calm.

The two-point-three mile course climbed and weaved through terrain that was alternately wooded and open. Trees were ablaze with autumn colors, which grew more vibrant with each passing day. Foxy had forgotten that New York possessed such rustic charm. October leaves stretched toward a hard blue sky and swirled and spun to the ground. There was the combination of biting air and heat from the sun so peculiar to fall. Of all the tracks she had seen in a decade of her life, Foxy favored Watkins Glen. There was something simple and basically American about it.

She watched the race begin through the lens of her camera. *The last one,* she thought, and let out a long breath as she straightened. Beside her, Charlie Dunning stared after the cars while he rolled the stub of a fat cigar around in his mouth.

"This'll do it, Charlie." Foxy smiled as he turned to her, squinting against the sun.

"Don't you get tired of taking pictures?" he demanded as he scowled at her camera.

"Don't you get tired of playing with cars and chasing women?" she countered sweetly.

"Those are both worthwhile occupations." He pinched her waist and snorted. "You're getting skinnier."

"You're getting cuter." Foxy rubbed his grizzled beard with her palm and winked.

"Wanna get married?"

"You're still a smart-aleck brat," he grumbled as he turned a rosy pink under his whiskers.

Grinning, Foxy dipped in his shirt pocket and pulled out a candy bar. "Let me know if you change your mind," she told him as she unwrapped the chocolate and took a bite. "I'm not getting any younger, you know."

With grumbles and mutters, Charlie moved away to lecture his mechanics.

"That's the first time Charlie's blushed in his life," Lance commented.

Foxy twisted her head and watched him approach. An odd thrill sped up and down her spine before it spread out at the base of her neck. His dark gray turtleneck was snug, showing off his lean torso. His mouth was cocked in a half smile. Abruptly she felt the memory of its pressure on hers. The sensation was so genuine, so vital, she was certain he must feel it too. As she looked at him it was as though a thin veil lifted from her eyes, and she saw him clearly for the first time: the dark gray eyes that saw so much and told so little, the well-shaped mouth that could give such pleasure, the firm chin and rawboned features that were so much more interesting than clean good looks. This was why Scott Newman had seemed so dull, why no boy or man she had ever known had measured up in her eyes. There was only one, had always been only one man in her heart.

I've never stopped loving him, she realized on a wave of alarm. *I never will.*

"You all right?" He reached for her as the color drained from her face. The gesture, coupled with the concern in his voice, snapped her back to reality.

"No . . . yes, yes, I'm fine." Foxy brushed a hand over her eyes as if to clear the mists. "I — I was daydreaming, I suppose."

"About wedded bliss with Charlie?" The careless brush of his hand through her hair sent tremors speeding through her.

"Charlie?" Blankly she glanced down at the chocolate bar in her hand. It was softening in the sunlight. "Oh, yes, Charlie. I was — I was teasing him." She wished desperately for a moment alone to pull herself together. Her mind was whirling with new knowledge. All of her senses seemed to be competing with each other for dominance.

Lance studied her with growing interest. "Are you sure you're all right?" His brow lifted in that habitual gesture and disappeared under his hair. "You look rattled."

Rattled? she thought, nearly giggling at the understatement. I'm going under for the third time. "I'm fine," she lied, then forced herself to smile. "How are you?"

Cars wound around the "Ss" and zoomed past. Absently she wondered how many laps she had missed while she had been in her trance. "Just fine," Lance murmured. There was a faint smile on his lips as he watched her. "Your chocolate's melting."

Dutifully Foxy took a bite of the bar. "What will you do after the race is over?" she asked, hoping she sounded only mildly interested.

"Relax."

"Yes." A portion of the tension slid out of her shoulders as she glanced around. It would be over in a matter of hours. "I guess we all will. It's been a long summer."

"Has it?" Lance retorted. Foxy wore a white Oxford shirt under a navy crew-neck sweater. Carelessly, Lance rubbed the collar between his thumb and forefinger while his eyes rested on hers. There was something proprietary in the casual gesture. "It doesn't seem very long ago that you popped out from under the MG in Kirk's garage."

"It seems like years to me," Foxy murmured as she turned back to the track. Cars hurtled by, and the noise was one continuous demand — roar and whine. She could smell oil and gas and heated rubber. "It doesn't seem to bother Pam at all," Foxy commented as she spotted the small blond figure near the edge of the pits. "I suppose it's easier if you're not personally involved with one of the drivers."

With a quick laugh, Lance took her chin and examined her face. "Do you need glasses or have you been off in space for the past few weeks?"

"What are you talking about?" Foxy was not ready to have him touch her and carefully backed away.

"Foxy, my love, Pam is very personally involved with one of the drivers. Take off your blinders."

Eyes narrowed against the sun, Foxy turned to study Pam's profile. She was watching the race steadily with her delicate hands tucked into the pockets of a spotless ivory blazer. Foxy turned back to Lance's amused face with a sharp glance. "You don't mean Kirk?" *Of course he means Kirk,* she realized even as she spoke. *I'd have seen it myself if I hadn't been so tangled up with Lance.* "Oh dear," she said on a sigh.

"Don't you approve, little sister?" Lance said dryly, then turned her back to face him. His hands remained light on her arms. "Kirk's a big boy now."

"Oh, don't be ridiculous." Foxy pushed her hair behind her back in a quick gesture of annoyance. "It's not a matter of approving, and in any case, Pam's wonderful."

"Then what's the problem?"

Foxy turned and gestured to where Pam stood. Her hair was rolled neatly at the nape of her neck with only a few wisps dancing gently around her composed face. "Just look at her," Foxy ordered impatiently. "That's how Melanie Wilkes would look today. Lord, she even sounds like her, with that quiet, cultured voice. Pam's tiny and fragile and should be serving tea in a drawing room. Kirk will swallow her whole."

"You've forgotten what a strong lady Melanie Wilkes was, Foxy." His fingers trailed lightly over her cheek. "Think about it," he advised before he turned and walked away.

For some moments, Foxy stood still. Being in love with Lance was not a new sensation, but now she loved as a woman and not as a child. This was no fairy-tale crush but a real, encompassing need. She knew now the agonies and joys of being in his arms, knew the heat and pressure of his mouth. She could never, as she had at sixteen, be content with making him the hero of her dreams. And after tomorrow, she remembered and shut her eyes against the painful reality, *I'll very likely never see him again.* Unable to deal with her situation, Foxy pushed it from her mind.

And now, there's Pam and Kirk, she reminded herself. Her loyalties at war, she walked over to the blond woman and stood beside her as the grid vibrated with passing cars.

"He's taken the lead a bit sooner than usual," Pam commented as she followed the flash of Kirk's car. "He wants badly to win this one." With a light laugh, she turned to Foxy. "He wants badly to win every one."

"I know . . . he always has." The calm blue eyes caused Foxy to take a long breath. "Pam, I know it's none of my business, but I'd . . ." With a sound of frustration, she turned back to the track and stuck her hands in her pockets. "Oh, I'm going to make a terrible fool of myself."

"You think I'm wrong for Kirk," Pam supplied gently.

"No!" Foxy's eyes grew wide with distress. "I think Kirk's wrong for you."

"How strangely alike the two of you are," Pam murmured, studying Foxy's earnest face. "He thinks so, too. But it doesn't matter, I know he's exactly right for me."

"Pam . . ." Foxy shook her head as she searched for the right words. "Racing . . ."

"Will always come first," Pam finished, then shrugged her slim shoulders. "Of course I know that. I accept that. The fact is, as much as it surprises even me, it's partly that which attracted me to him — the racing, his absolute determination to come out on top, his almost negligent attitude about danger. It's as exciting as it is frustrating, and I'm hooked. I think I'm going to be terrified, and then when the race starts, I'm not. I want him to win." She turned to Foxy with a brilliant smile. "I think I'm almost as bad as he is. I love him, I love who he is and what he is. Being second in his life is enough for me." Hearing her own words echo back to her, Foxy could do no more than stare out at the track. "I'm not trying to usurp your place with him," Pam began, and Foxy turned back quickly.

"Oh, no. No, it's not that. It's nothing like that. I'm glad for Kirk, he needs someone . . . someone who understands him the way you do." She ran her fingers through her thick mane of hair. It glowed like the russet leaves on the surrounding trees. "But I care about you, too." She made a frustrated gesture with her hands as if that would help her express herself. "He can be cruel by just forgetting."

"I don't bruise easily." Pam laid a hand on Foxy's shoulder. "Not as easily, I think, as you do." At Foxy's confused expression, she smiled. "It's easy for one woman in love to recognize another. No, no, don't start babbling a denial." She laughed as Foxy's mouth opened then closed. "If you need to talk, we will. I feel quite an expert on the subject."

"It's academic," Foxy told her with a restless movement of her shoulders. "Tomorrow we'll go our separate ways."

"You still have today." Pam gave Foxy's shoulder a quick squeeze. "Isn't that really all there is?"

It happened so suddenly. At first Foxy's brain rejected it. Even as Pam spoke, Kirk rounded the turn in front of them. She saw him swerve to avoid the abrupt fishtailing of the racer to his right, then waited for him to regain control. She saw the skid begin, heard its squeal echo through her head as she watched it grow wider and more violent. Part of her brain screamed in panic while still another kept insisting he would pull out of it. He had to pull out of it. The sound of the blowout was like a gunshot and just as lethal. Then there were columns of smoke and shrieking metal as the car slammed into the wall and careened away. Wheels and pieces of fiberglass rained in the air as the racer continued to spin wildly.

"No!" The cry was wrenched from Foxy as she darted toward the track. With one quick jerk, she freed herself from Pam's restraining hand and ran.

Jagged pieces of fiberglass flew with deadly abandon. A fear greater than any she had ever known filled her, blacking out all thoughts, all feelings. Her only reality was the twisting hulk of machine that held her brother in its bowels. Inches from the grid, her breath was cut off by a vise around her waist. The force lifted her off the ground, and she kicked uselessly in the air to free herself. She shook the hair from her eyes in time to see Kirk's car topple into the infield.

"For God's sake, Foxy, you'll kill yourself." Lance's voice was harsh in her ear as she writhed and struggled for freedom. In terror, she waited for the belching smoke to burst into flame.

"Let me go!" she shouted as she realized the vise around her waist was his arm. "It's Kirk, can't you see? I've got to get to him." Her breathing was ragged as she clawed at the imprisoning arm. "Oh God, I've got to get to him!" she shouted again, desperately fighting to free herself.

"There's nothing you can do." Lance jerked her back against him, cutting off her wind for a moment. Over her head, he could see members of the emergency team spraying the wreck with extinguishers while others worked to free Kirk from the cockpit. "There's nothing you can do," he said again. Her struggles ceased abruptly. She went so completely limp, he thought she had fainted until he heard her speak.

"Let me go." Foxy spoke quietly now, so that he barely heard her. "I won't do anything stupid," she added when he did not lessen his grip. "I'm all right, Lance, let me go."

Slowly he lowered her back to the ground and released her. She neither turned to him nor spoke, but watched in silence as they pulled Kirk from the wreckage. She gave no sign that she knew

159

Pam stood beside her. Behind them, the pits were like a tomb. The white flag fluttered in the autumn breeze.

Chapter Seven

The walls in the hospital waiting room were pale green. The floor was uncarpeted; an inconspicuous beige tile with tiny brown flecks disguised a day's collection of dust and dirt. On the wall opposite Foxy was a print of a Van Gogh still life. It was the sole spot of color in the drab little room. Foxy knew she would never see the print again without remembering the hours of torment and ignorance. Pam sat near the window, framed by drapes just darker than the walls. Occasionally she took sips of cold coffee. Charlie sat on a vinyl sofa and gnawed at the stub of a long-dead cigar. Lance paced. Unceasingly he prowled the small room, sometimes with his hands in his pockets, sometimes smoking. Once or twice, Foxy heard Pam murmur something to him, then caught the low rumble of his response. She did not hear the words, nor did she attempt to. They did not interest her. She felt the same nameless, unspeakable fear she had known in the first moments of consciousness after her own accident. She had been helpless then, and she knew she was helpless now. Lance had been right when he told her there was nothing she could do. Now Foxy accepted it. Anger and panic were buried under the numbing terror of the unthinkable. Her mind drifted and emptied as she stared at the Van Gogh print. Kirk's skid had begun more than three hours before.

"Miss Fox?"

With a jolt, Foxy was pulled back to the present. For a moment, she merely stared at the green-gowned figure in the doorway. "Yes?" she managed in a surprisingly strong voice as she rose to meet him. It floated through her mind that the doctor was very young. His mustache was dark but reminded Foxy of Kirk's. His surgical mask hung by its ties at his throat.

"Your brother's out of surgery." There was a quietness to his voice which, like his hands, he used for healing. "He's in recovery."

Cautiously Foxy held off relief and kept her gaze steady on his face. "How extensive are his injuries?"

The doctor heard and respected the control in her tone, but saw that her eyes were hurting and afraid. "He had five broken

162

ribs. His lungs collapsed, but they've been reinflated and the concussion's mild. The ribs will be painful, but since there was no puncture, the danger's minimal. His leg . . ." He hesitated a moment, and Foxy felt a fresh thrill of fear.

"He didn't . . ." She swallowed, then forced herself to ask. "He didn't lose it?"

"No." He took her hand for reassurance and found it ice cold but without a tremor. "But it's a complicated injury, we've had to do some reconstructing. It's an open, comminuted fracture, and there's some artery damage. We've realigned the bones, and the outlook is good that he'll have full use of the leg in a few months. Meanwhile, there's a risk of infection." After releasing her hand, the doctor allowed his gaze to sweep the people behind her before returning to Foxy. "He's going to be here for some time."

"I see." Foxy let out a shaky breath. "Is there anything else?"

"Minor burns and abrasions. He's a very lucky man."

"Yes." Foxy's agreement was solemn as she stared down at her hands. She joined them together, not knowing what else to do with them. "Is he conscious?"

"Yes." The doctor grinned and looked

younger yet. "He wanted to know who won the race." Foxy bit her bottom lip hard and continued to look straight ahead as he went on. "He'll be in a room in about an hour; you can see him then. Only one visitor tonight," he added firmly, again letting his eyes trail over the people behind Foxy. "The others can see him tomorrow. We're not giving him a phone for twenty-four hours."

Foxy nodded and spoke quickly. "Miss Anderson will stay to see him tonight then."

"Foxy," Pam began, shaking her head as she stepped forward.

"He'll want you," Foxy told her as their eyes met. "He'll be satisfied knowing I was here. You will stay, won't you?"

Feeling tears well up behind her eyes, Pam nodded quickly, then turned away. She had managed with a great deal of will-power to remain composed during the wait. Now, Foxy's simple generosity did what the hours of torture had not. Moving to the window, she stared out and let the tears have their freedom.

"The desk has my number," Foxy told the doctor. "Will you see that I'm called if there's any change before morning?"

"Certainly. Miss Fox," he added, recognizing the signs of shock and fatigue in her eyes. "He's going to be fine."

"Thank you."

"Charlie, wait around and take Pam back after she's seen Kirk," Lance ordered as he took Foxy's arm. "I'll take Foxy now." He turned to the doctor and spoke briskly. "There'll be reporters downstairs in the lobby. I don't want her to have to deal with them tonight."

"Take the service elevator down to the garage level. There's a cabstand near the entrance."

"Thanks." Without waiting for her assent, Lance began to lead Foxy down the corridor.

"You don't have to do this," she said. Her voice held no inflection at all as she allowed herself to be piloted.

"I know what I have to do," he tossed back and jammed the button on the service elevator. Behind them, the crepe soles of nurses' shoes made soft sounds against the tile.

"I didn't thank you before for stopping me from running out on the track." There was a quick ding of a bell before the doors slid open. Foxy made no protest as he pulled her into the empty car. "It was a stupid thing to do."

"Stop it, damn it! Just stop it." He whirled and took her by the shoulders. His fingers pressed tightly into her flesh. "Scream, cry, take a punch at me, but stop acting like this."

Foxy stared up into the furious heat of his eyes. Her emotions refused to surface. Her defenses remained sealed, as if they knew it was still too soon to allow anything to escape. She spoke quietly and her eyes were dry. "I already did all the screaming I'm going to do. I can't cry yet because I'm still numb, and I don't have any reason to take a punch at you."

"It was my car, isn't that enough?" he demanded. The doors opened, and he took her hand before he stalked out. Their footsteps echoed hollowly in the garage as he pulled her toward the entrance.

"Nobody forced Kirk into that car. I'm not blaming you, Lance. I'm not blaming anyone."

"I saw the way you looked at me when they pulled him out."

Fatigue was pouring over Foxy as Lance nudged her into a cab. Turning her head to face him, she made herself speak clearly. "I'm sorry. Maybe I did blame you for a minute. Maybe I wanted to blame you or anyone else who was handy. I thought he was dead." Because her voice trembled slightly, she paused until she was certain she could continue. "I've tried to be prepared for something like this every day of my life. But I wasn't prepared at all. It doesn't seem to make any difference that I've seen him crash before." Foxy sighed and leaned back against the seat. The streetlights came through the cab window to dance on her closed lids. "I don't blame you for what happened, Lance, any more than I blame Kirk for being who he is. Maybe this time he'll have had enough."

No answer came from Lance but the click and hiss of his lighter. Not having the energy to open her eyes, Foxy kept them closed and took the rest of the brief journey in silence. When they arrived at the motel, they found Scott Newman pacing the corridor in front of Foxy's room. He wore the disheveled look of an executive who has just left a hassle-filled board meeting.

"Cynthia." Giving Lance a quick nod, he held out both hands to her. "The hospital said you were on your way back. How's Kirk? They tell you next to nothing over the phone."

"He's going to be fine," Foxy told him, letting him squeeze her hands. She gave him a shortened version of the doctor's report.

"Everybody's been worried; they'll be glad to hear he's going to be all right. How about you?" He gave her an encouraging smile. "I thought you might need me."

"What she needs is some rest," Lance said shortly.

"It was very considerate of you to wait." Foxy smoothed over Lance's rudeness and added a smile which cost her some concentrated effort. "I'm fine, really, just a bit tired. Pam stayed behind to keep Kirk company for a while."

"The press is itching for the full story," Scott commented as he released her hands and straightened the knot in his tie. "We took a look at the replay. There's no doubt that Kirk had to swerve to avoid a crash with Martell, and that's when he lost it. Defective steering in Martell's racer is the verdict. A bad break for Kirk. Perhaps you'd like to give them a statement or pass one on through me."

"No," Lance answered before Foxy could respond. "Leave it. If you want to be useful, tell the switchboard not to pass any calls through to this room unless it's the hospital." His voice was curt and annoyed. "Give me the key, Foxy," he ordered.

"Of course." Scott nodded as he watched Foxy dig in her bag. "I'm sure I can hold them off at least until morning, but —"

"Come on to my room in a couple hours." Lance cut him off and snatched the key from Foxy's hand. "I'll give you enough for a press release. Just see that you keep her out of it. Understand?" Lance jerked open the door.

The fury registered. Scott agreed with another nod before turning to Foxy. "Let me know if there's anything I can do, Cynthia."

"Thank you, Scott. Good night," she managed before Lance shut the door in his face. Bone weary, she moved to a chair and sank into it. "You were very rude," she commented absently as she rubbed at a headache near her temple. "I don't recall that I've ever seen you be quite that rude before."

"Maybe if you took a look in the mirror, you'd understand why." The fury was still in his voice. Foxy watched him calmly from behind the numbing shield of shock and fatigue. "You're standing there getting paler by the minute. I swear the only color in your face right now is in your eyes. And he rambles on like an idiot about press releases." Lance made a gesture of disgust with his hand. "He's got the brains of a soft-boiled egg."

"He's a good manager," Foxy murmured, fighting against the building ache in her head.

"And a great human being," Lance added sarcastically.

"Lance," Foxy began with the first stirrings of curiosity, "were you protecting me?"

When he turned on her, she watched his temper boil in his eyes. Her curiosity increased as she watched him control it. "Maybe," he muttered, then turned to the phone. Foxy heard him mumble a series of instructions but paid no attention to the words.

Odd, she thought, *he seems to be making a habit of protecting me. First in Italy, and now here. It certainly doesn't seem to make him very comfortable, though.* She continued to study him after he had hung up the phone. Instantly he began to pace the room just as he had paced the waiting area in the hospital.

"Lance." He stopped when she quietly said his name. Foxy held out her hand, realizing suddenly how grateful she was that he was there. She wasn't ready to be alone yet. She wasn't feeling strong and capable and indestructible, but tired and vulnerable and afraid. Lance stared at her a moment without moving, then crossed to her to take the offered hand. "Thank you." Her eyes were dark and grave as they clung to his. "It's just occurred to me that I wouldn't have made it through all this without knowing you were there. I didn't even realize that I needed you, but you did. I want you to know how much it means to me."

Something flickered over his face before he raked his free hand through his hair. It was an uncharacteristic gesture of frustration, which reminded Foxy that he was as weary as she. "Fox," he began, but she continued quickly.

"You won't go away tomorrow, will you?" Knowing she was being weak did not prevent her from asking. She needed him, and her hand tightened on his. "If you could just stay for a couple of extra days, just until things settle. I can lie," she continued in a voice which was growing desperate. "I can walk right in that hospital room tomorrow and look at Kirk, look right in his eyes and lie. It's a trick I've learned over the years; and I'm good at it. He'll never have to know how much I hate him being in there. But if you could stay, if I could just know you were there. I know it's a lot to ask, but I . . ." She stopped, then pressed both hands to her eyes. "Oh, Lord, I think the numbness is wearing off." She heard the knock at the door, but took deep steadying breaths, leaving Lance to answer it. In a moment, she heard him move back to her.

"Foxy." He spoke her name gently and took her wrist until she had lowered her hands. Her eyes were young and devastated. "Drink this." He held out a glass filled with the brandy room service had delivered. Though she took it obediently, she only stared down into the amber liquid. Lance watched her for a moment, then crouched down until their eyes were level. "Fox." He waited until she had shifted her gaze from the brandy to him. "Marry me."

"What?" Foxy stared at him, saw the familiar intentness in his eyes, then squeezed her own shut. "What?" she said again, opening them.

Lance urged the brandy toward her lips. "I said, marry me."

Foxy drank the entire contents of the glass in one swallow. Her breath caught on the burn of the brandy, and the small sound thundered in the absolute silence of

172

the room. For several long seconds, she stared into his eyes trying to penetrate the impenetrable. She sensed that under the calm lay a whirlpool of energy, a power that would escape at any instant. He held something, she was unsure what, on a very tight leash. Tension gripped tight in her throat. She tried to swallow it and failed. Her eyes remained steady on his, but her voice was only a whisper. She was afraid. "Why?"

"Why not?" he countered then took the empty glass from her nerveless fingers.

"Why not?" Foxy repeated. She lifted her hand to make some helpless gesture, but he caught it in his own. Her fingers trembled as he brought them to his lips. Steadily he watched her.

"Yes, why not?"

"I don't know, I . . ." He had succeeded in distracting her with the unconventional proposal. She ran her free hand through her hair and tried to think properly. "There must be a reason, I just can't think."

"Well, if you can't think of any substantial reason against it, marry me and come to Boston."

"Boston?" Foxy echoed him blankly.

"Boston," Lance agreed, and for the first

time, a faint smile touched his lips. "I live there, remember?"

"Yes, of course." Foxy rubbed a line between her brows and struggled to concentrate. "Of course I remember."

"We could leave when you were confident that Kirk was settled. More than likely, he'll be staying here for the next couple of months, but there's no need for you to be here." Lance's voice was practical, his face absolutely calm. Frustrated and unsure, Foxy shook her head. *I'm hallucinating. Hallucinations don't hurt,* she reminded herself, then quickly shook off the argument. It was easier to believe it was an illusion than to believe Lance was asking her to marry him in the same tone he might ask her to fetch him a cup of coffee.

"Lance, I . . ." Foxy hesitated, then decided to evade the issue rather than face it head-on. "I don't think I'm taking all this in properly. I'm still a little fuzzy." She swallowed and tried to match his casual tone. "Let me think about it. Give me a day or two."

Lance inclined his head. "That sounds reasonable," he agreed as she rose to move away from him. "No," he said, causing her to turn and gape at him.

"What did you say?"

"I said no, you can't think about it for a day or two." In one quick gesture, he had her firmly by the shoulders and had abolished the distance between them. Foxy saw that his eyes were no longer calm but turbulent. He had held her like this before, she remembered, and had looked at her in precisely the same way. Years ago, she reflected, confused and foolishly disoriented, in the empty garage at Le Mans. Was he going to shout at her again? she wondered. Her brows drew together as she tried to keep the past and present separate.

"What do you want?" she asked, struggling with her feelings for him.

"You." He pulled her yet closer as his eyes burned into hers. "I'm not about to let you walk out of my life, Fox, and I've waited for you long enough." His mouth lowered swiftly but was gentle on hers. Even so, she could feel the imprisoned passion in the grip of his hands. The kiss was thorough, possessive. "Did you really think I'd calmly walk out that door and give you a couple of days to think it over?" His mouth closed over hers again, preventing any response she might have made. Once again, he drew her away, this time to stare down into her bemused eyes. "Do you think I could want you the way that I do, then walk away after you've told me you need me?"

"Lance, I didn't mean to . . ." Foxy shook her head as she searched for some scraps of common sense. "You shouldn't feel obligated, I was grateful. . . ."

"The hell with grateful," he declared, then grabbed her hair with both hands. "I'm not interested in some nice, patient emotion like gratitude. That's not what I want from you." Foxy saw the determination in his face, heard the fire in his voice. Her blood began to heat in response. "I don't give a damn if the timing's wrong, or that I'm pressing you when your defenses are down. I'm a selfish man, Foxy, and I've wanted you for longer than I care to think about. I'm going to have you."

Her pulse was beating so quickly, she was giddy. She steadied herself, placing her hands on his arms. "Lance . . ." Her voice would not behave but insisted on coming out in breathless whispers. "What you're talking about isn't what's necessary for marriage. That's a big step, a lifetime commitment, I don't know . . ."

"I love you," he said and stopped her speech cold. Her lips trembled open to form words which would not come. "I want to spend my life with you, and I'm not going back to Boston without you. I can't give you the candlelight and soft words that might smooth the road because I haven't the time or patience for them right now. I'll have to make it up to you later." His hands moved from her hair to her shoulders to her waist, but he brought her no closer. "Foxy, you drive me out of my mind." As she watched, she saw both demand and doubt flicker in his eyes. "You love me, too, I know you do."

"Yes." She rested her cheek against his chest and sighed. "Yes, I love you. Hold me," she murmured, finding again she fit perfectly into his arms. "I need you to hold me." For the next few moments, she allowed herself the incredible luxury of being held and cherished by the man she loved. It's all happening so fast, she thought, then pushed away the fears and listened to the steady drum of Lance's heart. *He loves me.* "Lance." Tilting her head, Foxy brought her lips to his. Instantly his mouth answered hers, passion for passion, wonder for wonder, until their bodies were heated and entwined. Lance loosened his hold as she shivered from spiraling emotions.

"We can be married in a couple of days." He spoke calmly again, but his hands wandered up and down her back before they rested on her hips. "The paperwork will take that long. Then we'll go to Boston." His eye grew serious on her face. "Pam will be here for Kirk, you understand that, don't you?"

"Yes." Foxy closed her eyes a moment and tried to block out the rushing image of the accident. "Yes, that's for the best. I want to go," she told him as she opened her eyes. "I want to be with you." Her nerves were jumping inside her stomach, refusing to grow steady, and she met his mouth desperately. Foxy felt his hunger and matched it. "Stay with me tonight," she whispered as she buried her face against his neck. "I don't want you to go."

Slowly Lance drew her away and scanned her face. Her cheeks were still pale, her eyes like smoke against her skin. Already there were faint shadows haunting them. "No." He shook his head as he brushed the back of his hand down her cheek. "You're too vulnerable tonight, I've already taken advantage of that. You need sleep." With this, he swept her up in his arms and carried her to the bed. Foxy's body responded to the weightlessness by floating with the fatigue. After he laid her on the mattress, he sat beside her. "Do you want anything?"

"Tell me again."

Lance lifted her hand and turned the palm to his lips. "I love you. Will you sleep?"

"Yes, yes, I'll sleep." Foxy could feel the weariness pressing down on her. She closed her eyes and immediately began to dream. Lance's lips were a soft promise on hers.

"I'll come for you in the morning," he murmured. Dimly she felt the bed shift as he stood. She was asleep before the door closed behind him.

Chapter Eight

Sunlight fell fresh and brilliant over Foxy's face. She moaned as it began to penetrate her slumber. Her mind gently floated to the surface, noticing small, inconsequential things: the rapid ticking of her travel alarm on the stand beside the bed, the vague itch between her shoulder blades, the uncomfortable warmth of the spread that lay on top of her. She had huddled under it during the night when she awakened cold and frightened in the dark. She did not remember the nightmare yet, the vivid clarity in which she had relived Kirk's crash. She had awakened, panting for breath, cold as ice, with terror ripping away all thought of sleep. She did not remember yet that the tears had finally come in torrents until her eyes were raw and her ribs ached from the strain. She had wept herself numb, then had fallen into a fitful sleep, plagued with doubts about her unconventional engagement to Lance. Perhaps he had proposed out of a sense of duty. Foxy had tried to recapture the feeling she had experienced when he had told her he loved her, but she was cold and miserable. She had huddled under the blanket and wished for morning.

Now that it was here, she found the light annoying and the spread stifling. She shifted crossly, still half asleep, and wished the spread would disappear without her having to move. As her consciousness swam reluctantly closer to the surface her memory began to merge with it. Her mind clear, she sat up abruptly and rested her face on her knees.

Pull yourself together, Foxy, she ordered, drawing her breath slowly in and out of her lungs. *You had a bad night; now shake it off and get down to business. Lance will be here soon.* Lifting her head, Foxy narrowed her eyes and stared at her left hand, trying to imagine an engagement ring on the third finger.

"I'm going to marry him," she said aloud, just to hear how the words would sound. Her stomach shivered, announcing the state of her nerves. It came to her abruptly that she knew absolutely nothing about the man who lived in Boston and ran a multimillion-dollar business. The Lance Matthews she knew was a cocky ex-driver who played a mean hand of poker and knew how to tear down an engine. The only hint she had seen of the other side of him had been on their date in Monte Carlo. It was, she reflected, not enough. She was going to marry him without knowing the whole man. Did he belong to the country club? Did he play golf on Saturdays? Foxy tried to imagine Lance swinging a nine iron and got nowhere. Shutting her eyes, she let the reckless side of her push away the doubts. *This is no time to sit around thinking,* she told herself. *What does it matter if he plays golf or backgammon or if he's into yoga? What does it matter if he wears a three-piece suit and carries a briefcase or if he wears jeans and sneakers?* Biting down on her lips, Foxy wondered when she had sewn this particular patchwork of thought together. *I've got to get up and put myself together so that I don't look like a zombie when he gets here.*

Throwing off the spread, Foxy rose from the bed and discovered that every muscle in her body was taking revenge on her for the restless night. *A hot shower,* she reflected, and began to strip off the clothes she had slept in. *I'm not nervous, I'm just groggy.* When Lance knocked at her door thirty minutes later, Foxy was just completing her attempt to camouflage the results of the wakeful night.

She wore a plain yellow shift, with her hair neatly coiled at her neck. Lance studied her face carefully before speaking. Her eyes were freed now from shock but were still haunted by shadows. He took her chin in his hand and frowned. Her fragile looks were intensified by the violet smudges under her eyes. Weeping had left them faintly swollen and weary.

"You've been crying," he accused, making Foxy realize that all her attempts with base and blusher and mascara had been for nothing. His voice was taut, and she could feel the tension in his fingers. It added to her own. "Didn't you sleep?" he demanded.

"Not very well," she admitted and wondered why he seemed so angry. "I woke during the night. It all seemed to hit me at once."

Lance's frown deepened. "I should have stayed."

"No." She shook her head, searching his eyes for the reason for the roughness in his voice. "I needed to be alone to get it out of my system. I'm better now."

Something flickered in his eyes before they became unfathomable. "Have you changed your mind?"

Foxy knew he was speaking of their marriage and felt a quick thrill of alarm. She forced herself to speak calmly. "No."

Lance nodded and released her chin. "Fine. We'll take care of the paperwork before we go by the hospital. Ready?"

Foxy frowned but stepped into the corridor, closing the door at her back. "When we see Kirk," she began as they walked toward the steps, "I'd like to tell him about our plans myself . . . when the time's right."

Lance's brow lifted and fell. "Fine."

Miffed by his tone and by his cool self-possession, Foxy tilted her face to his and spoke coldly. "Maybe I should've asked if you'd changed your mind."

"I'd have let you know if I had," he returned as they stepped into the sunlight.

"Undoubtedly," she agreed. Saying nothing, Lance led her to the sleek blue Porsche he had rented that morning. For the first time since her screaming fear of the previous afternoon, Foxy began to feel the full emotion of anger. "Are you going to have your lawyers draw up a contract? I want to be certain to read the fine print."

"Save it, Foxy," Lance warned and opened the passenger door.

"No." She stood back and glared. "I don't know why you're acting like this. Maybe you're just a miserable human being in the mornings. I'll get used to it, I suppose. But you'd better get used to the fact that I say what I want when I want. If you don't like it, you can —"

Her tirade was cut off as he slammed the door shut and pulled her roughly into his arms. His mouth came down hard on hers. Angry and dominant, his lips bruised hers while she stood too surprised to protest or respond. He held her, ravishing her mouth until she was breathless. Then, with a suddenness that left her gasping, he set her aside. "And I know how to shut you up when I don't want to hear it."

Foxy managed one indignant huff. "You're a maniac," she told him as he opened her door again.

"All right," he agreed. Then, without giving her a chance for further comment, he nudged her into the car.

For the first time, Foxy noticed two young girls standing on the sidewalk giggling. Furious and embarrassed, she folded her arms and clamped her lips shut. She would not give him the satisfaction of either arguing or submitting herself to his idle conversation. In utter silence, they drove off to secure a marriage license.

A scant two hours later, after speaking only when unavoidable, they walked into Kirk's hospital room. Foxy did her best not to register any shock at the sight of the bandages and plaster. His leg was surrounded by an external fixture rather than a cast. To Foxy's eyes it looked like an erector set built by a clever teenager. Surrounded by white sheets and bandages, tubes and metal, Kirk lay propped up in bed. He was scowling at Pam with the look of a man who has just finished giving a heated speech. Instantly Foxy sensed the tension and glanced from one to the other. She thought it best to employ tact and make no comment. Because she had known Kirk would hate them, she hadn't brought any flowers. Empty-handed, she crossed to the bed and gravely studied him.

"You're a mess," she concluded, making her voice lightly scornful. Her stomach trembled at the amount of bandages and the terrifyingly foreign-looking apparatus around his leg. As she had hoped, the scowl faded and a grin took its place.

"You're cute, too. Hi, Lance. I think I might have dented a fender on your car."

"Scraped the paint, too," he said easily

as his hands disappeared into his pockets. Watching him, Pam noted that he was uncomfortable in hospital rooms. Foxy, she mused, was putting up a front Kirk would see through if it occurred to him to look. But of course it wouldn't. "I'd keep clear of Charlie for a while," Lance advised as he glanced over to find Pam's eyes on him. Her face was composed, but he could detect the signs of a sleepless night. He had seen the expression she wore before, on wives, parents, and lovers of countless other drivers. A quick, silent understanding passed between them before he looked back at Kirk.

"I heard Betinni took first and hooked the championship." Hampered by the position, Kirk's shrug was awkward. "He's a good driver. We've been passing off the lead all season." He shifted a bit, and Foxy caught the brief wince of pain. Knowing sympathy would only earn her a growl, she turned to Pam.

"Well," she said with a smile a shade too bright, "I don't suppose he's been giving you any trouble."

"On the contrary." Pam glanced at Kirk, then back to his sister. "He's been giving me a great deal."

"Pam." Kirk's irritated tone held a

warning. She ignored both.

"He's ordered me back to Manhattan. He's very annoyed because I'm not going."

Unsure what to say, Foxy looked from Pam to Kirk, then to Lance. "Well," she said and cleared her throat.

"He seems to think I'm being quite unreasonable," Pam added in the same mild tone.

"And stupid," Kirk tossed out. His scowl was back, deeper than before.

"Oh yes." Pam smiled gently. "And stupid. I'd forgotten that."

"Look," Kirk began, and Foxy recognized the dangerous pitch in his voice. "You've got no reason to hang around here."

"I've got a hospital fetish," Pam returned.

"Damn it, I don't want you!" Kirk shouted, then cursed at the pain that followed his outburst.

Firmly Lance took Foxy's arm as she started to move forward. "Keep out of it," he ordered quietly.

"Too bad," Pam retorted. Her voice was soft, but she stood like a general facing the enemy, her shoulders straight. The sun streamed through the window behind her, haloing her hair. "You're not getting rid of me. I love you."

"You're crazy," Kirk threw back, fidgeting in the bed.

"Very likely."

He narrowed his eyes at her careless response. In the strong sunlight, her skin looked like alabaster. He felt the need rise surprisingly fast. "I'm not letting you stay," he ground out in defense.

"What're you going to do?" Pam countered with a shrug. "Kick me back to Manhattan with your good leg?"

"I will as soon as I can get up," Kirk muttered, furious that he had to lay flat on his back to argue with a woman half his size.

"Yeah?" The slang came with elegant ease from Pam's delicately tinted lips. She walked over and gave his mustache a hard tug that brought out a sound of surprised protest. "Remind me to be scared later. Now as I see it I've got three choices. I can murder you, jump off a bridge, or I can cope. I come from a long line of copers. You, on the other hand," she added with a pat on his cheek, "simply have no choice at all. You're stuck with me."

"Think so, huh?" Kirk's mouth twisted into a reluctant grin. "Guess you're pretty tough."

"You guess right," she agreed, then bent to kiss him lightly. Kirk grabbed a handful of her hair and took the kiss deeper.

"We're going to settle this when I can stand up," he muttered, but pulled her back to kiss her again.

"I'm sure we will," Pam said with a smile as she sat on the edge of the bed. Foxy noted that his hand sought hers.

He loves her, she realized suddenly. *He really loves her.* Her eyes fastened on Pam with a look of respect and hope. *Maybe,* she thought rapidly, *maybe she's the answer. Maybe he's finally found an alternative.*

"Well." Pam smiled into Foxy's bemused face. "Is there any news from the outside world?"

"News?" Foxy repeated, trying to reorganize her thoughts.

"Earthquakes, floods, wars, famine," Pam prompted with a laugh. "I feel I've been neatly cut off for the past twenty-four hours."

"There hasn't been any of those that I know of," Foxy answered with a glance at Kirk. *This is the time,* she told herself. *This is the time to tell him.* Suddenly she felt ridiculously nervous and awkward. "Lance and I," she began, then her eyes sought his for reassurance. Taking a deep breath, she looked back at Kirk and spoke quickly. "Lance and I are going to be married." Instantly Foxy saw the surprise and puzzlement cover Kirk's face. His brows drew together as he stared at her.

"Well!" Pam rose quickly and hugged Foxy. "This is news. The best kind." Glancing over Foxy's head, she met Lance's eyes. "You're a very lucky man."

"Yes," he returned, unsmiling. "I know."

"Married?" Kirk interrupted. "What do you mean, married?"

"The usual definition," Foxy told him as she moved to his bedside. "You've heard it before, it's still quite popular."

"When?" he demanded shortly.

"As soon as the blood tests and paperwork are taken care of," Lance put in casually. After strolling over to the bed, he slipped an arm around Foxy's shoulders. Kirk watched the gesture, then lifted his eyes to Lance's face. "What's the matter?" Lance asked him with a grin. "Did you want us to get your permission?"

"No," Kirk mumbled uncomfortably. Looking up into Foxy's face, he remembered the little girl. "Yeah," he admitted with a sigh. "Maybe. I could have used a little warning, anyway."

"You're hardly in any shape to beat him

up now," Foxy pointed out. Lance's arm around her eased away her tension, and her eyes laughed down at Kirk.

Kirk studied his best friend and then his sister. When he held out his hand, Foxy slipped hers into it. "You sure?"

Foxy turned her head until she faced Lance. *He's the only man I've ever loved,* she mused. *It's not a fantasy anymore, but real. Am I sure?* she asked herself, keeping both her mind and heart open. She took her time studying his familiar face, then answered the question she thought she saw in his eyes. "Yes," she said and smiled. "I'm sure." Rising on her toes, she met his mouth and felt the morning's nerves drain away. "Very sure." Her hand was still warm in Kirk's. "Don't worry about me," she told Kirk as she turned back to him.

"It's a new habit I've gotten into, but be happy and I won't worry," he countered, foolishly feeling as if something precious was being stolen from him. "I guess you're all grown up."

"I guess so," she said softly and returned the pressure of his hand.

"Give me a kiss," he ordered. After Foxy raised her head again, Kirk fastened his eyes on Lance. An essential male understanding passed between them. They knew each other as well as brothers ever do, but now they were joined deeper by the woman between them. Perhaps if they had not been close, had not been intimate with each other's thoughts over the years, it would have been simpler. The very quality of their friendship made it complex. "Don't hurt her," Kirk warned as he kept possession of Foxy's hand. "Are you going to live in that house in Boston?"

"That's right," Lance answered. Foxy watched them, knowing they said more than she could translate.

Abruptly Kirk's expression softened and a smile appeared. "I'm not going to be in any shape to walk down an aisle to give her away." He squeezed the hand he held in his, lingering over it a moment before he offered it to Lance. "Keep her happy," he commanded as Foxy's hand passed from one man to the other.

Chapter Nine

Three days later, Foxy sat in Lance's rented Porsche as it ate up the miles between New York and Massachusetts. Her hands lay in her lap but were rarely still. She continued to twist the plain gold band around and around the third finger of her left hand. *Married,* she thought yet again. *We're actually married.* It had been so quick, so lacking in emotion — a few moments in front of a blank-faced judge, a few words spoken. An unruffled fifteen minutes. It had been almost like a play until the ring had slipped onto her finger. That made it real. That made her Mrs. Lancelot Matthews.

Cynthia Matthews, she mused, trying out the sound in her mind. *Or perhaps,* she reflected, *I could try for more elegance with Cynthia Fox-Matthews.* She nearly laughed aloud. *Elegance needs more than a hyphen. Foxy Matthews,* she decided with a mental nod. *That'll just have to be good enough.*

"You're going to wear a ridge into your finger before we get to Rhode Island." Lance spoke quietly, but Foxy jumped in her seat as if he had shouted. "Nervous?" he asked with a laugh in his voice.

"No." Not wanting to confess what silliness her mind had been engaged in, she prevaricated. "I was just thinking . . . Kirk looked much better, didn't he?"

"Um-hum." Lance switched on the wipers as a light rain began to fall. "Pam's the best medicine he can get."

"Yes, she is." Foxy shifted in her seat so that she had a clear view of his profile. *My husband,* she thought and nearly lost the thread of the conversation. "I've never known anyone else who could handle Kirk so well. Except you."

"Kirk needs a co-driver who can't be intimidated into backing off," Lance told her, glancing toward her briefly. "You've always handled him in your own way. Even when you were thirteen, you could do it without letting him know he was being handled."

The faintest frown line appeared between Foxy's brows. "I never considered it handling exactly. . . . And I didn't realize anyone else noticed."

"There isn't anything about you I

haven't noticed over the years." Lance turned to her again with a deep, quiet look. Foxy's pulse hammered erratically.

Will he always be able to do this to me? she wondered. *Even after the novelty of marriage wears off, will he be able just to look at me to turn me into jelly? It hasn't changed in ten years, will it change in ten more?* Lance's voice broke into her thoughts, and she twisted her head to look at him again. "I'm sorry, what?"

"I said it was a nice gesture for you to give Pam your bouquet. Of course, it's rather a shame you don't have some small remembrance."

Foxy started to speak, then flushed and fumbled in her bag for her brush. Buried at the bottom was the white velvet ribbon she had removed from the spray of orchids Lance had given her for a bridal bouquet. The thought that he might think her sentiment foolish held her tongue. She had the brush in her hand before she remembered her hair was pinned up. Hastily she stuffed the brush back in her bag. Rain pattered lightly on the windows and blurred the autumn landscape.

"I suppose it was a bit cut and dried, wasn't it?" Lance commented. "Ten minutes in front of a judge, no friends or traditional trappings, no tears or rice." He glanced at her again, his brow lifted under his hair. "I suppose you're feeling a bit cheated."

"No, of course not." Though her mind had wandered once or twice to the complicated beauty of a traditional wedding, she didn't feel cheated so much as curious. *Would she feel married if the wedding had included veils and organ music? Would she have this awkward sense of it not being quite real if there had been a ceremony ending with old shoes and rice?* "Besides," she said with a shake of her head. "I don't have any great Aunt Sarah to weep softly in the back pew." The thought of family had her worrying her wedding band again.

"You did specify plain gold with no stones or markings?"

"What?" Foxy followed Lance's brief glance to her hands. "Oh, yes." Guiltily she dropped her right hand to her side. "Yes, it's exactly what I wanted."

"Does it fit?"

"Fit? Why yes, it fits."

"Then why the devil do you keep twisting it on your finger?" The annoyance in his tone was sharp.

Well aware it was justified, Foxy sighed. "I'm sorry, Lance. It all seems to be happening so fast, and going to Boston . . ." She bit her lip, then confessed. "I'm nervous about meeting your family. I haven't had a great deal of experience with families."

Lance lay his hand on hers a moment. "Don't judge the way of families by mine," he advised dryly. "They're not the type you see on a Christmas card."

"Of course," Foxy concluded with a wry grin, "that's supposed to reassure me."

"Just don't let them bother you," Lance advised with a careless shrug. "I don't."

"Easy for you to say," she retorted, wrinkling her nose at him. "You're one of them."

"So are you." Lifting her hand, Lance ran his thumb over her wedding band. "Remember it."

"Tell me about them."

"I suppose I'll have to sooner or later." With this, he drew out a cigar and punched in the car lighter. "My mother is a Bardett — that's an old Boston family. I believe they gave Paul Revere directions."

"How patriotic."

"The Bardetts are notoriously patriotic," he returned before he touched the glowing lighter to the tip of his cigar. "In any case, my mother enjoys being both a Bardett and a Matthews, but more than anything else, she enjoys committees."

"Committees?" Foxy repeated. "What sorts of committees?"

"All sorts of committees, as long as they're suitable for a Bardett-Matthews. She loves to organize them, attend them, complain about them. She's a snob from the top of her pure white coiffure to the tip of her Italian shoes."

"Lance, how dreadful of you."

"You said you wanted to hear about them," he countered easily. "Mother loves doing charitable work. It reads well in the society pages. She also feels anyone poor enough to require aid should have the good taste not to ask for it until she has a chance to organize the committee. But snob or not, she does a lot of good despite her motives, so it hardly matters."

"You're being very hard on her." Foxy frowned at the tone of his voice as she remembered her own mother: a happy, disorganized, loving woman with Kirk's penchant for ragged sneakers.

Lance gave Foxy a curious, sidelong glance. "Perhaps. She and I have never seen things the same way. My father used to find her committees amusing and harmless. I'm not as tolerant as he was." Foxy's frown deepened, and he gave her his crooked smile. "Don't worry, Fox, you won't see any blood spilled. We don't get along, but we're quite civilized about it. Bardetts, you see, are always civilized."

"And the Matthews?" Foxy asked, becoming intrigued.

"The Matthews have a tendency to produce a black sheep every generation or so. A couple of hundred years back, a Matthews ran off and married a serving wench from a local tavern. Spoiled the blood a bit." He grinned as if pleased with the flaw, then drew on his cigar. "But for the most part, the Matthews are every bit as . . . upstanding as the Bardetts. My grandmother is all dignity. According to the stories that drop from time to time, she never batted an eye when my grandfather had his affair with the countess. As far as she was concerned, it didn't happen. Her daughter, my aunt Phoebe, is exactly as the countess said: dull. She hasn't had an original thought in fifty years. There's an alarming amount of aunts, uncles, cousins, and in-laws."

"They don't all live in Boston, do they?"

"No, thank heaven. They're spread over the States and Europe, but a large clutch huddle in Boston and Martha's Vineyard and thereabouts."

"I suppose your mother was surprised when you told her about our getting married." Foxy caught herself before she twisted the ring again.

"I haven't told her."

"What?" Incredulous, she turned to stare at him. "You didn't tell her?"

"No."

Foxy started to demand why, then thought of the reason herself. *He's ashamed of me.* Swallowing, she twisted back to stare at the gray autumn rain. Cynthia Fox of Indiana doesn't measure up to the Bardetts and Matthews of Boston. "I suppose," she said in a tight voice, "you could keep me hidden in an attic room. Or we could forge a pedigree."

"Hmm?" Preoccupied, Lance glanced at her averted head, then back at the road. After passing a slow-moving truck, he tossed his cigar out the window.

For several moments, Foxy tried to hold her tongue and temper. She failed. "We could tell them I'm a deposed princess from some Third World country. I won't speak any English for the first six months." She rounded on him, hurt and furious. "Or I could be the daughter of some English baron who died and left me penniless.

After all, it's the lineage that's important, not the money."

Her tone captured Lance's attention. Looking over, he caught the sheen of angry tears in her eyes. Instantly his brows drew together. "What are you babbling about?"

"If you don't think I'm good enough to pass as Mrs. Lancelot Matthews, then you can just . . ." Her suggestion was lost as he whipped the car to the shoulder of the road. Before she could catch her breath, he had her arms in a punishing grip.

"Don't you ever let me hear you say that again, do you understand?" His face was furious, but Foxy tilted her chin and met it levelly.

"No, no, I don't understand. I don't understand anything." To her humiliation, tears began to well up in her eyes and spill out onto her cheeks. The weeping surprised both of them; her because it began so suddenly, not giving her an opportunity to control it, and him because he had never seen her cry before.

"Don't," Lance ordered roughly, then gave her a brisk shake. "Don't do that."

"I will if I want to." Foxy swallowed and let the tears fall.

Lance swore before he let her go. "All right, go ahead. We'll swim back to Boston, but I want to know what brought on the flood."

Foxy fumbled in her purse for a tissue and found none. "I don't have a tissue," she said miserably, then wiped at the tears with the back of her hand. With another well-chosen oath, Lance pulled his handkerchief from his jacket pocket and stuffed it into her hand. "It's silk," she said and tried to give it back to him.

"I'll strangle you with it in a minute." As if to prevent himself from doing so, Lance gripped the steering wheel. "We're not moving," he said in a firm voice, "until you tell me what's gotten into you."

"It's nothing, nothing at all," she claimed as she dampened the white silk. Foxy was thoroughly disgusted with herself, but her temper forced her to continue. "Why should it bother me that you haven't even told your family we're married?"

For a few moments, there was only the sound of the drizzling rain and Foxy's sniffles. The car became still except for the monotonous back-and-forth movement of the windshield wipers. "Do you think," Lance began in even, precise tones, "that I didn't tell my family of our marriage because I'm ashamed of you?"

"What else should I think?" Foxy tossed

back. "I don't suppose a Fox from Indiana is very impressive."

"Idiot!" The word vibrated in the small closed car. Foxy's sob was transformed into a gasp. Fascinated, she watched Lance struggle to control what appeared to be a violent surge of temper. When he spoke, it was too soft and too controlled. "I didn't tell my family because I wanted a couple of days of peace before they descend on us. As soon as they know we're married, the whole social merry-go-round gets started. A honeymoon would have been the ideal answer, but I explained to you it's impossible until I straightened out a few things. I've been away from the business for several months. I felt after the circuit and Kirk's accident, we both could use a few days of quiet. It never occurred to me you'd see it as anything else."

With a quick gesture of his hand, Lance put the car in first gear and merged back into the traffic. The silence was complete and unbearable. Foxy crumpled Lance's handkerchief into a tight ball and wished for a way to begin the conversation over again.

The days since Kirk's accident had been jumbled together into a mass of time rather than distinct minutes and hours.

She knew she had slept and eaten, but could not have told how many hours her eyes had been closed or what food she had tasted. Her marriage seemed steeped in unreality. *But it is real,* she reminded herself. *And Lance is right. I'm an idiot.*

"I'm sorry, Lance," she murmured, lifting her eyes to his profile.

"Forget it." His answer was curt and unforgiving. Recognizing the dismissal in his tone, she turned back to the view of misty rain.

Are all brides so insecure? she wondered, closing her eyes. *This isn't like me. I'm acting like a different person, I'm thinking like a different person.* Weariness began to close over her, and she let her mind drift. *I'll feel better once we're settled in. A few days of quiet is exactly what I need.* She let the pattering rain lull her to sleep.

Foxy moaned and stirred. She no longer heard the steady hum of the Porsche beneath her but felt a quiet swaying. She felt a cool spray on her face and turned her head away from it. Her cheek brushed something warm and smooth. The scent that teased her nostrils was instantly familiar. Opening her eyes, she saw Lance's jawline. Gradually she realized she was being carried. She nuzzled her face into his shoulder as the rain continued to fall half-heartedly. A gloomy dusk was settling, bringing with it a thin fog.

Along with Lance's scent she could detect the fragrance of damp leaves and grass, an autumn smell she would soon begin to associate with New England. His footsteps were nearly soundless, swallowed by the mists swirling close to the ground. There was something eerie and surreal about the dimming light and silence. Disoriented, Foxy shifted in his arms.

"Decide to join the living again?" Lance asked. He stopped, heedless of the drizzle and looked down at her.

"Where are we?" Totally confused, Foxy twisted her head to peer around. Almost at once, she saw the house. A three-story brownstone rose in front of her. Its walls were cloaked in ivy, dark green and glistening in the rain. Wrought-iron balconies circled the second and third stories, and they, too, were tangled with clinging ivy. The windows were tall and narrow. Even in the gloom, the house had an ageless elegance and style. "Is that your house?" Foxy asked. As she spoke she let her head fall back in order to see the roof and chimney.

"It was my grandfather's," Lance answered, studying her reaction. "He left it to me. My grandmother always preferred their house in Martha's Vineyard."

"It's beautiful," Foxy murmured. The rain that washed her face and dampened her hair was forgotten. She felt an immediate affection for the aged brownstone and tenacious ivy. *He had roots in this house,* she thought, and fell in love. "It's really beautiful."

"Yes, it is," Lance agreed as his eyes roamed her face.

Foxy looked up to meet his gaze. She smiled, blinking raindrops from her lashes. "It's raining," she pointed out.

"So it is." He kissed her, lingering for a moment. "Your lips are wet. I like the way the rain clings to your hair. In this light you look very pale and ethereal." His eyes were the color of the mist that grew thicker and seemed to be spun into threads around them. "If I let you go, will you vanish?"

"No," she murmured, then combed her fingers through the damp hair that fell over his forehead. "I won't vanish." A quick surge of need for him throbbed through her, causing her to shiver.

"I suppose you're real enough to catch a chill from standing in the rain." He tightened his grip on her and began to walk again.

"You don't have to carry me," she began.

Lance climbed nimbly up the front steps. "Don't you think we should do something traditional?" he countered as he maneuvered a key into the lock of the door. Pushing it open with his shoulder, he carried Foxy over the threshold and into the darkened house. "Welcome home," he murmured, then captured her lips in a long, quiet kiss.

"Lance," she whispered, incredibly moved. "I love you."

Slowly he set her on her feet. For a moment, they stood close, their faces silhouetted by the darkening sky. Before they closed the door, Foxy decided, there should be nothing between them. "Lance, I'm sorry about making that scene in the car."

"You've already apologized."

"You were angry enough for two apologies."

He laughed and kissed her nose, changed his mind and took her mouth again. It seemed that he could draw from a kiss more than she had known she had to offer. "Anger is the handiest weapon against tears," he told her as he ran his hands up and down her arms. "You threw me, Fox. You always do when you forget to be invincible." He lifted his finger to run it along her jawline, and his eyes were dark as he watched the journey. "Perhaps I should have explained things to you, but I'm simply not used to explaining myself to anyone. We're both going to have some adjustments to make." He took both her hands in his, then lifted them to his lips. "Trust me for a while, will you?"

"All right." She nodded. "I'll try."

After releasing her hands, Lance closed the door, shutting out the damp chill. For an instant, the house was plunged into total darkness, then abruptly the entrance hall streamed with light. Foxy stood in its center and turned around in a slow circle. To her left was a staircase, gleaming and uncarpeted. Its oak banister looked smooth as silk. To her right was a mirrored clothes stand that had once reflected the face of Lance's great-great grandmother. He watched as she made a study of Revere candlesticks and a gilt-framed Gainsborough. The light from the chandelier showered down on her, catching the glint of rain in her hair. She had a wraithlike quality in the simple green dress she had chosen to wear as a bride. It had long narrow sleeves and a high mandarin collar. Its skirt fell straight and unadorned from a snug waist. Her only jewelry was the plain gold band he had placed on her finger. She looked as untouched as springtime, but the sensuality of autumn was in her movements.

"I wouldn't have pictured you in a place like this," Foxy said after completing her circle.

"Oh?" Lance leaned against the wall and waited for her to elaborate.

"It's beautiful," she went on in a voice touched with wonder. "Really beautiful, but it's so . . . settled," she decided, then looked back at him. "I suppose that's it. I've never thought of you as settled."

"I enjoy being settled now and again," was his careless answer. Foxy thought that in the trim gray suit he looked at ease amid the ivy and brownstone. Yet there was something in his eyes, she realized, that would never quite be tamed. Expert tailoring and priceless antiques would never alter the man he was. Knowing she was mad to prefer the sinner to the saint, Foxy was nevertheless glad.

"But I should be prepared to pack at a moment's notice?" she asked, giving him a smile a great deal like her brother's.

"How fortunate I am to have married a woman who understands me." His grin was crooked and familiar and still managed to send her pulses racing. He moved toward her, then wound one of the curls that framed her face around his finger. "And an exceptional-looking creature as well; quite bright, quick with her tongue, impulsive enough to be fascinating, and with a voice that constantly sounds like she's just been aroused."

Foxy flushed with a mixture of amusement and embarrassment. "Sounds like you made quite a deal."

"Oh, I did," Lance agreed but his grin faded and he studied her with serious eyes. "A smart businessman knows when to make his pitch." As quickly as it had grown grave, his expression lightened. Bemused, Foxy watched the changes. "Hungry?" he asked suddenly.

Intrigued, Foxy shook her head. "No, not really." She remembered the long hours he had spent driving, "I suppose there must be a can or something around I could open."

"I think we might do better." Taking her hand, Lance led her down the hallway. The rooms to the right and left were dark and mysterious. "I called Mrs. Trilby yesterday.

She does the housekeeping and so forth. I told her I was coming in and to have things ready. I'm not fond of dustcovers and empty pantries." He passed through a door at the end of the hall. As he turned the switch light spilled into the kitchen.

"Oh, it's wonderful!" Foxy cried as she moved into the room. "Does it work?" she demanded, going immediately to the small arched fireplace that was built into one wall.

"Yes, it works." Lance smiled as she bent closer to peer inside.

"I love it," she said with a laugh as she straightened. "I'll probably want a fire in it in August." She ran her finger over a pine trestle table, which stood in the bow of a bay window. "The only fire I have in my kitchen is when I burn the bacon."

"This is your kitchen," Lance reminded her. He watched her as he loosened the knot in his tie, then slipped it off. There was something intensely intimate in the casual gesture. Foxy felt a quick thrill and turned to walk the room.

"I'm not very domestic," she confessed. "I don't even know where I keep the coffee."

"Try the counter behind you," Lance suggested as he turned to find what Mrs.

Trilby had tucked into the refrigerator. "Can you cook?"

"Name it," Foxy challenged, then located the coffee. "I can cook it."

"We'll skip the Beef Wellington due to lack of time and imminent starvation. How about a couple of omelets?"

"Kid stuff." Foxy peeked over her shoulder. "Do you cook?"

"Only if I fall asleep at the beach."

"Get me a skillet," she ordered, trying to look disgusted.

The Lancelot Matthewses enjoyed their wedding supper of omelets and coffee at the kitchen table. Outside, the darkness was complete, with the rain still pattering and the moon a prisoner of the clouds. Time was lost to Foxy. It might have been seven in the evening or three in the morning. The feeling of timelessness was soothing, and wanting to prolong it, she ignored the watch on her wrist. Beneath her light conversation, her nerves were struggling to reach the surface. She chided herself for having them, attempted to ignore them, but they remained, under the veneer of confidence. She toyed with the rest of her eggs as Lance divided the last of the pot of coffee between them.

"That's why you're so thin," he commented. When Foxy looked up blankly, he went on. "You don't take enough interest in food. You lost weight during the season. I watched it slide off you."

Foxy shrugged away the pounds but dutifully applied herself to the rest of her eggs. "I like to eat in restaurants as the exception rather than the rule. I'll gain it back in a couple weeks." She smiled up at him. "I do have a growing interest in a hot bath, though."

"I'll take you up," he said and rose. "Then I'll go out and get the bags. The rest of the luggage should arrive by tomorrow."

Foxy rose, too, and began to stack the dishes. Though she knew it was foolish, she felt her nerves rise with her. "You don't have to take me up, just tell me which bath to use. I'll find it."

He watched her back as she set the dishes in the sink. "The second door on the right's the bedroom, the bath's through there. Leave the dishes," he ordered.

Foxy started to refuse, but his hand on her shoulder gently persuaded her to forget her qualms. She needed a few moments alone to collect her wits. "All right," she agreed, then turned with a nod. "I won't be long. I imagine you'd like a bath after the driving you did today."

"Take your time." They left the kitchen together and walked down the main hall. "I'll use another bath."

"Fine," Foxy said as they parted at the end of the hall. *How polite we are,* she thought as she fled up the stairs. *How terrifyingly married.*

In the bedroom, a pair of French doors opened out onto a balcony. The walls were covered with a rich cream wallpaper with dark trim along the floor and ceiling. The furniture was a mixture of periods and styles; Hepplewhite, Chippendale, Queen Anne, and the result was both exquisite and natural. Set into the far wall was a white brick fireplace with a marble mantel; there were logs waiting to be lit within it. Foxy decided Mrs. Trilby must be efficient. The bed was a high four-poster and was covered with a midnight-blue silk counterpane. An heirloom, she knew instantly, probably priceless. She caught her bottom lip between her teeth. This was the sort of thing she would have to learn to deal with — more, to live with.

I'm being an idiot. I married Lance, not his money, not his family. Bride's nerves. I wouldn't feel so awkward and tense if I'd had more experience. Foxy's gaze strayed to the bed again before she took a deep breath and looked down at her hands. Her wedding band glinted back at her. Ignoring the fluttering in her stomach, she began to undress. In her slip, she walked into the bath and discovered more proof of Mrs. Trilby's efficiency. Fresh towels were laid out along with a collection of fragrant soaps, oils, and bath salts. The tub itself was sunken, large enough for two, and Foxy's skin tingled at the thought of languishing in it.

As the hot water began to run she experimented with scents and oils. The room grew rich with steam and fragrance. She began to enjoy herself. Thirty minutes later, she stepped out of the tub, her muscles loose, her skin pink and scented. Choosing a mint-green towel, she wrapped it like a sarong around her body. Lulled by the bath, she hummed lightly as she pulled the confining pins from her hair. It tumbled in a confused mass past her shoulders, and she ran her fingers through it in a vain attempt to set it to rights. *There'll be a brush and a robe in the bags,* she told her reflection. *Surely Lance has brought them up by now.* Leaving her hair carelessly tangled, Foxy opened the connecting door and walked into the bedroom.

The room was lit by the warm glow of china lamps and a crackling fire. It was the scent and sound of the burning wood that caused Foxy to glance toward the fireplace. She was halfway into the room before she saw him. With a small sound of surprise, she clutched at the towel that was tucked loosely over her breasts. Dressed in a black kimono-style robe, Lance stood beside a round, glass-topped table. He paused in the act of opening a split of champagne and studied every inch of his wife. With her free hand, Foxy pushed at her steam-dampened curls.

"Enjoy your bath?" he asked, opening the champagne without taking his eyes from her.

"Yes." Making a quick search, Foxy spotted her cases. "I didn't hear you in here," she said, knowing her voice was not quite its normal pitch. "I was just going to get my brush and a robe."

"Why?" Deftly he poured two glasses of the sparkling wine. "I like you in green." Foxy's fingers tightened on the towel as he smiled. It was the wicked, devilish smile that always pulled at her. "And I like your hair when it's not quite tamed. Come." He held out a glass. "Have some champagne."

It was not as Foxy had planned it. She

knew she should have been dressed in the peignoir Pam had given her. She should have been alluring and confident and ready for him. It had not been in her plans to greet her husband on their wedding night clad in only a bath towel with her hair flying every which way and a look of stunned surprise on her face. She obeyed him, however, accepting the wine in the hope that it would soothe the sudden dryness in her throat. As she started to lift the glass to her lips, he reached out and took her wrist. Her pulse throbbed desperately under his fingertips.

"No toast, Foxy?" he said softly, the smile still lingering on his lips. His eyes remained on hers as he took a step closer and touched his glass to hers. "To a well-driven race."

She lifted her glass warily, watching him as she sipped. The champagne was ice cold and thrilling on her tongue.

"Only one glass tonight, Fox," Lance murmured. "I don't want your mind clouded."

Her heart hammering, Foxy turned away. "This is a lovely room." She hastily cleared her throat and moistened her lips. "I've never seen so many antiques in one place."

"Are you fond of antiques?"

"I don't know," she answered as she moved around the room. "I've never had any. You must like them." The last word was only a whisper as she turned around and found him directly behind her. There was something eerie about the soundless way he moved. She would have taken a quick step in retreat, but his hand circled her neck.

"It appears there's only one way to get you to hold still." With the merest pressure of his fingers, he brought her to her toes and firmly covered her mouth. Foxy felt the room dip and sway. His tongue teased the tip of hers before it traced her lips. "Would you like to discuss my Hepplewhite collection?" he asked. From her limp fingers, he took the half-filled glass of champagne.

Foxy opened her eyes. "No." Even the short word was difficult to form as her gaze strayed to his mouth. In an instant he was kissing her again, and the passion built, shuddering through her. She was clinging to him without having been aware of moving at all. The towel slipped unnoticed to the floor. With a low sound of pleasure, Lance buried his mouth against the curve of her throat while his hands ran over her heated skin. She felt the pain of desire and pressed closer to him. "Lance," she murmured as the blood drummed in her head. "I want you. Love me. Love me now." The words were lost under his mouth as it returned urgently to hers. "The light," she said breathlessly as he lowered her to the bed.

His eyes were dark and compelling. "I want to see you."

His body fitted itself to hers. He did not love gently. She had not expected gentleness, she had not expected patience. She had expected quick heat and urgent demands, and she was not disappointed. His hands moved roughly over her, exploring before they possessed. From her lips, his mouth trailed down along her throat, hungry always hungry, as it journeyed to her breast. Foxy moaned with trembling pleasure as he flicked his tongue over her nipple. The ache of desire spread from her stomach. His hands were bruising, arousing as they wandered down her rib cage, lingering at her waist and hips as his mouth continued to ravish her breast.

She began to move under him, a woman's instinct making her motions sensual and inviting. Lean and firm, his hands massaged the sensitive skin of her inner thigh, and her muscles went lax, her joints fluid. She learned that he made love as he had raced — with intensity and absorption. There was a ruthless, steady dominance in him, a power that demanded much more than submission. Surrender would have been too tame a response. More, she discovered her own power. He needed her. She could feel it in the urgency of his hands, taste it in the hunger of his mouth. She heard it as he spoke her name. They were tangled together, flesh against flesh, mouth against mouth while it seemed the only reality was dark, moist kisses and heated skin. The faint scent of wood smoke added something ageless and primitive.

As her body tingled under his hands she began to make her own explorations. She discovered the hard, rippling muscles which his leanness had disguised. As she moved her hands to his hips Lance groaned against her mouth and took the kiss deeper. His hands grew wild, desperate, and she tumbled with him into a world ruled by sensation. The pleasure was acute, so sharp, it brought with it a hint of pain. There seemed to be no part of her that he did not wish to know, to enjoy, to conquer. She locked her arms tightly around his neck, burying her mouth against his throat. His taste filled her until champagne seemed a poor substitute. Here was something dark and male she had yet to learn, and she traced the tip of her tongue over his skin, exploring, discovering. Passion was building beyond anything she had imagined possible. Both emotionally and physically, her response was absolute. She was his.

Her breath was clogging in her lungs, passing through her lips as moans and sighs. Desire reached a turbulent peak when she whispered his name. "Lance." His mouth took hers with fresh desperation, cutting off her words. He shifted on top of her, urging her legs apart with the movement.

The pleasure she had thought already at its summit, increased. Passion came in hot, irresistible waves, overpowering her with its tumultuous journey until all need, all sensation focused into one.

The dawn approached slowly. She was still wrapped tightly in his arms when the hiss of rain lulled her to sleep.

Chapter Ten

Foxy felt content. A dull red mist behind her lids told her the sun was falling on her face. With a small sigh, she allowed sleep to drift slowly away. She remembered the ease of Saturday mornings when she had been a young girl. Then she would lie in bed, dozing blissfully, knowing there was nothing but pleasure in the day ahead. There would be no worries, no time schedules, no responsibilities. School and Monday morning were centuries away. Foxy drifted on the edge of consciousness with the sensation of being both protected and free — a combination of feeling that had not been hers for a decade. She inched closer to it and clung.

There was a weight around her waist that added to her sense of security. Beside her was warmth. She snuggled yet closer to it. Lazily her lids fluttered open, and she looked directly into Lance's eyes. The past was whisked away as the present took over, but the sensation she woke with remained.

Neither she nor Lance spoke. She saw by the clearness of his gaze that he had been awake for some time. There was no hint of sleep in his eyes. They were as sharp and focused as hers were soft and heavy. His hair was tousled around his head, reminding her that it had been her fingers that had disturbed it short hours before. They continued to watch each other as their mouths moved closer to linger in a whisper of a kiss. The thought that they were naked and tangled together seeped through Foxy's drowsy contentment. The arm around her waist was firm in its possession.

"You looked like a child as you slept," he murmured as his mouth journeyed over her face. "Very young and untouched."

Foxy did not want to tell him that her thoughts had been childlike as well. As his fingers traced her spine she began to feel more and more as a woman. "How long have you been awake?"

His hand roamed with absentminded intimacy over her hip and thigh. Reminded that his touch the night before had not been absentminded, she felt her drowsiness swiftly abating. "Awhile," he said as he tightened his arm to bring her yet closer. "I considered waking you." His eyes roamed to her sleep-flushed cheeks, to the rich confusion of her hair against the pillowcase, to the full softness of her untinted mouth. "I rather enjoyed watching you sleep. There aren't many women who can manage to be both soothing and exciting the first thing in the morning."

Foxy arched her brows deliberately. "You know a great deal about women first thing in the morning?"

He grinned, then nuzzled the white curve of her neck. "I'm an early riser."

"A likely story," Foxy murmured, feeling her contentment mixing with a more demanding sensation. "I suppose you're hungry." She felt the tip of his tongue flick over her skin.

"Oh yes, I have quite an appetite this morning." He caught her bottom lip between his teeth. Desire quickened in Foxy's stomach. "You have the most appealing taste," he told her as he teased her lips apart. "I'm finding it habit forming. Your skin's amazingly soft," he went on as his hand moved to cup her breast. "Especially for someone who appears to be mostly bone and nerve." He ran his thumb over its peak and watched her eyes cloud. "I don't think I'm going to get enough of you anytime soon."

He was leading her quickly into passion with quiet words and experienced hands. His touch was no longer that of a stranger and was all the more arousing for its familiarity. She knew now what waited for her when all the doors were opened. She learned and enjoyed and shared. The morning grew late.

It was past noon when Foxy moved down the staircase toward the main floor. She moved slowly, telling herself that the day would last forever if she didn't hurry it. She wanted to explore the house, but firmly turned toward the kitchen. The other rooms would wait until Lance was with her. She had only taken two steps down the hall when the doorbell rang. Glancing up the stairs, Foxy concluded that Lance could hardly be finished showering and decided to answer the bell herself.

There were two women standing on the sheltered white porch. One look told Foxy that they were not door-to-door salespeople. The first was young, around Foxy's age, with warm brunette hair and a rosy complexion. She had a youthful beauty and frank, curious brown eyes. Her clothes were casual but expensive: a tweed suit with a fitted jacket and flared skirt softened by a silk blouse. Supreme confidence was in her every move.

The second woman was more mature but no less striking. Her hair was white and short, brushed back from a delicately pale face. She had few lines or wrinkles, and her not inconsiderable beauty depended more on her superb bone structure and cameo coloring than on the prodigal application of makeup. Her ice-blue suit matched her eyes; its simplicity cunningly announced its price. It occurred to Foxy in the instant they studied each other that her face was quite lovely but expressionless — like a painting of a lovely landscape executed without imagination.

"Hello." Foxy shifted her smile from one woman to the other. "May I help you?"

"Perhaps you'd be good enough to let us in." Foxy heard the distinct Boston cadence in the older woman's voice before she breezed into the hallway. More curious than annoyed, Foxy stepped aside to allow the younger woman to cross the threshold. Standing in the center of the hall, the matron stripped off her white kid gloves and surveyed Foxy's straight-leg jeans and loose chenille sweater. The air was suddenly redolent with French perfume. "And where," she demanded imperiously, "is my son?"

I should have known, Foxy thought as the cool blue eyes examined her. *But how totally unlike her he is. There's not even a shade of resemblance.* "Lance is upstairs, Mrs. Matthews," Foxy explained and tried a fresh smile. "I'm —"

"Well, fetch him then," she interrupted with an imperious movement of her hand. "And tell him I'm here."

It was not the rudeness as much as the tone of contempt that fanned Foxy's temper. Careful to guard her tongue, she spoke precisely. "I'm afraid he's in the shower at the moment. Would you care to wait?" She employed the tone of a receptionist in a dentist's office. From the corner of her eye, she caught the look of amusement in the younger woman's face.

"Come, Melissa." Mrs. Matthews flapped her gloves against her palm in annoyance. "We'll wait in the living room."

"Yes, Aunt Catherine." Her tone was agreeable but she flashed Foxy a look of mischief over her shoulder as she obeyed.

Taking a long breath, Foxy followed. She took care not to search the room like a newcomer, deciding that Catherine Matthews need not know she had seen little more than the bedroom of Lance's house. Her eyes fluttered over a baby grand piano, a Persian carpet, and a Tiffany lamp before moving back to the queenly figure that had settled into a ladder-back chair. "Perhaps you'd like something while you wait," Foxy offered. Hoping her tone was more polite than her thoughts, she tried the smile again. She was aware of the fact that an introduction was in order, but Catherine's air of scorn persuaded her to hold back her identity. "Some tea perhaps," she suggested. "Or some coffee."

"No." Catherine set her leather envelope bag on the table beside her. "Is Lancelot in the habit of having strange young women entertain his guests?"

"I wouldn't know," Foxy returned equably. Her backbone stiffened in automatic defense. "We haven't spent a great deal of time discussing strange young women."

"I'm quite certain that conversation is not why my son enjoys your companionship." Placing both hands on the ends of the chair's arms, she tapped a manicured finger against the polished wood. "Lancelot rarely chooses to dally with a young lady because of the prodigiousness of her vocabulary. His taste generally eludes me, but I must say, this time I'm astounded." With an arch of her brow, she gave Foxy a calculated look. "Where *did* he find you?"

"Selling matchbooks in Indianapolis," Foxy tossed out before she could prevent herself. "He's going to rehabilitate me."

"I wouldn't dream of it," Lance stated as he walked into the room. Foxy was instantly grateful to see that he was dressed much as herself: jeans, T-shirt, and bare feet. He gave Foxy a brief kiss as he moved past her to greet his mother. Bending down, he brushed the offered cheek with his lips. "Hello, Mother, you're looking well. Cousin Melissa." He smiled and kissed her cheek in turn. "I see you're lovelier than the last time."

"It's good to see you, Lance." Smiling, Melissa made a flirtatious sweep with her lashes. "Things are never dull when you're around."

"The highest of compliments," he replied, then turned back to his mother. "I imagine Mrs. Trilby told you I was coming in."

"Yes." She crossed surprisingly slender, youthful-looking legs. "I find it quite annoying to hear of my son's whereabouts from a servant."

"Don't be too annoyed with Mrs. Trilby," Lance countered carelessly. "She probably thought you knew. I intended to call you at the end of the week."

Catherine bristled at his deliberate misunderstanding of her meaning. When she spoke, however, her voice was cool and expressionless. Watching her, Foxy recalled Lance saying how the Bardetts were always civilized. *In their own fashion,* Foxy mused, thinking of her initial encounter. "I suppose I should be grateful that you intended to call me at all since you appear to be involved with your" — her eyes drifted to fasten briefly on Foxy — "guest." She lifted her brow, arching it into a smooth, high forehead. "Perhaps you would send her along so that we might have a private conversation. Since Trilby isn't here, she might make a pot of tea."

Foxy, knowing she would explode if she stayed, turned with the intention of locking herself into the bedroom until she could be trusted again.

"Foxy." Lance spoke her name mildly, but she recognized the underlying tone of command. Eyes flaming, she turned back. Lance casually crossed the room and slipped his arm over her shoulders. "I don't believe you've been introduced."

"Introductions," his mother cut in, "are hardly necessary or appropriate."

Lance inclined his head. "If you've finished insulting her, Mother, I'd like you to meet my wife."

There was total silence. Catherine Matthews did not gasp in alarm or surprise but merely stared at Foxy as if she were a strange piece of artwork in a gallery. "Your wife?" she repeated. Her voice remained calm, her face devoid of emotion. Folding her hands in her lap, she turned her eyes to her son. "When did this happen?"

"Yesterday. Foxy and I were married in the morning in New York. We drove up directly afterward for" — the grin flickered in his eyes as he kept them on his mother — "an informal honeymoon."

He's enjoying this, Foxy realized as she heard the amusement lace his voice. She knew, too, by the ice in Catherine's that she was not.

"One hopes Foxy is not her given name."

"Cynthia," Foxy put in distinctly as she grew weary of being referred to as an absent participant.

"Cynthia," Catherine murmured thoughtfully. She did not offer her hand or cheek for a token embrace or kiss; instead she carefully studied Foxy's face for the first time, obviously considering what could be done to salvage the situation. *I'm the situation,* Foxy realized with a quick flash of humor. "And your maiden name?" Catherine demanded with an inclination of her head.

"Fox," she told her with a mimicking nod.

"Fox," Catherine repeated, tapping her finger on the arm of the chair again. "Fox. The name is vaguely familiar."

"The race driver Lance sponsors," Melissa supplied helpfully. She stared at Foxy with undisguised fascination. "I suppose you're his sister or something, aren't you?"

"Yes, I'm his sister." The bold curiosity in her voice made Foxy smile. "Hello."

Mischief streaked swiftly over Melissa's face. Like Lance, Foxy noted, she was enjoying the encounter. "Hello."

"You met her on a — a . . ." Catherine's fingers waved as she searched for the proper term. "A race-car track?" The first hint of fury whispered through the words. Foxy stiffened again at the expression of contempt that was turned on her.

"I could do with some coffee, Fox, would you mind?" At Lance's calm request, she tossed her head back to flame at him. "Melissa will give you a hand," he continued, nearly cutting off her explosion. "Won't you, Melissa?" He addressed his cousin, but never took his eyes from his wife.

"Of course." Melissa rose obediently and crossed the room. Trapped, Foxy fought down the surge of temper. She turned, leaving Lance and his mother without another word. "Did you really meet Lance on a racetrack?" Melissa asked as the kitchen door swung behind them. There was no guile in the question, simply curiosity.

"Yes." Struggling with fury, Foxy managed to keep her tone level. "Ten years ago."

"Ten years? You had to have been a child." Melissa settled down at the table while Foxy scooped out coffee. Sunlight poured through the windows, making the drizzling rain of the day before only a memory. "Now, ten years later, he marries you." Elbows on the table, Melissa made a cradle out of her hands and set her chin on it. "It's terribly romantic."

As she felt her anger taper off Foxy blew out a long breath. "Yes, I suppose it is."

"I wouldn't worry too much about Aunt Catherine," Melissa advised, studying Foxy's profile. "She wouldn't have approved of anyone she hadn't handpicked."

"That's comforting," Foxy replied. Wanting to keep busy, she began to brew a pot of tea as well.

"There'll also be a large contingent of women between twenty and forty who'll want to murder you," Melissa added as she crossed her silk-covered legs. "There hasn't been a shortage of hopefuls for the title of Mrs. Lancelot Matthews."

"Marvelous." Foxy turned to Melissa and leaned back against the counter. "Just marvelous."

"You'll meet the bulk of them socially in the first few weeks," Melissa told her cheerfully. Foxy noted that like Catherine's, Melissa's nails were perfectly tended. "Of course, Lance will be there to guard against unsheathed claws at parties and dances, but you'll have to be alert during charity functions and those lovely luncheon meetings."

"I won't have time for much of that sort of thing," Foxy told her with undisguised relief. Turning away, she managed to locate an appropriate cream and sugar set. "I have my work."

"Work? Do you have a job?" The utter incredulity in her voice caused Foxy to turn back again and laugh.

"Yes, I have a job. Isn't it allowed?"

"Yes, of course, depending . . ." The tip of Melissa's tongue ran slowly along her teeth as she considered. "What do you do?"

"I'm a free-lance photographer." Leaving the kettle on to heat, Foxy joined her at the table.

"That might do well enough," Melissa

said with a thoughtful nod.

"What do you do?" Foxy countered, growing intrigued.

"Do? I . . ." Melissa searched for a word, then smiled with a gesture of her hand. "I circulate." Her eyes danced with such blatant good humor, Foxy was forced to laugh again. "I graduated from Radcliffe three years ago, then I took the obligatory Grand Tour. My French is flawless. I know who's tolerable and who's not in Boston society, how to get the best table at the Charles, where to be seen and with whom, where to buy shoes and where to buy lingerie, how to order creamed chicken for fifty Boston matrons, and where the skeletons are buried in the majority of closets. I've been mad about Lance since I was two, and if I wasn't his cousin and ineligible, I should certainly despise you. But I couldn't have married him in any case, so I'm going to like you very well and enjoy watching you twist a few noses out of shape."

She paused to catch her breath but not long enough for Foxy to get a word in. "You're fabulously attractive, particularly your hair, and I would imagine when you're suited up, you're devastating. Lance would never have chosen anyone with ordinary good looks. And of course, there's your tongue. You certainly set Aunt Catherine down a peg. You'll have to keep it sharp to get through the next weeks unscarred. But I'll help you. I enjoy watching people do things I haven't the courage to do. There now, your kettle's boiling."

Slightly dazed, Foxy rose to take it from the burner. "Are all Lance's relatives like you?"

"Heavens no. I'm quite unique." Melissa smiled with perfect charm. "I know a great number of the people in my circle are bores and snobs, and I haven't any illusions about myself." She shrugged as Foxy began to steep the tea in a porcelain pot. "I'm simply too comfortable to give them a black eye now and again as Lance does. I admire him tremendously, but I haven't the inclination to emulate him." Melissa tossed her hair casually behind her shoulder, and Foxy saw an emerald flash on her hand. "There are times Lance does things strictly to annoy the family's sensibilities. I believe he might have started racing with that in mind. Of course, he became quite obsessed with it for a while. And still, he's involved with designing and building cars rather than driving them . . ." Melissa trailed off, studying Foxy with thoughtful brown eyes.

Hearing the speculation in her voice, Foxy met the stare and spoke without inflection. "You're thinking perhaps he married me to again annoy the family's sensibilities."

Melissa smiled and shrugged her tweed-clad shoulders. "Would it matter? You took first prize. Enjoy it."

Both women turned as the prize strolled into the room. His eyes flickered over Foxy, then settled on his cousin. "Mother's anxious to get along, Melissa."

"Pooh." She wrinkled her nose as she rose. "I'd hoped all this would make her forget about the meetings she's dragging me to. I suppose she told you there's a party at Uncle Paul's tomorrow night. They'll expect you now."

"Yes, she told me." There was no enthusiasm in his voice, and Melissa grinned.

"I'm looking forward to it now. I expect Grandmother might even put in an appearance . . . under the circumstances. You really know how to keep them off balance, don't you?" Melissa winked at Foxy before she crossed over to Lance. "I haven't congratulated you yet."

"No," he agreed and lifted a brow. "You haven't."

"Congratulations," she said formally, then

rose on her toes to peck both of his cheeks. "I like your wife, cousin. I shall come back soon whether you invite me or not."

"You're one of the few I don't draw the bolt against." Lance gave her a quick pinch on the chin. "She'll need a friend."

"Don't we all?" Melissa countered dryly. "We'll go shopping soon," she decided as she turned back to face Foxy. "That's a quick way to get to know each other. I'll see you tomorrow night," she continued before she moved to the door, "for your trial by fire."

Foxy watched the door swing to and fro after Melissa. "I'm feeling a bit singed already," she muttered.

Lance crossed the room and cupped her chin in his hand. "You seemed to hold your own well enough." His eyes grew serious as he studied her face. "Shall I apologize for my mother?"

"No." Foxy closed her eyes for a moment, then shook her head. "No, it isn't necessary. And as I think back you did try to warn me." She opened her eyes and shrugged. "I suppose you knew she wouldn't approve."

"There's very little I do my mother approves of," he countered. He traced his thumb over her jawline while his eyes remained on hers. "I don't base anything I do on her approval, Foxy, least of all my marriage to you. Our lives are our own." His brows lowered into a frown, and he kissed her, hard and quick. "I asked you before," he reminded her, "to trust me."

With a sigh, Foxy turned away. The air seemed suddenly thick with the scents of coffee and tea. "It appears we didn't manage our few days of peace." Picking up the teapot, she poured the contents down the sink. She felt his hands on her shoulders and straightened them automatically. Nothing was going to mar her first full day as his wife. Whirling, Foxy threw her arms around his neck. "We still have today." All the anger melted along with her bones as Lance covered her offered mouth with his. "I don't think I want any coffee now," she whispered as their lips parted and met again. "Do you?"

For an answer, he grinned and drew away. Before she realized his intent, Foxy was slung over his shoulder. Laughing, she pushed the hair from her eyes. "Lance," she said with a mock shiver as he swung through the kitchen door. "You're so romantic."

Chapter Eleven

Foxy considered dressing for her first social evening as Mrs. Lancelot Matthews equal to dressing for battle. Her armor consisted of a slim tube top and loosely pleated evening pants in pale green. Standing in front of the full-length mirror, she adjusted the vivid emerald hip-length jacket and fastened it with a thin gold belt. Deliberately she set about arranging a more dramatic style for her hair.

"If they're going to stare and whisper," she muttered as she pinned up the back of her hair, "we'll give them something to stare and whisper about." Using her brush lightly, she persuaded her curls to fall in soft disorder around her face. "I wish I was built," she complained with a glare at her willowy reflection.

"I'm rather fond of your construction," Lance stated from the doorway. Startled, Foxy turned and dropped the brush. Looking casually elegant in a black suit of the thinnest wool, he leaned against the jamb. His eyes trailed over her in a lazy arch before returning to lock on hers. "Going to give them their money's worth, are you, Foxy?"

She shrugged carelessly, then stooped to retrieve her brush. As she turned away to place it on her dresser she felt his hands descend to her shoulders. "My mother got under your skin, didn't she?"

Foxy toyed with the collection of bottles and jars on the dresser's surface. "It's only fair," she parried. "I got under hers." She heard him sigh, then felt his chin rest atop her head. She kept her eyes lowered on her own restless fingers.

"I suppose I should have apologized for her after all."

Foxy turned, shaking her head. "No." With her own sigh, she offered an apologetic smile. "I'm pouting, aren't I? I'm sorry." Determined to change the mood, she stepped back a bit and held out her hands, palms up. "How do I look?" Below the fall of curls, her eyes were saucy and teasing.

Catching her wrist, Lance spun her into his arms. "Fantastic. I'm tempted to forgo dear Uncle Paul's little party. I'm very possessive of what's mine." His mouth lowered to rub against hers. "Shall we play truant,

Foxy, and lock the door?"

She wanted badly to agree; his mouth promised such delights. To keep the scales balanced, she drew her face away from the warmth of his lips. "I think I'd like to get it over with. I'd rather meet a cluster of them at one time than meet them in dribbles."

He brushed his fingers through her hair. "Pity," he murmured. "But then you always have been a brave soul. I believe you should have a reward for valor before the fact." He slipped his hand into his pocket, then held out a small black box.

"What is it?" Foxy demanded, giving him a curious look as she accepted it.

"A box."

"Clever," she muttered. After opening it, Foxy stared down at two shimmering diamonds shaped like exquisite tears of ice. "Lance, they're diamonds," she managed as she lifted wide eyes to his.

"So I was told," he agreed. The familiar crooked grin claimed his mouth. "You suggested once I buy you something extravagant. I thought these more appropriate than Russian wolfhounds."

"Oh, but I didn't mean for you to actually . . ."

"Not all women can wear diamonds," he said, moving lightly over her protest. "It takes a certain finesse or they look over-done or tawdry." As he spoke, he took the gems from the box and fastened them to her ears. His touch was smooth and practiced. Lifting her chin with his fingers, he critically studied the result. "Yes, it's as I thought, you're well suited. Diamonds need a great deal of warmth." He turned her so that she looked into the mirror. "A lovely woman, Mrs. Matthews. And all mine." Lance stood behind her, his hands on her shoulders.

The mirror reflected a pose of natural affection between husband and wife. Foxy's throat clogged with emotion. I'd trade a dozen diamonds, she thought, for a moment such as this. When her eyes met his in the mirror, her heart and soul were in them. "I love you," she told him in a voice that trembled with her feelings. "So much that sometimes it scares me." Her hands reached up to grasp his with a sudden desperation she neither understood nor expected. "I never realized love could scare you, making you think of all the what-ifs there are in life. This has all happened so fast that when I wake up in the mornings, I still expect to be alone. Oh, Lance." Her eyes clung to his. "I wish we could have been an island a little while longer. What are they going to do to us? All these people who aren't you and me."

Lance turned her until she was facing him and not his reflection. "They can't do anything to us unless we let them." Gently his mouth lowered to hers, but her head fell back, inviting more. His arms tightened as the kiss grew lengthy and intimate. "I think we'll be a bit late for Uncle Paul's party," Lance murmured as he changed the angle of the kiss, then teased the tip of her tongue with his.

Foxy pushed the jacket from Lance's shoulders, working it down her arms until it dropped to the floor. Slowly she moved her hands up the silk front of his shirt while her mouth answered his. She felt his response in the tensing of his muscles, in the strength of his hands as they moved to her hips. Locking her arms around his neck, she strained closer. His lips moved to her hair, then her temple, until they burrowed at her throat. His warm musky scent mingled with hers, creating a fragrance Foxy thought uniquely their own. She slipped out of her shoes. "Let's be very late for Uncle Paul's party," she murmured and sought his mouth again.

Foxy found her imagination had not

been sufficiently extravagant in its picture of Paul Bardett's party. Her first misconception had been the number of people. In attendance were more than double her most generous estimate. The elegant old brownstone on Beacon Hill was packed with them. They thronged the tiny elegant parlor with the Louis XVI furniture, strolled on the terrace under the Chinese lanterns, moved up and down the carpeted staircase. Foxy was certain that every exclusive designer from either side of the Atlantic was represented, from the most conservative sheath to the most flamboyant evening pajamas. During her seemingly endless introductions to the vast Matthews-Bardett clan, she was treated to smiles, handshakes, pecks on the cheek, and speculation. The speculation, as the kisses and the smiles, came in varying degrees. Sometimes it was vague, almost offhand, and other times it was frank, direct, and merciless. Such was the case with the senior Mrs. Matthews, Lance's grandmother. Even as Lance introduced them, Foxy saw the faded blue eyes narrow in appraisal.

Edith Matthews was not a flamboyant countess from Venice. Her sturdy, matronly figure was clad decently in a tasteful black brocade relieved only by a small ruching of white lace at the throat. Her hair was more silver than white, waved carefully away from a strong-boned face. Foxy studied her in turn, wondering if there had once been beauty there, masquerading now behind the mask of age. With the countess, she had been certain, the beauty was still very much alive in the vibrant green eyes. The clasp of Mrs. Matthews' hand was quick, firm enough though the skin was thin, and the eyes told Foxy only that she was being considered: acceptance was being withheld.

"It appears you've cheated us out of a wedding, Lancelot," she said in a quiet voice, raspy with age.

"There seems to be no shortage of them each year," he countered. "One shouldn't be missed very much."

She shot him a look under brows Foxy noticed were thin and beautifully arched. "There are those who have been rather looking forward to yours. Well, never mind," she went on, waving him away with a queenly flick of her fingers. "You will do things your own way. You'll live in the house your grandfather left you?"

Lance was smiling at the gesture she had used. It had been employed in exactly the same way for as long as he could remember. "Yes, Grandmother."

If she recognized the teasing lilt to his voice, she ignored it. "He would like that." She shifted her eyes to Foxy. "I have no doubt he would have liked you as well."

Accepting this as the highest form of approval she would receive, Foxy took the initiative. "Thank you, Mrs. Matthews." Impulsively she bent and brushed the wrinkled cheek with her lips. There were soft scents of lavender and talc.

The beautifully arched brows drew together, then relaxed. "I'm old," she said and sighed as if the thought were not unpleasant so much as unexpected. "You may call me Grandmother."

"Thank you, Grandmother," Foxy replied obediently and smiled.

"Good evening, Lancelot." Foxy's pleasure faded as she heard Catherine Matthews' greeting. "Good evening, Cynthia. You look lovely."

Foxy turned to face her and saw the practiced social smile. "Thank you, Mrs. Matthews." *Manners at ten paces,* Foxy reflected, and thought pistols might be preferable. She watched Catherine's eyes flicker, as dozens of others had that evening, over the diamonds on her ears.

"I don't believe you met my sister-in-law, Phoebe," she said smoothly. "Phoebe Matthews-White, Lancelot's wife, Cynthia."

A small, pale woman with a nondescript face and hair the color of a lead pencil held out her hand. "How do you do?" She pushed her gray-framed glasses more securely on her nose and squinted her bird-like eyes. "I don't believe we've met before."

"No, Mrs. Matthews-White, we haven't."

"How odd," Phoebe said with mild curiosity.

"Lancelot and Cynthia summered in Europe," Catherine put in as she gave Lance an arched look.

"Henry and I stayed at the cape this year," Phoebe confided, easily distracted from her curiosity. "I simply hadn't the energy for a trip to Europe this season. Perhaps we'll spend the holidays in St. Croix."

"Hello, Lance!"

Foxy turned to see a woman in delicate pink embrace her husband. Her photographer's eye detected a perfect model. She had what Foxy labeled the Helen of Troy look — classic delicacy with a sculptured, oval face. Her eyes were deep blue, round, and striking, the nose small and straight over a Cupid's bow mouth. Her figure was as classic as her face, richly curved and enticing in a simple silk sheath. Foxy saw the face in soft focus against the background of white satin — a study of feminine perfection. She knew the woman would photograph magnificently.

"I just learned you were back in town." The Cupid's bow brushed over Lance's cheek. "How bad of you not to have let me know yourself."

"Hello, Gwen. You're lovelier than ever. Hello, Jonathan."

Foxy glanced just beyond Gwen's right shoulder and saw the masculine version of her classic looks. These eyes, however, were not on Lance, but on her. His profile was magnificent, and her fingers itched for her camera.

"Catherine," Gwen said as she tucked her arm in Lance's. "You simply must persuade him to stay this time."

"I'm afraid I could never persuade Lancelot to do anything," Catherine returned dryly.

"Foxy." Lazily, Lance circled his fingers around her wrist. "I'd like you to meet Gwen Fitzpatrick and her brother Jonathan, old family friends."

"What a perfectly dreadful introduction," Gwen complained as her sapphire eyes roamed Foxy's face. "You must be Lance's surprise."

Foxy recognized the cool speculation and responded to it. "Must I?" She sipped at her glass of champagne. Still, she thought, the face is lovely regardless of the woman within. It has so many possibilities. "Have you ever modeled?" she asked, already formulating angles and lighting.

Gwen's brows arched. "Certainly not."

"No?" Foxy smiled, amused at the chipped ice in Gwen's tone. "What a pity."

"Foxy's a photographer," Lance put in and cast her a knowing glance.

"Oh, how interesting." Skillfully, she drenched the words in boredom before turning her attention back to Lance. "We were all simply stunned to hear you were married, and so suddenly. But then, you always were impulsive." Foxy struggled to remain amused. Again the round blue eyes shifted to her. "You must share your secret with those of us who tried and failed."

"You only have to look at her to learn the secret," Jonathan Fitzpatrick stated. Taking Foxy's fingers, he lifted them to his lips, watching her over her own knuckles. "A pleasure, Mrs. Matthews." His eyes were appealing and insolent. Foxy grinned, liking him instantly.

"How charming," Gwen murmured as she sent her brother a frosty glance.

"Hello, everyone." Stunning in red silk, Melissa popped up beside Foxy. "Lance, I simply must borrow your wife a moment. Jonathan, you haven't flirted with me once tonight. I'm terribly annoyed. You'll have to see if you can charm me out of the sulks as soon as I get back. Excuse us, won't you?" Beaming smiles in all directions, Melissa maneuvered Foxy through the crowd and onto a shadowed section of the terrace. "I thought you might like a breather," she commented as she adjusted the cuff of her sleeve.

"You really are unique," Foxy managed when she caught her breath. "You're also right." As she set the glass of champagne down on a white iron table, she heard the wind whispering through drying leaves. The approaching winter was in the air. Still, she preferred the light chill of fresh air to the growing stuffiness inside.

"I also thought a little road mapping might help you." Melissa carefully checked the cushion of a chair for dampness before sitting.

"Road mapping?"

"Or who's who in the Matthews-Bardett

circle," Melissa explained and daintily lit a cigarette. "Now." She paused again as she blew out a stream of smoke and crossed her legs. "Phoebe, Lance's aunt on his father's side — relatively harmless. Her husband is in banking. His main interest is the Boston Symphony, hers is 'doing what's proper.' Paul Bardett, Lance's uncle on his mother's side — very shrewd, occasionally witty, but his life revolves around his law practice. Corporate stuff, very dry and very boring if he corners you. You met my parents, Lance's cousins by marriage on his father's side." Melissa sighed and tapped the ash of her cigarette on the terrace floor. "They're very sweet really. Daddy collects rare stamps and Mother raises Yorkshire terriers. Both of them are obsessive about their respective hobbies. Now, about the Fitzpatricks." She paused and ran the tip of her tongue over her upper lip. "It's best if you know Gwen was the front runner in the 'Who Will Finally Bag Lance Matthews Contest.'"

"She must be very annoyed," Foxy murmured. She walked to the edge of the terrace where the shadows deepened. With sudden clarity, she was reminded of the night of Kirk's party when she had sought out the scent of spring; the first time Lance had kissed her, on the glider in the moonlight. "Were they . . ." Foxy shut her eyes and bit her lip. "Were they . . ."

"Lovers?" Melissa supplied helpfully, taking a sip at Foxy's wine. "I imagine. Lance seems quite the physical sort to me." Glancing over, she studied Foxy's back. "You're not the jealous type, are you?"

"Yes," Foxy murmured without turning around. "Yes, I think I am."

"Oh dear," Melissa said into the champagne. "That's too bad. In any case, that was Chapter One, this is Chapter Two. Oh, and as for Jonathan." Melissa finished the wine and gently crushed her cigarette under her heel. "He's a dangerous flirt and hopelessly charming and insincere. I've decided to marry him."

"Oh." Foxy turned back now and stared at her strange fountain of information. "Well, congratulations."

"Oh, not yet, darling." After rising, Melissa carefully brushed out her skirts. The pearls at her throat gleamed white in the moonlight. "He doesn't know he's going to ask me yet. I shouldn't think the idea will occur to him until around Christmastime."

"Oh," Foxy said blankly, then frowned at the empty glass Melissa handed her.

"You're perfectly free to flirt with him," she added generously. "I'm not the jealous type at all. I believe I'd like a spring wedding, perhaps May. A four-month engagement is perfectly long enough, don't you think? We'd best go back in," she said, linking her arm with Foxy's before she could answer. "I have to begin enchanting him."

Chapter Twelve

During the next week, Foxy established a routine. On a search through the house, she had located the perfect site for her darkroom. Her time was absorbed with the clearing out of a basement storage room, arranging for her equipment to be shipped from New York and altering the room to suit its new function. Lance's days were spent in his Boston office while Foxy spent hers relocating her career base. Before she could continue with the creative aspects of her work, there were practicalities to be seen to. There was cleaning, plumbing to be installed, equipment to be set up. During the transition, Foxy was grateful that Mrs. Trilby proved to be efficient indeed, and quite proprietary about the top three stories of the house. She left the basement to Foxy without a murmur of protest. But there was no doubt in Foxy's mind that the tiny, prim lady in crepe-soled shoes would have snarled like a tiger if she had interfered with the working routine of the living quarters. Foxy left the polishing of the Georgian silver to Mrs. Trilby while she set up her enlarger and bathing tanks. The arrangement suited them both.

Foxy alternated work in her darkroom with solitary explorations of the city. She shot roll after roll of film, recording her impressions and feelings with her camera. She became reacquainted with loneliness. It surprised her that after so many years of thoughtless independence, she should so strongly need another's company. Knowing Lance's business needed careful attention after his months on the road helped her to keep any complaints to herself. Complaints, in any case, were something she rarely uttered. Problems were made to be worked out, and she was accustomed to doing so for herself. The loneliness itself was fleeting, forgotten when she and Lance were together, dulled by her fascination with the city which was now her home. When loneliness threatened, she fought it. Work was her panacea, and Foxy indulged in it lavishly. Within a week, her darkroom was operable, and the prints of the racing season were half completed.

As she studied a set of drying work prints Kirk jumped into her mind. Had it only been three weeks since the accident? she mused as she brushed her hair away from her eyes. It seemed like a lifetime. Wasn't it, in essence? In some strange way, Kirk's accident had been the catalyst that had altered her life. The world she existed in now was far removed from the one she had known as Cynthia Fox. With an unconscious gesture, she fingered her wedding ring.

Hanging wet and glossy, a print of the white racer as it would never be again caught Foxy's attention. She had highlighted it, muting the background into a smudge of varied colors without shape. It had been an unconscious tribute to her brother as she had once thought of him — indestructible. Abruptly a flood of homesickness overwhelmed her. It was an odd sensation and a new one. There had been no truly consistent home in her life in over ten years. But there had been Kirk. Impulsively Foxy left her work in the darkroom and rushed up the steps to the first floor. Hearing the hum of the vacuum in the upstairs hall, she ducked into Lance's study.

Closing herself in the room, she dropped into the chair behind Lance's walnut desk and picked up the phone. In moments, the lines were clicking between Massachusetts and New York.

"Pam!" Foxy felt a quick rush of pleasure the instant she heard the quiet, southern voice. "It's Foxy."

"Well, if it isn't Mrs. Matthews. How are things in Boston?"

"Fine," Foxy replied automatically. "Yes, fine," she repeated, unconsciously adding a nod for emphasis. "Well." She sighed and settled back in the chair with a laugh. "Different certainly. How's Kirk?"

"He's doing very well." Pam's voice continued lightly. "Impatient, naturally, to get out of the hospital. I'm afraid you've missed him just now. He's down in X-ray."

"Oh." Her disappointment was clear, but Foxy pushed it away. "Well, how are you? Are you managing to keep Kirk in line and maintain your sanity?"

"Just barely." Pam's laugh was easy and familiar. Foxy smiled with the pleasure of hearing it. "He'll be sorry he missed your call."

"I missed him all of a sudden," Foxy confessed with a small shake of her head. "Everything's moved so fast in the past few weeks, sometimes I almost feel like someone else. I think I needed him to remind me I was still the same person." She stopped and laughed again. "Am I rambling?"

"Only a tad. Kirk's not only reconciled to your marriage now, but quite pleased about it. I think he's talked himself into believing he arranged the entire thing between races." Pam waited a beat, then continued in the same tone. "You are happy, Foxy?"

Knowing Pam had meant the question seriously and not as casual conversation, Foxy took a moment to answer. She thought of Lance, and a smile coaxed her lips upward. "Yes, I'm happy. I love Lance, and on top of that, I'm lucky enough to love the house and Boston. I suppose I've been a bit lost, especially since Lance is back at his office. Everything here is so different, at times I feel I've stepped through the looking glass."

"Boston society can be a wonderland of sorts, I imagine," Pam replied. "Have you been spending your time chasing white rabbits?"

"I've been working, my friend," Foxy countered in a tone that reflected her raised brows. "My darkroom here is now fully operable. I'll be sending you the prints in a week or so. I'll send you numbered work prints. If you need more copies, or want something enlarged or reduced, give me the number."

"Sounds good. How many prints do you have so far?"

"Finished?" Foxy's brow furrowed as she considered. "A couple hundred if you count the ones I have drying."

"My, my," Pam remarked. "You have been a busy one, haven't you?"

"Photography has become not only my career but my salvation. It saves me from luncheons." There was a smile in her voice now as she settled back into the deep cushion of the chair. "I went to my first, and my last, earlier this week. Nothing and no one will induce me to go through that again. I'm simply not cut out for *functions*."

"Ah well," Pam comforted with a cluck of her tongue. "They will probably carry on without you. I take it you've met Lance's family by now."

"Yes. He has a cousin, Melissa, who's really a character. I like her. His grandmother was rather sweet to me. For the rest" — Foxy paused and wrinkled her nose — "there's been everything from casual friendliness to rank disapproval." Pam could all but hear the shrug in her voice. "I'm looking at this first round of social obligations and introductions as kind of a pledge week. After it's done, I'll know them, and they'll know me, and that will be that." She grinned. "I hope."

"Lance's mother is a . . . formidable lady," Pam commented.

"Yes," Foxy agreed, surprised. "How did you know?"

"My mother and she are slightly acquainted," she answered. Foxy was reminded that Pam had been born and bred in the world she had found herself thrust into by marriage. "I met her myself once when I was covering a story on art patrons." Pam recalled her impression of an elegant, aristocratic woman with cool eyes and beautiful skin. She remembered no warmth at all. "Just keep your feet planted, Foxy. It'll all settle in a few months."

Toying with the brass model of a Formula One that served as a paperweight, Foxy sighed. "I'm trying, Pam, but I do wish Lance and I could just lock the doors for a while. Our honeymoon was interrupted before it had really begun. I'm selfish enough to want a week or two alone with him while I'm getting used to being a wife."

"That sounds more reasonable than selfish," Pam corrected. "Maybe you'll be able to get away once he's finished designing this new car for Kirk. From what I gather, it's a bit complicated because of some new safety features Lance is working on."

"What car?" Foxy demanded softly as she felt her blood turn cold.

"The new Formula One Lance is designing for Kirk. Hasn't he told you about it?"

"No, no he hasn't." Foxy's voice was normal but her eyes were dull and lifeless as she stared down at the polished surface of Lance's desk. "I suppose it's for next season."

"That's why they're pushing to move it along," Pam agreed. "It's practically all Kirk can talk about. He's hoping to fly into Boston as soon as he's out of here so that he can be in on it before it's a finished project. The doctors seem to feel his avid interest in the car is a good motivation for getting him back on his feet quickly." Pam rambled on while Foxy stared without seeing anything. "There's no doubt he's cooperating so well with his therapist because he wants to walk out of here by the first of the year."

"If he's not on his feet," Foxy put in slowly, "they can lift him out of his wheelchair and strap him into the cockpit." Though it cost her some effort, she managed to keep her voice carefully level. "I'm sure Lance would have no objections."

"I wouldn't be surprised if Kirk tried to arrange it." Pam made a sound that was half laugh, half sigh. "Ah, well. What I would like, if you can do it, are some shots of the new car. Seeing as you have an in with the head man, you should be able to get close enough to take a shot or two. I'd especially like a few at the test track when it's progressed that far."

Foxy shut her eyes on the headache that was beginning to throb. "I'll do what I can." *Will I never get away from it?* she wondered and squeezed her eyes tighter. *Never?* "I have to get back to work, Pam. Give Kirk my love, will you? And take care of yourself."

"Be happy, Foxy, and give our best to Lance."

"Yes, I will. Bye." With studied care, Foxy replaced the phone on its cradle. The cold shield over her skin remained, stretching out to extend to her brain. There was a void where her emotions might have been. Anger hovered on the edge of her consciousness, but failed to penetrate. Kirk's accident replayed in her head, not with the smooth motion of a movie, but with the quick, staccato succession of a slide show. Each frame was distinct and horrible.

There were countless grids in her memory, countless wrecks. They came back to her in a montage of cars and drivers and pit crews all jumbled together in a throbbing mass of speed. She sat, swamped by the largeness of Lance's chair, and remembered all of ten years as the light shifted with evening. Outside, the temperature began to drop with the sun. When the door to the study opened, Foxy turned her eyes to it with little interest.

"Here you are." Lance strolled into the room, leaving the door open behind him. "Why are you sitting in the dark, Fox? Don't you get enough of that in your fortress in the basement?" Moving to her, he cupped her chin in his hand and kissed her. The gesture was casual and somehow possessive. When he received no response, he narrowed his eyes and studied her face. "What is it?"

Foxy looked up at him, but her eyes were shadowed in the dimming light. "I just talked to Pam."

"Is it Kirk?" The quick concern in his voice melted the shield that covered her. Under it was the boiling fury of betrayal. She struggled to remain objective until she understood. "Are you concerned about his health?" she asked, but drops of anger burned through the words.

Frowning at the tone, Lance traced her jaw with his finger and felt the tension. "Of course I am. Has there been a complication?"

"Complication," she repeated tonelessly as her nails bit into her palms. "That depends on your viewpoint, I suppose. Pam told me about the car."

"What car?"

The blatant curiosity and puzzlement in his voice snapped her control. Knocking his hand from her face, Foxy rose, putting the chair and her temper between them. "How could you begin designs on a car while he's still in the hospital? Couldn't you even wait until he can walk again?"

Understanding replaced the puzzlement on Lance's face. He made no attempt to close the distance between them, but when he spoke, his voice was patient. "Fox, it takes time to design and build a car. Work was begun on this months ago."

"Why didn't you tell me?" She tossed the words at him, more annoyed than soothed by the patience in his tone. "Why were you keeping it from me?"

"In the first place," he began, frowning

as he watched her. "Designing cars is my business, and you're aware of it. I've designed cars for Kirk before, you're aware of that, too. Why is this different?"

"He was nearly killed less than a month ago." Foxy gripped the supple leather of Lance's chair.

"He crashed," Lance said calmly. "He's crashed before. You and I both know that there's always the chance he'll crash again. It's a professional risk."

"A professional risk," she repeated while fresh fury grew in her eyes. "Oh, how like you! That makes it all neat and tidy. How marvelous it must be to be so impersonally logical."

"Be careful, Foxy," Lance said evenly.

"Why are you encouraging him to go back to it?" she demanded, ignoring his warning. "He might have had enough this time. He had Pam now, he might . . ."

"Wait a minute." Though shadows washed the room, Foxy had no need to see his face clearly to recognize his anger. "Kirk doesn't need any encouraging. Accident or no accident, he'll be back on the grid next season. It's no use trying to delude yourself, Foxy. Neither a wreck nor a woman is going to keep Kirk out of a cockpit for long."

"We'll never be sure of that now, will we?" she countered furiously. "You'll have one all ready for him. Custom fit. How can he resist?"

"If I didn't, someone else would." Lance's hands slipped into his pockets as his voice became dangerously quiet. "I thought you understood him . . . and me."

"All I understand is that you're planning to put him into another car, and he's not even able to stand up yet." Her voice became desperate and she dragged an impatient hand through her hair. "I understand that you might have used your influence to persuade him to retire, and instead —"

"No." Lance interrupted her flatly. "I won't be held responsible for what your brother chooses to do with his life."

Foxy swallowed hard, struggling not to cry. "No, you don't want the responsibility, I can understand that, too." Bitterness spilled over and colored her words. In the dimming light, her eyes glittered both with anger and despair. "All you have to do is draw some lines on paper, balance some equations, order some parts. You don't have to risk your life, just your money. You've plenty of that to spare." Her mind began to spin with a cascade of thoughts and accusations. "On a different level, it's a bit like the casino in Monte Carlo." Foxy raked her hands through her hair again, then gripped them together, furious that they were trembling. "You could just sit back and watch the action, like some . . . some overlord. Money doesn't mean very much to someone who's always had it. Is that how you get your satisfaction?" she demanded, too incensed to realize that his very silence was ominous. "By paying someone to take the risks while you sit back in safety and watch?"

"That's enough!" He moved like lightning, giving her no chance to evade him. In an instant, he had pulled her from behind the chair until he towered over her. "I don't have to take that from you. I did my time on the grid and quit because it was what I wanted to do." Temper was sharp in his voice, hard in the fingers that gripped her arms. "I retired because I chose to retire. I'll race again if I choose to race again. I don't justify my life to anyone. I pay no one to take risks for me."

Fear over the thought of Lance taking the wheel again coated her anger. Her voice trembled as she fought to suppress even the possibility from her brain. "But you're not going to race again. You're not —"

"Don't tell me what I'm going to do."

The words were clipped and final.

Foxy swallowed her terror and spoke with a desolate calm. Once again, she felt herself being shifted to the backseat. With Kirk, she had accepted the position without thought, but now, waves of anger, frustration, and pain spilled through her. "How foolish of me to have thought my feelings would be important enough to matter to you." She started to move past him, but he stopped her by placing his hands on her shoulders. The gesture itself was familiar enough to bring an ache to the pit of her stomach.

"Foxy, listen to me." There were hints of patience in Lance's voice again, but they were strained. "Kirk is a grown man, he makes his own decisions. Your brother's profession has nothing to do with you anymore. My profession has nothing to do with us."

"No." Calmly she lifted her eyes to meet his. "That's simply not true, Lance. But regardless of that, Kirk will drive your car next season, and you'll do precisely what you want to do. There's nothing I can do to change any of it. There never has been with Kirk, and now my position's been made clear with you. I'm going upstairs now," she told him quietly. "I'm tired."

The room was dark now. For some moments he studied her in complete silence before taking his hands from her shoulders. Without speaking, she took a step back, then moved around him and walked from the room. Her footsteps were soundless as she climbed the stairs.

Chapter Thirteen

Morning came as a surprise to Foxy. She had lain awake for hours, alone and unhappy. Her conversation with Pam played over in her mind, and the argument with Lance came back to haunt her. Now she awoke, unaware of having fallen asleep, and the morning sun was streaming onto the bed. Lance's side of the bed was empty. Foxy's hand automatically reached out to touch the sheets where he would have slept. Some warmth still lingered on the spot, but it brought her no comfort. For the first time since their wedding night, they might have slept in separate beds. They had not woken tangled together, to drift into morning as they had drifted into night.

The heaviness that lay on Foxy did not come from sleep but from dejection. Arguing with Lance was certainly not a novel occupation to her, but this time Foxy felt the effects more deeply. *Perhaps*, she thought as she stared at the ceiling, *it's be-*

cause now that I have more, I have more to lose. He's probably still downstairs. I could go down and . . . No. Foxy interrupted her own train of thought with a shake of her head. No, there was too much here to be resolved over morning coffee with Mrs. Trilby hanging over his shoulder. *In any case, I could use the day to sort things out.*

Mechanically Foxy rose and showered. She took her time dressing, though her choice of cords and a rag sweater were simple. As she dressed, she mentally outlined her schedule. She would work on the racing prints until eleven, then she would walk to the public gardens and continue on her new project. Satisfied with her agenda, she moved downstairs. There was no sign of Lance, and though she told herself it was for the best, she lingered by the hall phone a moment, undecided. No, she told herself firmly. *I will not call him. We can't discuss anything rationally over the telephone. Is there anything to discuss?* she wondered and frowned at the phone as if it annoyed her. Lance seemed clear enough on his opinion of our positions last night. *I won't accept it,* she told herself staunchly, still staring at the phone. *I will not accept it. He can't go back to racing.* She swallowed the iron taste of fear that had risen to her throat. He couldn't have meant that. Squeezing her eyes tight, Foxy shook her head. *Don't think about it now. Go to work and don't think about it.* She took a deep breath and turned her back on the phone.

After confiscating a cup of coffee from the kitchen, Foxy closeted herself in her darkroom. The prints still hung on the line as she had left them. Without consciously planning to do so, she pulled the print of Kirk's racer down and studied it. *A comet,* she thought, remembering. *Yes, he is a comet, but doesn't even a comet have to burn out sometime? There'll be other pictures of him next year, but someone else will have to take them. Maybe Lance will arrange for that, too.* A sharp, frustrated sound escaped her. *I can't think about all of this anymore.* She pulled down the dry prints, then began to work on a fresh roll of film. Time passed swiftly and in such absolute silence that she was jolted when a knock sounded on the door. Foxy frowned as she went to answer it. Mrs. Trilby had never ventured into her territory.

"Melissa!" she exclaimed as her frown flew into a smile. "What a nice surprise."

"It's not dark," Melissa said with a small pout as she moved passed Foxy and into the room. "Why is it called a darkroom if it isn't dark? I'm disillusioned."

"You came at the wrong time," Foxy explained. "I promise it was quite dark in here a couple of hours ago."

"I suppose I'll have to take your word for it." Melissa slowly walked down the line of new prints Foxy had hanging. "My, my, you really are a professional, aren't you?"

"I like to think so," Foxy answered wryly.

"All so technical," Melissa mused as she wandered around the room and scowled at bottles and timers. "I suppose this is what you studied in college."

"I majored in photography at USC. Not Smith," she added with a lift of brow. "Not Radcliffe, not Vassar, but at that little-known institution, the state college."

"Oh, dear." Melissa bit her lip but a small portion of the smile escaped. "Some of the ladies have been giving you a bad time, I take it."

"You take it right," Foxy agreed, then wrinkled her nose. "Well, I suppose I'm just a nine days' wonder. They'll forget about me soon enough."

"Such sweet naïveté," Melissa murmured as she patted Foxy's cheek. "I'll let you hold on to that little dream for a while. In any case," she continued, briskly brushing a speck from her pale blue angora sweater. "There's a dance at the country club Saturday. You and Lance are coming, aren't you?"

"Yes." Foxy didn't bother to suppress her sigh. "We'll be there."

"Buck up, darling. The obligations will taper off in a few months. Lance had never been one to socialize more than is absolutely necessary. And" — she smiled her singularly charming smile — "it's such a marvelous excuse to go shopping." Melissa gave the room another sweeping glance. "Are you all done in here?"

"Yes, I've just finished." Foxy glanced at her watch and gave a satisfied nod. "And right on schedule."

"Well then, let's go shopping and buy something fabulous to wear Saturday night." She linked her arm with Foxy's and began to lead her from the room.

"Oh no." She stopped long enough to close the darkroom door behind her. "I went on one of your little shopping safaris last week. You invaded every shop on Newbury Street. I haven't taken my vitamins today, and anyway, I have a dress for Saturday. I don't need anything."

"Good grief, do you have to *need* it before you buy it?" Melissa turned back from her journey to the stairs and gaped. "You only bought one little blouse when we went shopping before. What do you think Lance has all that lovely money for?"

"For a multitude of things, I'm sure," Foxy replied gravely. Still, a smile tugged at the corners of her mouth. "But hardly for me to spend on clothes I have no need for. In any case, I use my own money for personal things."

Melissa folded her arms and studied Foxy with care. "Why, you're serious, aren't you, pet?" She looked puzzled as she lifted her shoulders. "But Lance has simply hoards of money."

"I know that. I often wish he didn't." As she started to climb the stairs to the first floor Melissa took her arm.

"Wait a minute." Her voice had altered from its brisk good humor. It was quiet now, and serious. "They really are giving you a bad time, aren't they?"

"It doesn't matter," Foxy began, using a shrug to toss off the question.

"Oh, but I think it does." Melissa's hand was surprisingly firm on Foxy's arm. She kept Foxy facing her on the narrow stairway. "Listen to me a minute now. I'm going to be perfectly serious for a change. This business about you marrying Lance for his money is just typical nonsense,

Foxy. It doesn't mean anything. And not everyone is saying it or thinking it. There are some morons who carry on about status and bloodlines, of course, but I never pay much attention to morons." She smiled when she paused for breath, but her eyes remained grave. "You've already won over a great many people, people like Grandmother, who's no pushover. And you've done that by simply being yourself. Surely Lance has told you how many people are pleased with his taste in wives."

"We don't discuss it." Foxy dragged her hand through her hair with a sound of frustration. "That is, to be more exact, I haven't said anything about his less friendly relations. It hardly seems fair to hound him with complaints."

"Is it fair for you to stand quiet while a scattered few toss rocks at you?" Melissa countered, lifting a brow uncannily as Lance did. "Martyrdom is depressing, Foxy."

Foxy grimaced at the title. "I don't think I care much for that." Shaking her head, she gave Melissa a rueful smile. "I suppose I'm being too sensitive. There've been so many changes all at once, and I'm having a hard time juggling everything."

Melissa linked her arm with Foxy's again

as they mounted the stairs. "Now, what else is there?"

"Does it show?"

"I'm very perceptive," Melissa told her carelessly. "Didn't you know? My guess is that you and Lance had a tiff."

"Your term is a bit mild," Foxy murmured as she pushed open the door to the first floor. "But we'll go with it."

"Who's fault was it?"

Foxy opened her mouth to blame Lance, closed it again on the thought of blaming herself. She gave up with a sigh. "No one's, I suppose."

"That's the usual kind," Melissa said briskly. "The best cure is to go out and buy something fabulous to boost your ego. Then, if you want to make him suffer, you can be coolly polite when he gets home. Or" — she gestured fluidly with her hand — "if you want to make up, you send Mrs. Trilby home early and have on as little as possible when he gets here."

"Melissa." Foxy laughed as she watched her retrieve her coat and purse from the hall stand. "What a lovely way you have of simplifying things."

"It's a gift," she said modestly, studying her reflection in the antique mirror. "Are you going to be fun and come shopping with me, or are you going to be horribly industrious?"

"I think," Foxy mused thoughtfully, "I've just been insulted." On impulse, she leaned over and kissed Melissa's cheek. "You tempt me, but I'm very strong-willed."

"You're actually going to work this afternoon?" The look she gave Foxy was filled with both admiration and puzzlement. "But you even worked this morning."

"People have often been known to work an entire day," Foxy pointed out, then grinned. "It can get to be a habit . . . like potato chips. I'm starting a series of photographs on children, so I'm off to the park."

Melissa frowned as she slipped into her short fur jacket. "You make me feel quite the derelict."

"You'll get over it," Foxy comforted as she ran a curious finger down the soft white pelt.

"Of course." Melissa swirled around and kissed both of Foxy's cheeks. "But for a moment, I feel guilty. Have a nice time, Foxy," she said as she swung out the door.

"You too," Foxy called over the quick slam. With a laugh, she pulled her own suede jacket from the closet. In a lighter frame of mind, she swung her purse over one shoulder and her camera case over the other. As she turned she all but collided with Mrs. Trilby. "Oh, I'm sorry." *Crepe-soled shoes,* Foxy thought with an inward sigh, *should be outlawed.*

"Are you going out, Mrs. Matthews?" Mrs. Trilby stood stiffly in her gray uniform and white apron.

"Yes, I have some work planned this afternoon. I should be back around three."

"Very good, ma'am." Mrs. Trilby stood expressionless in the archway as Foxy moved to the front door.

"Mrs. Trilby, if Lance . . . if Mr. Matthews should call, tell him I . . ." Foxy hesitated, and for a moment the unhappiness and indecision was reflected on her face.

"Yes, ma'am?" Mrs. Trilby prompted with the slightest softening of her tone.

"No," Foxy shook her head, annoyed with herself. "No, nothing. Never mind." She straightened her shoulders and sent the housekeeper a smile. "Goodbye, Mrs. Trilby."

"Good day, Mrs. Matthews."

Foxy stepped outside and breathed in the crisp autumn air. Though her MG had been shipped from Indiana and now sat waiting in the garage, Foxy opted to walk. The sky was piercingly blue, empty of clouds. Against the unrelieved color, the bare trees rose in stark supplication. Dry leaves whirled along the sidewalk and clung to the curbs. Now and then, the wind would whip them around Foxy's ankles until they fell again to be crunched underfoot. The crisp perfection of the day lifted her spirits higher, and she began to formulate an outline for the project she had in mind.

Mums were still stubbornly beautiful throughout the public gardens. There were flashes of rich color along the paths where rosy-cheeked children darted and played. The afternoon was fresh and sharp. Babies were rolled along in carriages or strollers by their mothers or uniformed nannies. Toddlers practiced the art of walking on the leaf-carpeted grass.

Foxy moved among them, sometimes shooting pictures, sometimes striking up a conversation with a parent, then charming her way into the shot she wanted. She had learned from experience that photography was more than knowing the workings of a camera or the speed of film. It was the ability to read and portray an image. It was patience, it was tenacity, it was luck.

She lay on her stomach on the cool grass, aiming her Nikon at a two-year-old girl who wrestled with a delighted bull terrier puppy. The child's blond, rosy beauty was the perfect foil for the dog's unabashed homeliness. A pool of sunlight surrounded them as they tussled, finding each other far more interesting than the woman who crawled and scooted around them snapping a camera. The dog yapped and rushed in circles, the child giggled and captured him. He escaped to be cheerfully captured again. At length, Foxy sat back on her heels and grinned at her models. After a quick exchange with the girl's mother, she stood, prepared to load a fresh roll of film.

"That was a fascinating performance."

Glancing up, Foxy found herself facing Jonathan Fitzpatrick. "Oh, hello." She tossed her hair behind her back, then brushed a stray leaf from her jacket.

"Hello, Mrs. Matthews. A lovely day for rolling in the grass."

His smile was so blatantly charming, Foxy laughed. "Yes, it is. Nice to see you again, Mr. Fitzpatrick."

"Jonathan," he corrected and plucked another leaf from her hair. "And I'll call you Foxy as Melissa does. It suits you. Now, may I ask what it is you're doing, or is it a government secret?"

"I'm taking pictures, of course." With a grin, Foxy continued to load her camera. "I make a habit of it, that's why I'm a photographer."

"Ah yes, I did hear that." As she bent her head over her work, the sunlight shot small flames through her hair. With admiration, Jonathan watched them flare. "Professional, are you?"

"That's what I tell the publishers." Finished, she closed the camera and gave Jonathan her attention again. The resemblance to his sister was striking, yet she felt no discomfort with him as she had with Gwen. He was, she thought on another quick study, an exact opposite of Lance: fair and smooth and harmless. Instantly annoyed with her habitual comparisons, she gave him her best smile. "I'm working on a project with children at the moment."

Jonathan studied her, taking in the easy smile, the large gray-green eyes, the face that became more intriguing each time it was seen. He completed his examination in a matter of seconds and decided Lance had won again. This was no ordinary lady. "May I watch awhile?" he asked, surprising them both. "I have the afternoon free. I was just crossing to my car when I spotted you."

"Of course." She bent to retrieve her camera case. "But I'm afraid you might find it boring." Turning, she began to walk in the direction of the Mill Pond.

"I doubt that. I rarely find beautiful women boring in any circumstances." Jonathan fell into step beside her. Foxy cast him a sidelong look. He had the smile of the boy next door and the profile of an Adonis. Melissa, Foxy mused, is going to have her hands full.

"What do you do, Jonathan?"

"As I please," he answered as he slipped his hands into the pockets of his leather jacket. "Theoretically, I'm an executive in the family business. Import-export. In reality, I'm a paper shuffler who charms wives when necessary and escorts daughters."

Humor sparkled in Foxy's eyes. "Do you enjoy your work?"

"Immensely." When he looked down with his easy grin, she decided he and Melissa were ideally suited for each other.

"I enjoy mine as well," she told him. "Now stand out of the way while I do some."

There was a bench by the pond where a willow dipped into the mirrorlike water. A woman sat reading while a chubby toddler in a bright red jacket tossed crackers to paddling ducks. Nearby, an infant snoozed in a stroller in a square of sunshine. A forgotten rattle hung limply in the curled fingers. After exchanging a quiet word with the woman on the bench, Foxy set to work. Taking care not to disturb him, she captured the delight of the toddler as he threw his crumbs high in the air. Ducks scrambled for the free meal. The boy squealed with pleasure and tossed again, sometimes sampling a cracker himself while the ducks vied for the soggy offering. She translated the sound of his laughter onto film.

Using sun and shade, she expressed the peace and innocence of the fat-cheeked infant. Changing angles, speeds and filters, she altered moods and heightened emotions, until, satisfied, she stopped and let the camera hang by its strap.

"You're very intense while you work," Jonathan commented as he moved up to join her. "You look very competent."

"Is that a compliment or an observation?" Foxy asked him, then snapped on her lens cover.

"A complimentary observation," Jonathan countered. He continued to study her profile as she secured her equipment. "You fascinate me, Foxy Matthews. I find you one more reason to envy Lance."

"Do you?" She looked up, revealing a guileless interest that surprised him. "And are there many others?"

"Scores," he said promptly, then took her hand. "But you're at the top of the list. Is it true your brother's Kirk Fox and that Lance snatched you from the racing world?"

"Yes." Foxy was immediately on guard. Her tone cooled. "I grew up at the race-track."

Jonathan lifted a brow. "I've struck a nerve. I'm sorry." He ran his thumb absently across her knuckles. "Would it help if I said I'm curious, not critical? Lance's racing career also fascinates me, and I've followed your brother's as well. I thought you might have some interesting stories to tell." His voice, Foxy noted, was not like Gwen's; it was far too honest.

"I'm sorry." She sighed and moved her shoulders. "That's the second time today I've been overly sensitive. It's a bit difficult being the new kid on the block."

"You were a bit of a surprise." His touch was so light that Foxy had forgotten he still held her hand. "There are those who require everything well planned and predictable. Lance seems to prefer the unique."

"Unique," Foxy murmured, then shot Jonathan a direct, uncompromising stare. "I don't have any money, I haven't a pedigree. I spent my adolescent years around garages and mechanics. I didn't go to an exclusive college, and all I've seen of Europe is what I could squeeze in between time trials and races."

Watching her, Jonathan observed the tiny flecks of unhappiness in her eyes. Sunlight flickered through the willow leaves to catch the highlights of her hair. "Would you like to have an affair?" he asked casually.

Stunned, Foxy stepped back, her eyes huge. "No!"

"Have you ever ridden on the swan boat?" he inquired just as easily.

Her mouth opened and closed twice in utter confusion. "No," she managed cautiously.

"Good." He took her hand again. "We'll do that instead." He smiled, keeping her fingers tightly in his. "All right?"

Warily Foxy studied his face. Before she realized it, a smile began to tug at the corners of her mouth. "All right," she agreed. *Melissa will never be bored,* she decided as she let Jonathan lead her away.

"Would you care for a balloon?" His voice took on a formal note.

"Yes, thank you," she returned in a matching tone. "A blue one."

The next two hours were the most carefree Foxy had spent since she had begun her social duties as Mrs. Lance Matthews. With Jonathan, she glided on the Mill Pond, tucked in a swan boat with tourists and sticky-fingered preschoolers. They walked through the gardens eating ice cream with Foxy's balloon trailing on its string at their backs. She found him undemanding, easy to talk to, a tonic for depression.

When Jonathan pulled up in front of the brownstone, Foxy's mood was still light. "Would you like to come in?" She shifted the strap of her case onto her shoulder. "Perhaps you could stay for dinner."

"Another time. I have a dinner engagement with Melissa."

"Tell her hello for me." With a smile, Foxy opened her door. "Thank you, Jonathan." On impulse, she leaned across the seat and kissed his cheek. "I'm sure it was much more fun than an affair, and so much simpler."

"Simpler anyway," he agreed, then brushed a finger down her nose. "I'll see you and Lance on Saturday."

"Oh, yes." Foxy made a face before she slid from the car. "Oh, tell Melissa I totally approve of her plans for May." She laughed at his puzzled face, then waved him away. "She'll know what I mean." Slamming the door, she shivered once in the cooling air before moving up the path to the house. The front door opened as she reached for the knob.

"Hello, Foxy." Lance stood in the doorway. With a quick scan, he took in her smile, bright eyes, and blue balloon. "Apparently you've had an enjoyable afternoon."

Her buoyant mood left no place for remnants of anger from yesterday's argument. They could talk and be serious later, now she wanted to share her pleasure. "Lance, you're home early." She was glad to find him waiting and smiled again.

"Actually, I believe you're home late," he countered as he shut the door behind her.

"Oh?" A look at her watch told her it was nearly five. "I didn't realize, I suppose I lost track of the time." With the balloon tied jauntily to its strap, Foxy set down the camera case. "Have you been home long?"

"Long enough." He studied her autumn-kissed cheeks. "Want a drink?" he said as he turned and walked back into the drawing room.

"No, thank you." His coolness seeped through Foxy's elated spirits. She followed him, calculating the best way to bridge the gap before it widened further. "We didn't have any plans for this evening, did we?"

"No." Lance poured a generous helping of scotch into a glass before he turned back to her. "Do you intend to go out again?"

"No, I . . ." She stopped, paralyzed by the ice in his eyes. "No."

He drank, watching her over the rim. The tension that had flown from her during the afternoon returned. Still, she could not yet bring herself to speak of Kirk or racing. "I ran into Jonathan Fitzpatrick in the public gardens," she began, unbuttoning her jacket in order to keep her hands busy. "He brought me home."

"So I noticed." Lance stood with his back to the wide stone fireplace. His face was cool and passive.

"It was beautiful out today," Foxy hurried on, fretting for a way out of the polite, meaningless exchange. Warily, she watched

Lance pour another glass of scotch. "There seem to be a lot of tourists still, but Jonathan said they slack off during the winter."

"I had no idea Jonathan was interested in the tourist population."

"I was interested," she corrected, then pulled off her jacket with a frown. "It was crowded in the swan boats."

"Did Jonathan take you?" Lance asked mildly before he tossed back the contents of his glass. "How charming."

"Well, I hadn't been before so he —"

"It appears I've been neglecting you," he interrupted. Foxy's frown deepened as he lifted the bottle of scotch again.

"You're being ridiculous," Foxy stated as her temper began to rise. "And you're drinking too much."

"My dear child, I haven't begun to drink too much." He poured another glass. "And as for being ridiculous, there are some men who would cheerfully beat a wife who spends afternoons with other men."

"That's a Neanderthal attitude," she snapped. She tossed her jacket into a chair and glared at him. "It was perfectly harmless. We were in a public place."

"Yes, buying balloons and riding on swans."

"We had an ice cream cone as well," she supplied and jammed her hands into her pockets.

"Your tastes are amazingly simple." Lance glanced briefly into his glass before lifting it and swallowing. "For someone in your current position."

Her shocked gasp was trapped by the obstruction in her throat. Absolutely still, she stood while all color drained from her face. Against the pallor, her eyes were dark with hurt. Swearing richly, Lance set down his glass.

"That was below the belt, Fox, I'm sorry." He started toward her, but she backed away, throwing out her hands to ward him off.

"No, don't touch me." She took quick, deep breaths to control the tremor in her voice. "I've had to listen to the innuendos, I've had to put up with the knowing smirks and tolerate the sniping, but I never expected it from you. I'd rather you had beat me than said that to me." Turning quickly, she fled up the stairs. Before she could slam the bedroom door, Lance caught her wrist.

"Don't turn away from me," he warned in a low, even voice. "Don't ever turn away from me."

"Let go of me!" she shouted, trying to pull away from him. Before she thought about what she was doing, she swung out with her free hand and slapped him.

"All right," he said between his teeth as he locked both her arms behind her back. "I had that coming, now calm down."

"Just take your hands off me and leave me alone." She struggled for release but was only caught tighter.

"Not until we settle this. There are some things that have to be explained."

"I don't need to explain anything." She tossed her head to free her eyes from her hair. "Now take your hands off me, I can't bear it."

"Don't push me too far, Foxy." Lance's voice was as dark and dangerous as his eyes. "I'm running low on self-control, particularly after last night. Now calm down, and we'll talk."

"I don't have anything to say to you." Cold with fury, she stopped struggling and stared up at him. "I had my say yesterday, and you've had yours tonight. It looks like we understand each other well enough."

"Then we won't talk," Lance said harshly before his mouth came down on hers. With an iron grip, he handcuffed her wrists so that her frantic movements were useless. There was something calculating as well as brutal in the kiss. She recognized the same ruthlessness she knew him to be capable of in racing. Knowing her struggles were futile, she forced her body to go limp and her mouth to remain passive. "Ice won't work," Lance muttered and lifted her off her feet. "I know how to melt it."

As he began to carry her to the bed Foxy's passive acceptance disappeared. "No!" Desperately she tried to free herself from his arms. "Lance, don't, not like this." She pushed hard against his chest and felt herself falling. Her small cry of alarm was knocked from her as she hit the mattress. Before she could roll away, he was on top of her.

His body molded itself to hers. As she turned her head his hand locked on her jaw, holding her face still as his mouth took hers again. Quickly, as though her struggles were nonexistent, he began to undress her. There was determination without passion in his movements. He didn't look for partnership now, but for capitulation. Foxy's body heated to his touch even as she fought for freedom. Her sweater and jeans were tossed carelessly to the floor and the thin chemise she wore was no barrier against his hands. Her nipples were taut against the silk as he sought the sensitive hollow of her throat with his lips and tongue. She continued to struggle even as his hand moved down the silk to the flatness of her stomach. His fingers moved roughly over the top of her leg where the chemise ended.

Desire surged through her, weighing on her limbs as she pushed and twisted. She knew she needed to escape not only from him but from herself. Her movements brought only more arousal. With his tongue, he traced the peak of her breast through the chemise, catching it then between his teeth as her fingers dug into his shoulders. He exploited her weaknesses, explored the secrets only he knew until the fire kindled and flared. She responded. She arched against him now not in protest, but in answer. Hungrily her mouth sought his as her fingers fumbled with the buttons of his shirt. His skin was hot against her palms, his muscles tight.

Abruptly, his mood altered. His cool control vanished as a thunderous urgency took its place. Hooking his hands in the bodice, he ripped the chemise down the front in one sharp gesture. Foxy heard him curse her as his breathing grew as labored as hers. His hands were wild now, bruising over her naked skin while his mouth was hard and demanding. Control was lost for both of them. There was only sensation, only need, only the dark pleasure of damp flesh and deep kisses. But even as he took her, even as she gave herself without reservation, Foxy knew neither of them had won.

Chapter Fourteen

It started raining early Saturday morning. Then the cold arrived and turned the rain to snow before afternoon. Alone, with the house rattling around her, Foxy watched it fall in thin sheets. The ground was still warm, and the snow melted even as it landed. It poured down quickly enough, but left no trace. *There'll be no snowmen built today,* Foxy mused and hugged her elbows. *I wonder where he could have gone.*

Lance had already left when she awakened, and the house was empty. Foxy knew that what had passed between them the night before had cost them both dearly. In the end, he hadn't taken her in anger, and she had given herself willingly. Desire had won over both of them but misunderstanding remained in its wake. Discovering herself alone in a cold bed had shot a shaft of gloom over her, which grew only sharper as the hours passed. The morning hours spent in her darkroom had been productive but had done nothing to alleviate her dilemma.

What's happening to my marriage? she asked herself as she stared out at the stubbornly falling snow. *It's barely begun, and it seems to be going nowhere. Like the snow out there,* she mused, and lay her fingers on the windowpane. It just keeps disappearing. Could it be as fragile as an early snow, and as fleeting? Foxy shook her head and cradled her elbows. *I won't let it be.* The sound of the phone had her whirling around. *Lance,* she thought instantly and raced to answer it.

"Hello," she said with anticipation ripe in her voice.

"Hiya, Foxy. How are things in the real world?"

"Kirk." Her disappointment was outweighed by her pleasure. She dropped down on an ottoman and pushed the disappointment aside. "It's good to hear your voice." Even as she said the words, she realized how true they were. Her pleasure increased and turned to happiness. "How are you?" she demanded. "Have you talked them into letting you out? Where's Pam?"

"I think marriage has slowed you down," he commented gravely. "Can't you think of anything to say?"

Laughing, Foxy tucked her feet under her. "Just answer any or all of the above questions, but start with the first one. How are you?"

"Pretty good. Healing. They might be persuaded to let me out in a couple weeks if Pam's willing to cart me back and forth for therapy." She could tell from the sound of his voice that his injuries were hardly uppermost in his mind. *Professional risks.* She remembered Lance's words and bit down hard on her bottom lip.

"I imagine she could be persuaded," Foxy managed to say naturally. "I'm glad you're better." *I worry about you,* she told him silently, then smiled and shook her head. *He wouldn't like to hear that.* "I suppose you're getting bored."

"I passed bored last week," he returned dryly. "I'm getting so good at the *Times* crossword puzzles, I've started doing them in ink to show off."

"You were always cocky. Shall I send you some paste and colored paper to keep you busy?" She kept her tongue in her cheek as she heard him snarl.

"I'll let that pass because I'm good-natured." Kirk ignored her laughter and continued. "So, tell me about Boston. Do you like it there?"

"It's beautiful." As she answered, Foxy glanced out the window. Flakes were falling in a white curtain and vanishing. "It's snowing now, and I suppose it'll turn cold, but I've done a lot of exploring. I'm rather anxious to see how Boston looks in the winter."

"How about Lance's family," Kirk demanded. "I can get a weather report from the newspaper."

"Well, they're . . ." She fumbled for words, hesitated, and ultimately laughed. "They're different. I feel a bit like Gulliver, finding himself an oddity in a world where the rules are all different. We're getting used to each other, and I've made a couple of friends." She smiled, thinking of Melissa and Jonathan. Remembering Catherine, she felt the smile slip a bit, and with a shrug began to trace a pattern on the ottoman with her fingernail. "I'm afraid his mother doesn't care for me."

"You didn't marry his mother," Kirk pointed out logically. "I can't imagine my sister letting herself get pushed around by a few Boston bluebloods." He spoke with such easy confidence that Foxy was forced to smile again.

"Who me?" she countered, accepting the strange compliment. "They grow 'em tough in the Midwest, you know."

"Yeah, you're a real Amazon." The rough affection in his tone made her smile sweeten. "How's Lance?"

"He's fine," she answered automatically. Nibbling on her lips, she added, "He's been busy."

"I imagine the plans for the new car have him pretty tied up just now." She heard the excitement creep into Kirk's voice and schooled herself to accept it. "It sounds like a beauty. I'm itching to get up there and see how it's going. Lance is a damn genius at a drawing board."

"Is he?" Foxy asked with a curious frown.

"It's one thing to come up with ideas, Fox. I have a few of those myself. It's another to be able to put them to practical use." He spoke with a hint of envious amusement, causing Foxy to consider another aspect of her husband.

"Strange, he doesn't seem the type for drawing boards and calculators, does he?"

"Lance isn't any type at all," Kirk corrected. "You should know that better than anyone."

Foxy paused a moment in thought. Her frown deepened, then softened into a smile. "Yes, of course, you're right. And I do know it, I've needed someone to remind me though. It's also nice to hear from my brother that my husband is a genius."

"He was always more interested in the mechanics than the race," Kirk added absently. "So, how are you?"

"Me?" Foxy shook her head to bring her attention back to Kirk. "Oh, fine. You can tell Pam I have the prints finished and I'll be sending them up to her."

"Are you happy?"

She heard the same seriousness in his tone she had heard when Pam had asked the identical question. "What sort of question is that to ask a woman who's only been married a few weeks," she countered lightly. "You're not supposed to come down to happy for at least a month."

"Foxy," Kirk began.

"I love him, Kirk," she interrupted, voicing some of her thoughts for the first time. "It's not always easy and it's not always perfect, but it's the only place for me. I'm happy and I'm sad, and I'm a hundred other things I wouldn't be if I didn't have Lance."

"Okay." She could almost see his nod of acceptance. "As long as you have what you want. Listen, I really called to let you know. Well, I thought I should tell you first. . . ."

Foxy waited a full ten seconds. "What?" she demanded on an exasperated laugh.

"I asked Pam to marry me."

"Thank goodness."

"You don't sound surprised," he complained.

A grin of pure pleasure spread over Foxy's face. "Only that such a nifty driver could be so slow. When are you getting married?"

"An hour ago."

"What?"

"Now you sound surprised," Kirk stated, satisfied. "Pam wouldn't wait until I could stand up, so we got married right here in the hospital. I tried to call you before, but nobody answered."

"I was down in my darkroom." With a sigh, she drew her knees up to her chest. "Oh, Kirk, I'm happy for you. I'm not sure I believe it."

"I'm not sure I do either. She's not like anyone else in the world." Foxy heard the tone, recognized it, and blinked tears from her lashes.

"Yes, I know what you mean. Can I talk to her?"

"She's not here, she's out making arrangements for this place we're going to rent while I'm having my leg prodded. We're hoping to be in Boston by the first of the year so that I can keep an eye on Lance and my car, but we'll stay near the hospital till then."

"I see." *He'll never change,* she told herself and shut her eyes briefly. I was a fool to think differently. Everything Lance said the other night was true. Kirk will race as long as he's capable of racing. Nothing and no one could stop him. She clearly remembered the things she had said to Lance in the dimming light of the library. Guilt all but smothered her. Foxy switched the phone to her other ear and swallowed. "I'll be glad to have you and Pam here, even if it's only until the season starts." Understanding made acceptance easier.

"Will you be coming to Europe?"

"No." Foxy shook her head and made the break. "No, I won't be coming."

"Pam said she didn't think you would. Listen, they're coming in to poke at me again. Tell Lance that Pam and I expect him to break out some champagne when we get into town. The French stuff."

"I'll do that," she promised, relieved that he had let her go without a second thought. "Take care of yourself."

"Sure. Hey, I love you, Foxy."

"I love you, too." After cradling the phone, Foxy drew her knees closer and wrapped her arms around them. As she watched, the snow grew thinner until it was little more than a fine mist.

He doesn't need me anymore, she reflected before she realized the thought had been in her mind. It struck her as odd that she had not fully understood Kirk's need for her until it no longer existed. Their need for each other had been mutual, even when she had been a child. The link between them was strong, perhaps because of the tragedy that had left them only each other. *There'll always be something special between us,* Foxy brooded. *But he has Pam now, and I have Lance.* Resting her chin on her knees, Foxy wondered if Lance needed her. Loved her, yes, wanted her, but did Lance Matthews with his casual self-sufficiency, his easy wealth and supreme confidence *need* her? Was there something special about her that completed his life, or was she simply overly romantic and foolish in wanting to believe it was true? She found, to her surprise, that the answer mattered very much.

Abruptly Foxy's senses tingled. Lifting her head, she looked up to see Lance standing in the doorway. Moving quickly, she unfolded herself from the ottoman and stood. As she met his eyes every speech she had rehearsed, edited, and rerehearsed that morning vanished from her mind. Foolishly she tugged her sweatshirt over the hips of her jeans and wished she had worn something more dignified.

"I didn't hear you come in," she said, then cursed herself for the inanity.

"You were on the phone." It was his quiet, measuring look. He stood watching her without a flicker in his eyes to hint at his thoughts. Nerves began to dance in her stomach.

"Yes, I . . . It was Kirk." She tugged her fingers through her hair, unable to keep them still, and inadvertently betrayed her tension.

In silence, Lance continued to scan her face. He came no further into the room when he spoke again. "How is he?"

"Fine. He sounds wonderful actually. He and Pam were married this morning." While making the announcement, Foxy began to wander around the room. She fiddled with priceless pieces of bric-a-brac and toyed with Mrs. Trilby's careful arrangement of fall flowers.

"That pleases you?" Lance asked,

studying her restless movements before he crossed to the bar. He lifted a bottle of scotch, then set it down again without pouring any.

"Yes. Yes, very much." Taking a deep breath, she prepared to plunge into an apology for blaming him for Kirk's decision to continue racing. "Lance, I . . . Oh." As she turned, she found him directly in front of her. She backed up a step, surprised, and his brow lifted at her action. While Foxy dealt with feeling awkward and unsettled, Lance slipped his hands in his pockets.

"Apologies aren't my strong suit," he stated as she searched for a way to begin again. "In this case, however, I don't think it's possible to avoid the need for one." His face was closed against her searching gaze. His eyes were on hers, but they did not speak to her. "I apologize both for the things I said to you and for what happened. That hardly makes up for it, but you have my word, nothing like that will happen again."

His stilted formality only added to Foxy's strain. She knew nothing she had planned to say could be said to the polite stranger who stood before her. Dropping her eyes, she studied the pattern in the Aubusson rug. "No absolution, Foxy?" Hearing the softness in his voice, she lifted her eyes again.

The strain, she noted, was not all on her side. She saw the signs of a restless night in his face and was compelled to offer comfort. She lifted a hand to his cheek. "Please, Lance, let's forget about it. We've both said things these past couple of days that shouldn't have been said." Her eyes and mouth were grave as her palm brushed over his cheek. "I don't like apologies either."

Lance lifted his fingers and twined the tip of a curl around them. "You always were a strange mixture of tiger and kitten. I think I'd forgotten how disarmingly sweet you can be." His eyes were no longer silent as he looked at her. "I love you, Foxy."

"Lance." Foxy flung her arms around him and burrowed her face into his neck. At last, the tension inside her uncurled. "I've missed you," she murmured against his neck. "I didn't know where you'd gone, and the house seemed so empty."

"I went into the office," he told her as he slipped his hands under her shirt to caress the warm length of her back. "You should have called if you were lonely."

"I almost did, but I thought . . ." She

sighed and closed her eyes, wonderfully content. "I didn't want it to seem as if I was checking on you."

"Idiot," he muttered, then tilted her head back and kissed her briefly. "You're my wife, remember?"

"You have to keep reminding me," she suggested and smiled. "I don't feel like a wife yet, and I don't know the rules."

"We make our own." This time when he kissed her, it was long and lingering. In instant response, her bones liquified. Her mouth clung to his, avid and sweet while his quiet moan of pleasure warmed her skin.

"I want champagne tonight," she murmured against his ear. "I feel like a celebration."

"For Pam and Kirk?" Lance questioned before he came back to her mouth.

"For us first," Foxy countered, drawing away far enough to smile at him. "Then for Pam and Kirk."

"All right. But tomorrow I want to go to the movies and eat popcorn."

"Oh yes!" Her face lit with pleasure. Her eyes danced. "Yes, something either terribly sad or terribly funny. And I want a pizza afterward with pepperoni."

"A very demanding woman." Lance

laughed as he took her hand and lifted it to his lips. Suddenly his fingers tightened on hers. Sensing a dramatic change of mood, Foxy stared down at their joined hands. Slowly Lance turned hers to the side and examined the light trail of mauve shadows on her wrist. "It seems I owe you yet another apology."

Distressed that the stiffness was back in his manner, Foxy moved toward him. "Lance, don't. It's nothing."

"On the contrary." The coldness in his voice halted her. "It's quite a lot."

"Don't! I can't stand it when you're like this." Filled with frustration, Foxy paced around the room. "I can't deal with you when you're formal and polite." She whirled to face him, then whirled back to roam the room again. "If you're going to be angry, then at least be angry in a way I can understand. Shout, swear, break something," she invited with an inclusive sweep of her hand. "But don't stand there like a pillar of the community. I don't understand pillars."

"Foxy." A reluctant grin teased Lance's mouth as he watched her storm around the room. "If you knew how difficult you make things."

"I'm not trying to make things difficult."

She lifted a pillow from the couch and hurled it across the room. "I'm trying to make thing simple. *I'm* simple, don't you understand?"

"You are," Lance corrected, "infinitely complex."

"No, no, no!" Foxy stomped her foot, furious that they were talking in circles again. "You don't understand anything!" Angrily she tossed her hair behind her back. "I'm going upstairs," she announced and marched from the room.

Going directly to the bath, Foxy turned on the water and let it steam. Carelessly she tossed a mixture of powders and scents into the tub and stripped. *He's an idiot,* she decided as she plopped into the oversized tub. Bubbles rose and frothed around her. *And so am I.* Seething with impotence, Foxy picked up a sponge and began to scrub.

I could probably stop loving him if I really put my mind to it. She scowled at the sponge then squeezed it mercilessly. *I'm going to stop loving him and work on hating him. Once I start hating him,* she concluded, *I won't be an idiot anymore.* As the door opened she glanced up sharply.

"Mind if I shave?" Lance asked casually as he strolled into the room. He had slipped out of his jacket and now wore only his shirt and slacks. Ignoring her glare and not waiting for her assent, he opened the medicine chest.

"I've decided to hate you," Foxy informed him after he had removed the shaving lotion and begun to lather his face.

"Oh?" She watched his eyes shift in the mirror until they met hers. It infuriated her that they were amused. "Again?"

"I was good at it once," she reminded him. "I'm going to be even better at it this time."

"No doubt." The razor stroked clean over his cheek. "Most things improve with age."

"I'm going to hate you perfectly."

"Good for you," Lance told her as he continued to shave. "One should always aim high."

Beyond control, Foxy hurled the wet sponge and hit Lance between the shoulder blades. She felt a surge of satisfaction almost immediately followed by a surge of alarm. *He won't,* she decided grimly, *let me get away with that one.* Still, her eyes challenged his. Slowly Lance set down the razor and bent to pick up the sponge. Foxy's trepidation grew as he turned and walked to the tub. *He wouldn't drown me,* she thought, fending off a few pricks of doubt. Even as she debated the matter, Lance sat on the edge of the tub. She realized with some disgust that she had backed herself neatly into a corner.

Lance made no comment, only dropped the sponge back into the water with a plop. Distracted, Foxy glanced down. Before she realized his intent, his hand was on her head and she was sliding under the hot, fragrant water. Sputtering, she surfaced. Her hair dripped and frothed over her shoulders and into her face as she wiped the bubbles from her eyes.

"I do hate you!" she choked, pushing at her sopping hair. "I'm going to thrive on hating you! I'm going to invent new ways to hate you!"

Lance gave her a calm nod. "Everybody should have a hobby."

"Oh!" Incoherent with fury, Foxy tossed as much water into his face as she could manage. She braced herself for another dunking. To her utter amazement, Lance rolled into the tub in one smooth, unexpected motion. Bubbles spewed over the side. Her shock was transformed into hysterical giggles. "You're crazy," she concluded as she tried to keep herself from submerging under the rocking water.

"How can I hate you properly if you're crazy?" Their bodies tangled together effortlessly. Her skin was slick and fragrant from the oil, and his hands slid over it, bringing her closer. His wet clothes were little more than nothing between them. "You're drowning me," Foxy protested as he shifted her. She swallowed bubbles and giggled again. "I knew you were going to drown me."

"I'm not going to drown you," Lance corrected. "I'm going to make love with you." He gripped her waist and nudged her up until her chin cleared the water. His fingers lingered, spreading over her stomach while his hand cupped her breast. There was a gentleness in his touch he rarely used. "Since you were sharing your sponge and water, I figured you wanted me to join you." He grinned as Foxy pushed dripping hair from his eyes. "I didn't want to be accused of being stuffy."

"You're not stuffy," she said softly. Her eyes reflected regret as they met his. "Lance . . ."

"No more apologies tonight." He closed his mouth over hers to shut it off before it could be formed. He took his hands on a slow, easy journey of her body, pausing and lingering, seducing with a quiet touch.

"We should talk," Foxy murmured, but the words were faint and without conviction. Her sigh was more eloquent.

"Tomorrow. Tomorrow we'll be sensible and talk and sort things through." As he spoke, his lips roamed over her face. His hands sought and touched and enticed. "I want you tonight. I want to make love with my wife." He moved his lips to her neck, tasting, before he caught the lobe of her ear between his teeth. Foxy shuddered and drew him closer. "Then I want to take her out and get her a little drunk before I bring her home and make love with her all over again."

His mouth returned to hers, demanding, then possessing, then demanding again. All sensible thoughts floated from Foxy's mind.

Chapter Fifteen

Foxy began her work day much later in the morning than was her habit. It was nearly eleven before she had finished sorting and cataloging the prints. As she slid them into a thick envelope for mailing she thought over the last few months. For a moment, as she brought it all back into her mind, she could almost smell the hot scent of fuel, hear the high squeal of tires and roaring engines. Shaking her head, she began to seal the envelope. *I'm finished with all that now. It's behind me.*

Briskly she began to develop the film she had taken of children in the park and around Boston. In the back of her mind, the idea for a book was germinating, a collection of photographs of children. Instinct told her that some of the shots were exceptional. *More time,* she mused, *more variety. I'll have to haunt a few more playgrounds.* Patiently she worked through the morning and early afternoon, letting her fingers act as her eyes when the room was dark. Still, her mind continued to drift to Lance.

Foxy knew the night spent in lovemaking had not solved any of their true problems. Again and again, her thoughts returned to the possibility of Lance going back to racing. Again and again, she closed off the idea. *Coward,* she accused herself as she stood in the dark. *You have to think about it, you have to deal with it. I don't know if I can.* She pressed her fingers against her eyes and took a deep breath. *I have to talk to him. Sensibly. Isn't that what he said? Tonight we'll talk sensibly.* She reflected that they had done little of that since he had asked her to marry him in her motel room near Watkins Glen. It was time, she decided, to find out what each of them wanted from the other, and what each was willing to give.

Locked in the darkroom with a red bulb casting its pale light, Foxy discovered one of the answers for herself. As she moved prints from tray to tray and images formed on the paper, she began to understand fully what she had been looking for. The faces of children looked back at her, some smiling, some caught in temper tantrums or tears. There were sleeping infants, moon-faced toddlers, sharp-eyed preschoolers. Foxy hung the prints with a growing sense of serenity. She wanted children. She wanted a family and all that went with it. The home, the normality, the commitment of a structured family was something she found she wanted and perhaps had been afraid to ask for. A permanent home with the man she loved . . . Lance's children . . . family traditions. *Her* family's traditions.

Would Lance feel the same way? Foxy pushed the hair from her face and tried to think of the answer. She discovered that as long as she had known him, as intimate as they had been, she did not know. *We will have to talk about it,* she told herself as she studied the drying prints. *We will have to talk about a number of things.*

A glance at her watch told her she still had a few afternoon hours left. It was time, she thought, to finish her commitment to Pam and the racing shots. After gathering up her gear, she went upstairs to put a call through to Lance's office. The quick, efficient voice of his secretary answered.

"Hello, Linda, it's Mrs. Matthews. Is Lance busy?"

"I'm sorry, Mrs. Matthews, he's not in. Would you like to leave a message or is there something I could do for you?"

"Well, no, I . . . Yes, actually," Foxy decided with another glance at her watch. She wanted to get this done today. "He's working on a new car, a new Formula One for next season."

"Yes, the one your brother will drive."

"That's right. I'd like to get some pictures if I can."

"That shouldn't be a problem, Mrs. Matthews, if you don't mind a bit of a drive. Mr. Matthews and the crew have the car out at the track today for some testing."

"That's perfect." Foxy picked up the pad and pencil by the phone. "You'll have to give me directions. I haven't been out there yet."

Thirty minutes later, Foxy pulled up near the familiar sight of the oval track. As she stepped from the car the brisk breeze caught at her hair and blew open her unbuttoned jacket. The roaring sound of the engine reached her ears. Shielding her eyes with her hand, she watched the low red blur whiz around the track. The smell of hot rubber and fuel filled the air. *It never changes,* she thought and slipped the strap of her camera around her neck. She recognized Charlie with a group of men, wondered fleetingly where Lance might be, then set to work.

Foxy moved quickly. After choosing the best position for the shots, she selected a lens and set the camera. With quick turns of the controls and shifts of her own body, she snapped shot after shot. It was, she observed, a fast one. The car seemed like a ball of flame as it rounded a curve and sped down the straightaway. *It will suit Kirk,* she mused, easily able to picture him in the cockpit. *And Kirk will suit it.* Foxy straightened, pushing her hair behind her ears as she stood.

"Can't keep you away from the track, huh, kid?"

Turning, Foxy grinned into Charlie's scowling face. "I can't keep away from you, Charlie," she corrected. She plucked the smoldering cigar from his mouth and gave him a loud, smacking kiss. He shuffled his feet as she handed it back to him.

"Got no respect," he grumbled. He cleared his throat, then squinted at her. "You getting along all right?"

"I'm getting along just fine," she told him. Moving with an old habit, she rubbed her palm over his grizzled beard. "How about you?"

"Busy," he growled, but colored under his fierce frown. "Between your brother and your husband I got no time."

"Price you pay for being the best."

Charlie sniffed, accepting the truth. "Kirk'll be ready for the car when it's ready for him," he prophesied. "Shame we don't have two," he mused as he shifted his narrowed eyes back to the track. "Lance knows how to handle a machine."

Foxy started to make some comment when the full meaning of Charlie's statement sunk in. Her eyes flew to the track and locked on the speeding car. Lance. The iron taste of fear rose in her throat. She shook her head, trying to deny what her mind screamed was the truth. "Lance is driving?" she heard herself ask. Her voice sounded thin and hollow to her ears, as if it had traveled down a long tunnel.

"Yeah, regular test driver's sick." Charlie's answer was casual before he shuffled off. Foxy was left alone as the roaring sound of the engine droned on.

As she watched, the car did a quick fishtail on a curve, then straightened without any slackening of speed. Foxy's brow felt like ice. Queasiness knotted her stomach, and for a moment the bright sunlight dimmed. She chewed on her bottom lip and let the pain overwhelm the faintness. She stood helplessly while dozens of the crashes she remembered passed vividly in front of her mind's eye. *Not again,* she thought in desperation. *Oh God, not again.* He drove as he had always driven, with complete control and determination, not a comet, but a ruthless, cunning tyrant. Foxy began to shiver uncontrollably in the quick autumn breeze. *It'll be hot in the cockpit,* she thought as her fingers went numb on the strap of her camera. *Desperately hot, and all he sees is the track, all he hears is the engine. And the speed's like a drug that keeps pulling him back.*

Fear kept her frozen even after she heard the whine of the slowing engine. She stood straight and still as Lance pulled up near the group of men. Unstrapped, he unfolded himself from the cockpit, pulling off his helmet as he stood. He peeled off the balaclava then ran a hand through his hair. She had seen him make the same gestures after countless races on countless grids. Pain began to work its way through the cold fear. Her breath became irregular. Lance was grinning down at Charlie, and his laughter carried to her. His brow lifted at something Charlie said, and his eyes followed the careless gesture of the older man until they found Foxy.

For a moment, they only watched each

other; husband and wife, man and woman, two people who had known each other for a decade. She saw his expression change, but took no time to decipher it. Tears were coming too quickly for her to prevent them. *I've lost,* she thought, and pressed her hands against the sides of her face. As Lance pushed his way through the group of men Foxy turned and ran toward her car. He called her name, but she wrenched open the door and tumbled inside. The only coherent thought in her mind as she turned the key was escape. Seconds later, she was racing away from the track.

It was nearly dark when Foxy turned down the street toward the brownstone. Streetlights flickered on. Lance's car sat at the curb rather than in the garage, and she pulled her MG behind it. Foxy turned off the engine, and rested her forehead for a moment against the wheel. The two hours she had spent driving had calmed her but left her enervated. She took this time to gain back some strength. With slow, careful movements, she stepped from the car and moved up the walk. Even as she reached for the knob, the door opened. From either side of the threshold, they watched each other.

Lance studied her as if seeing her for the

first time — thoroughly, carefully, with no smile to interfere with his concentration. His eyes were guarded but searching. The familiar stillness was on him. She was reminded of the first night, at Kirk's party, when she had opened the door to find him outside. He had looked at her in precisely the same way. *Will I ever get over him?* she wondered almost dispassionately as she met him look for look. *No,* she answered her own question. *Never.*

"Fox." Lance held out a hand to bring her inside, but she ignored it, moving around him. Carefully she set down her camera case but did not remove her jacket before she walked into the parlor. Without speaking, she moved to the bar and poured a snifter of brandy. Her decision had been made during her two-hour drive, but following through now was not going to be easy. Foxy swallowed brandy, shut her eyes as it burned her throat, then swallowed more. Lance stood in the doorway and watched her.

"I've been down to your darkroom looking for you." He frowned at the absence of color in her cheeks and dipped his hands in his pockets. "I saw the pictures you had drying. They're extraordinary, Foxy. You're extraordinary. Every time I think I know who you are, I find another part of you." When she turned to face him fully, he came into the room. "I owe you an explanation for this afternoon."

"No." Foxy shook her head as she set the snifter down on a table. "You told me before your profession had nothing to do with me." Her eyes lifted and held steady on his. "I don't want an explanation."

He took a step closer. The shadows in the room shifted with the movement. "Well then, Foxy, what do you want?"

"A divorce," she said simply. Feeling the pressure of emotions rising in her throat, she spoke quickly. "We made a mistake, Lance, and the sooner we fix it, the easier it should be for both of us."

"You think so?" he countered. His eyes were level with hers.

"It should be easy enough to arrange," she returned, evading the question. "I'd like you to do it since you have lawyers and I don't. I don't want any settlement."

"Another drink?" Lance asked, and turned to the bar.

His casual tone had her eyeing him warily. "Yes," she answered, wanting to appear as composed as he. The room grew quiet save for the clink of glass against glass. With the decanter in hand, Lance crossed to Foxy and filled the snifter again. The sun slanted low in the window and fell at their feet. Foxy sipped, wondering with a flash of giddyness if they should toast their divorce plans.

"No," Lance said, then drank.

"No?" Foxy repeated, wondering now if he had seen into her mind.

"No, Foxy, you can't have a divorce. Can I interest you in something else?"

Her eyes widened, then narrowed at his arrogance. "I'll have a divorce. I'll get a lawyer of my own and sue you for one." She slammed down her glass. "You can't stop me."

"I'll fight you, Fox," he countered with easy assurance as he placed his glass beside hers. "And I'll win." Reaching out, he grabbed a handful of her hair. "I'm not going to let you go. Not now, not ever. I told you before, I'm a selfish man." Giving her hair a tug, he tumbled her into his arms. "I love you and have no intentions of doing without you."

"How dare you?" Furious, Foxy pushed against him. "How dare you think so much of yourself that you give no thought to my feelings? You don't know anything about love." She kicked out in frustration as her struggles got her nowhere.

"Foxy, you're going to hurt yourself." Lance locked his arms around her and lifted her off her feet. For a moment, she fought against him, then subsided. She shut her eyes, infuriated that she had to surrender on any level.

"Let go of me." Her voice came from between her teeth, but was quiet and even.

"Will you listen to me now?"

She jerked back her head, wanting to refuse. Her eyes were bright with anger and hurt. "I don't have much choice, do I?"

"Please."

The one simple word knocked her off balance. The word was in his eyes as well. Defeated, Foxy nodded. When Lance released her, she stepped away, moving to the window. The early moon was white and full and promising. Its light fell in showers over the naked trees and glittered over scattered leaves. Foxy thought nothing had ever seemed so lonely.

"I had no idea you were coming out to the track today."

Foxy gave a quick laugh, then rested her forehead against the glass. "Did you think what I didn't know wouldn't hurt me?"

"Fox." The tone of his voice persuaded her to turn and face him. "I didn't think at all, that's the point." He made a quick, uncharacteristic gesture of frustration. "I test the cars from time to time, it's a habit of mine. It didn't occur to me until I turned and saw you standing there how it would affect you."

"Would it have made a difference?"

"Damn it, Foxy!" His voice was hard and impatient.

"Is that an unreasonable question?" she returned. She began to wander about the room as she found standing still was impossible. "It doesn't seem like one to me. It seems perfectly justified. I've discovered something about myself in the past month. I can't be second with you." Foxy paused, taking a deep breath. "I have to be first, I can't ride in the backseat with you the way I've always done with Kirk. It's not at all the same thing. I want — need something solid, something permanent. I've been waiting for it my whole life. This house . . ." She made a helpless gesture as her thoughts came almost too quickly for the words to keep pace. "I want what it stands for. It doesn't matter if we leave it a dozen times a year to go to a dozen different places, as long as it's here to come back to. I want stability, I want commitment, I want a home, children. Your children." Her voice quivered with her feelings, but she turned, dry-eyed, to look up at him. "I want it all, everything."

Foxy turned away again and swallowed. She took two long breaths, hoping they would steady her. "When I saw you in that car this afternoon . . ." Emotions swamped her, and she shook her head before she could continue. "I can't explain what it does to me. Perhaps it's unreasonable, but I can't control it." Pressing the heel of her hand between her eyes, Foxy tried to speak calmly. "I can't live like that again. I love you, and sometimes I can't quite believe that we're together. I don't want you to be anything but what you are. And I know the things I want might not be what's important to you. But when I think about you going back to racing, I . . ."

"Why should I go back to racing?" The question was calm and curious.

Foxy moved her shoulders hopelessly. "You said you might the day I found out about Kirk's new car. I know it's important to you."

"Do you think I would do that to you?" This time the tone of his voice brought Foxy's eyes to his. "Have you been thinking that all this time?" He moved to her, then placed both hands on her shoulders. "I'm not interested in racing again.

But if I were, I'd manage to do without it. I'm more interested in my wife, Fox." He shook her, but the gesture was more caress than punishment. "How could I consider racing when I know what it does to you? Can't you see you are first in my life?"

She opened her mouth to speak, but only managed to shake her head before he continued. "No, you probably don't. I don't suppose I've made things very clear. It's time that I did." He rubbed her shoulders lightly before he dropped his hands. "In the first place, I pressured you into marriage, taking advantage of Kirk's accident. I've had some bad moments because of that. Let me finish," he told her as she started to protest. "I wanted you, and that night you looked so lost. I snatched you into marriage and rushed you up to Boston without giving you any of the frills you were entitled to. The truth is, I was afraid you might get away, and I told myself I'd make it up to you after we were married."

"Lance," Foxy interrupted and lifted a hand to his cheek. "I don't need frills."

"Is this the woman who once compared a garage to Manderley?" he countered. He took her fingers to his lips, then let them go. "Maybe I need to give them to you, Foxy. Maybe that's why I was devoured with jealousy at the thought of you spending the afternoon in the park with Jonathan. I should have been with you. I rushed you into being my wife and never bothered to discuss the finer points." With his hands in his pockets, he turned away and roamed about the room. "It's difficult to be patient when you've been in love for nearly ten years."

"What?" Foxy stared at him, then slowly lowered herself to the arm of the sofa. "What did you say about ten years?"

Lance turned to her with his tilted smile. "Maybe if I had explained myself in the beginning, we could have avoided some of these problems. I don't know when I started loving you. It's hard to remember a time when I didn't. You were an adolescent with fabulous eyes and a woman's laugh. You nearly drove me out of my mind."

"Why . . . why didn't you tell me?"

"Fox, you were little more than a child. I was a grown man." With a laugh, he ran his hand through his hair. "Kirk was my best friend. If I had touched you, he would have killed me with perfect justification. No, I couldn't sleep that night at Le Mans because this sixteen-year-old girl was making me crazy. In the garage when I turned around and you all but fell into my arms, I wanted you so badly it hurt. Badly enough that I took my defense in cruelty. Driving you away from me was the only decent thing to do. God, you terrified me."

Shaking his head, he lifted Foxy's neglected drink. "I knew I had to give you time to grow up, time to form your own life. The six years I didn't see you were incredibly long. It was during that time that I started building cars and moved into this house." He turned and looked at her again. "I always pictured you here. It seemed right somehow. You belonged here with me, I felt it. I've never made love to another woman in this house." He set down the glass, and his eyes grew dark and intense. "There's never been anyone but you. Shadows, substitutes at best. I've wanted other women, but I've never loved anyone else. I've never needed anyone else."

Foxy swallowed, not certain she could trust her voice. "Lance, do you need me?"

"Only for day-to-day living." He moved to her, then ran a hand down her hair. "I've learned a few things in the past weeks. You can hurt me." He traced a finger down the side of her throat as his eyes met hers. "I'd never considered that possibility. What you think of me matters. I've never given a damn what anyone thought of me before. You become more important to me in dozens of ways every day. And my need for you doesn't soften." He smiled slowly. "And you still terrify me."

Foxy returned his smile, feeling the blanketing warmth of contentment. "I suppose this sort of marriage will never be completely smooth and settled."

"I shouldn't think so."

"I suppose it'll always be somewhat tempestuous and demanding."

"And interesting," Lance added.

"I suppose when two people have been in love for as long as we have, they can be quite stubborn about it." She lifted her arms. "I've always loved you, you know, even through all the years I tried not to. Coming back to you was coming home. I want you to kiss me until I can't breathe."

Even as she spoke, Lance's mouth claimed hers. "Foxy," he murmured at length and rested his cheek against hers.

"No, no, I'm still breathing." Thirsty, her mouth sought his until he abandoned his gentle caress. Wild, turbulent, electric, their lips met over and over as the room grew soft with dusk. "Oh, Lance." Foxy held him tightly a moment, then lifted his face and combed her fingers through his hair. "How could we both be such idiots and not tell each other what we were feeling?"

"We're both new at marriage, Fox." He rubbed his nose against hers. "We just have to practice more."

"I feel like a wife." She wrapped her arms around his neck and pulled him close. "I feel very much like a wife. I like it."

"I think a wife should have a honeymoon," Lance murmured as he began to enjoy the privileges of a husband. "I should have told you that I've been spending a great deal of extra time at the office so that I could manage a couple of weeks away. Starting now. Where would you like to go?"

"Anywhere?" she asked, floating under the drugging power of his hands.

"Anywhere."

"Nowhere," she decided as she slipped her hands under his sweater. His back was taut and warm under her palms. "I've heard the service is great here." She smiled up at him when he lifted his face. "And I love the view." Reaching up and behind, Foxy found the phone and tugged it over her head. "Here, call Mrs. Trilby and tell her we've gone to . . . . Fiji for two weeks.

Give her a vacation. We'll lock the door and take the phone off the hook and disappear."

"I married a very smart woman," Lance concluded. He took the phone, dropping it on the floor with the receiver off. "I'll call her later . . . much later." Lowering his mouth, he rubbed it gently over Foxy's. "You did say something about children, didn't you?"

The eyes that were beginning to close opened again. "Yes, I did."

"How many did you have in mind?" he asked as he kissed the lids closed again.

"I hadn't thought of a number," Foxy murmured.

"Why don't we start with one and work from there?" Lance suggested. "An important project like this should be started immediately, don't you think?"

"Absolutely," Foxy agreed. Dusk became night as their mouths met again.